Bite Thy Neighbor

by

Esmae Browder

This is a work of fiction. Names, characters, places, and incidents are either the product of the author's imagination or are used fictitiously, and any resemblance to actual persons living or dead, business establishments, events, or locales, is entirely coincidental.

Bite Thy Neighbor

COPYRIGHT © 2017 by Esmae Browder

Cover Art by Debbie Taylor

The Wild Rose Press, Inc.
PO Box 708
Adams Basin, NY 14410-0708

Visit us at www.thewilderroses.com

Publishing History
First Scarlet Rose Edition, 2017
Print ISBN 978-1-5092-1571-3
Digital ISBN 978-1-5092-1572-0

Published in the United States of America

Some neighbors desire more than a cup of sugar...

"You're the one I've been waiting for," Adam whispered. "And I've waited a long time."

I was unable to fight being aroused by this sexy man with the fierce, dark eyes. His lips were a pale red, and as I looked at them, my mind instantly pictured us in a heated lip lock, our tongues ravishing each other. All my senses jumped to high alert.

"I don't know what you mean," I whispered back, unable to keep the shake out of my voice. "You don't know me. And...and I'm a married woman."

"Married?" he scoffed and grabbed my hand, kissing it lightly. "That doesn't matter when it comes to destiny."

Damn. His lips on my skin set my heart skipping. I started to feel a little tingle between my legs.

"Destiny?" I asked, shifting slightly.

"Don't play dumb with me, my sweet Maisy." Adam smiled and then stood in front of me so quickly I didn't see the actual movement. "You can't deny the passion you feel for me," he said, going to his knees. "I've been in your dreams. I know your desires."

He put a hand on my bare leg, sliding it up to my thigh as light as a feather.

"That's not possible." I shivered, wondering if he would slip that hand higher and discover how vulnerable I was without panties. "You're teasing me."

"Am I?"

Dedication

To my neighbors. You keep life interesting!

Chapter One

Jensen and I had vowed to stop being assholes to the neighbors a few months ago.

My husband was sincere in this promise, but I had my fingers crossed.

We sat on two lawn chairs in the driveway of our home as was our custom most Friday evenings in the summer. The faint, purple light of twilight brought out the lightning bugs, and the soft June wind had turned from insanely hot to about bearable.

Down the street, a woman unloaded groceries from the back of her pearly-white minivan while two kids clad in bathing suits ran through a sprinkler in her front yard. Their shouts of joy echoed down to us, blending in with the sounds of a few brave souls who had decided to wait until the evening to mow their lawns into pristine rows of green grass as designated by our picky Home Owners Association.

"Maisy, listen to me." Jensen's smooth Southern drawl reminded me of a Tennessee Williams play. "We really need to stop being assholes toward the neighbors."

"Speak for yourself." I tossed a smoldering cigarette stub into the perfectly trimmed bushes bordering our house. "I haven't done anything to be ashamed of. I can't help it if everyone else on the block hasn't followed my example and continues to act as if

1

nothing happened."

"How many times have I asked you not to toss your Friday night cigarette into the yard? When are you gonna give up the habit anyway?"

"One social smoke a week is not really a habit."

With a sigh, Jensen rose, retrieved the cigarette, stubbed it out against the bricks of our house, and dropped it in the garage trashcan. As he sat back down, I stole a glance at his tight butt perfectly framed in his cargo shorts.

Pushing a strand of blond hair out his eyes, he eyeballed me in a calculating way I found deceptively sexy. "Maisy, we really need to get a handle on this neighbor thing. Just because the cops went over to Jane and Michael's house that one time does not mean they are bad people."

I glanced over at the two-story house next to us. White shutters bordered the front windows and matched the mini fence they'd put around their flowerbeds which boasted of red and gold zinnias. "I never said they were *bad* people. I actually like Jane. I can't help it if their family suffers from Resting Bitch Face syndrome. They all have it. Even when they aren't pissed off, they look pissed off. The only thing that changes their expression is when Jane is drunk and Michael is high and running to us for help."

Accustomed to my cynical view of the world, Jensen rolled his green eyes.

"Hey, when your neighbor comes running into your garage with cops chasing him and drugs stuffed up his ass, it's hard to let that go." I rolled my eyes right back at him, frustrated by his naiveté. "Our five-year-old daughter could have seen him. What if she'd been outside, and he'd pulled a gun?"

"Now you're just being overly dramatic." Jensen scratched his head, leaving tufts of hair sticking up. "Michael doesn't own a gun. Besides, everyone else around here has moved on from that incident. He even went to rehab."

"The rest of the people living around us are just as bat shit crazy as the RBF family."

Jensen took a long sip from his beer, no doubt mulling the wisdom of my words.

We were both in shorts and T-shirts, but I have to admit, part of the reason I liked sitting outside with Jensen was so I could admire his strong, tan legs and the bulge of his biceps in the tattered old muscle shirt he wore. His hair was a silky mix of blond and brown, the kind you could spend hours running your fingers through.

Yep, my husband was a handsome man.

Too bad our marriage was one of convenience, an arranged match designed to please someone we'd both cared about. Jensen may have been my spouse and a hottie to boot—score!—but he didn't love me. He didn't have the same kind of dirty thoughts about me that I constantly had about him at the worst possible times.

Don't think about it right now. Thinking about it only makes you crazy.

I ignored the little pang of sadness rattling around in my heart at this truth, forcing myself to reflect on Jensen's decree that we no longer be assholes. I observed the cookie cutter homes of my other neighbors, wondering if this new edict covered their occupants as well.

Directly in front of me in the quaint, limestone one-story lived Zero to Sixty and Boy Genius. Of course, that's not her real name—it's actually Alexis—but I called her that due to her ability to go from completely sober to completely wasted after two sips of vodka tonic.

Zero to Sixty was popular with the other moms on the block because of her gregarious attitude and her willingness to hold the monthly wine party. Her husband, Boy Genius—real name, Greg—was gone a lot, traveling for work. Without him around, she was the wild and crazy red-headed party girl wearing low cut tops to show off her big boobs, and she always had a bottle of something alcoholic open to share with anyone who liked looking at them.

Oh, and just so you know…she does anal once every quarter.

Yeah. She told me that the first time I met her. I could feel my cheeks burning with embarrassment. Don't get me wrong…I like sex, but I've been going through a bit of a dry spell.

Flustered by her over share, I'd tried to keep my distance after that first meeting, but like the RBF family, Zero to Sixty also had kids my daughter, Rebecca's, age. Even though Zero's kids and the RBF family's kids were currently at some swanky summer camp, I was still forced into conversation with her from time to time. In fact, usually on Friday nights during the summer, she and Boy Genius would set up camp on their front porch like Jensen and I set up in the driveway.

But on the evening of the "no more assholes" conversation, she wasn't out yet.

On the right of us, another single story home housed more neighbors I avoided. The house featured the limestone brick we all had except the front yard was a standout, which made it a source of irritation to the HOA. Unkempt, bright-colored flowers lined the driveway and were strategically placed in the flowerbeds around the trees along with several smiling ceramic gnomes with bright red hats. The front window of the house had decorative shutters painted with intricate butterflies, which also dotted the front door, giving off a warm and friendly vibe—very sneaky in my opinion.

The SOS family lived there. You know what that stands for, right?

Sex Offender Siblings.

"I know what you're thinking." Jensen followed my gaze. "We don't have a *Flowers in the Attic* situation going on next door."

"More like *Petals in the Wind*," I muttered. "Or *Game of Thrones*. Their blond hair, blue eyed family is too perfect. I mean, Seth and Sophia look exactly alike. *Exactly*. If they aren't a brother and sister secretly living together as a married couple, then I will eat my shoe. And let's not forget, Seth is a registered sex offender!"

Jensen chuckled. "He got caught masturbating in his car by an overly ambitious bicycle cop. It's not like he was out hurting kids or vulnerable women."

"Maybe. But I still find their sibling love offensive. So I will call them the SOS family if I want to."

"Maisy, what am I going to do with you?" he asked. "You get more like your mother every day."

If there is one thing that makes me crazy, it's being

compared to that woman.

"You—"

He stopped me before the anger could unleash itself. "Don't get bent all out of shape," he said with a kind smile. "All I'm saying is that you both have a habit of making snap judgments. Sometimes those judgments get you in trouble. You know that better than anyone."

"I'm not crazy, just nosy." Thinking about Momma always made me see red. And I was terrified of turning out like her, a fact my oh-so-handsome husband knew.

"In your family, there seems to be a fine line between the two. Don't go looking for trouble, darlin'. You're a teacher. You're supposed to be more open-minded than everyone else."

"Momma's problems were much more complicated than that." I tried to keep the temper out of my voice, tried to keep control of my emotions, tried to ignore the little thump my heart gave when he called me "darlin" in that sexy way I liked so much. "And if you think I'm going to do anything like she did…"

Images of the foster homes I'd grown up in flitted through my mind, worn photographs of tumultuous times with strangers where my mentally incapacitated mother was nowhere to be found. There were no birthday parties or Thanksgiving dinners with family in those memories, no visits from Santa or Easter Egg hunts. I tried not to think about it too much. I'd never quite managed to forgive my mother for being the freak of the week and ruining my childhood.

Jensen cleared his throat and shifted in his chair, a sign he was letting the topic of my mother go before it spiraled out of control.

"Now that we've agreed to stop being assholes," he

said with a lazy grin, "I guess it's a good time to tell you that I have some neighborhood gossip."

"For the record, I've agreed to nothing, but tell me what the gossip is anyway."

"We are getting new neighbors."

I looked up and down the street. Had I missed a "For Sale" sign?

"Behind us," Jensen said.

"The Amityville House?" I glanced over my shoulder.

The house behind us was on a street called Lost Faith and certainly fit in on a street with such a depressing name. Two stories and made of limestone like all the others, the back of it was unique with big bay windows up high which reminded me of eyes—hence the Amityville reference—and beautifully carved French doors that opened out onto a covered back porch. Once upon a time, the backyard had been a gorgeous showpiece consisting of Japanese-style plants and a small pond with a rock waterfall.

Of course, I'd never been to the house or anything, but peeking through the holes of our back fence gave me a lot of information.

Unfortunately, the owner—a short Japanese man I'd called Mr. Miyagi—passed away six months ago. He fell down the stairs, twisting his neck. Naturally, I'd assumed a strange Japanese curse had fallen on the place and turned it into a haunted house where the walls dripped blood.

It was the only sensible thing to think.

"Well? Who bought the place?" I asked.

"I don't know who bought it," he said. "I happened to notice the 'For Sale' sign was gone when I passed it on my way home."

"And you waited this long to tell me?"

"Figured we should have the asshole talk first. We might want to keep it in mind when we meet these new people." He paused and took a deep breath. "I've been noticing the other kids aren't playing with Rebecca as much. Do you think it's because we aren't that social with the neighbors?"

I shrugged but couldn't quite meet his eyes, afraid to admit he might be right.

"Maisy," he said with rare sternness. "We don't want Rebecca left out because of our biases."

"I'm not biased."

He raised an eyebrow.

"Okay, maybe I'm a little biased." Guilt pricked at my heart. The thought of Rebecca being excluded from all the normal things she was supposed to experience as a kid hurt. My childhood experiences wouldn't be hers. I wouldn't let them.

"All I'm saying is that we should stop being assholes to the neighbors. Instead of ignoring their requests to come over or throwing cigarette butts into their yard, maybe we should acknowledge that we're not perfect." Jensen gave me a pleading look that was always hard for me to say no to.

I wasn't perfect, but I was a hell of a lot better than most of the weirdoes living around us.

"C'mon," he prodded. "Do it for Rebecca. Next time Sophia asks you over for coffee, accept the invitation. And didn't Alexis just ask you to go to Wine Night tomorrow at her house?"

"I don't remember. I usually don't listen when she talks."

"It's summer. Summer can be lonely for kids if they have no one to play with. Think back to the summers before Pops took you in. Do you want that for Rebecca?"

Damn. Jensen was good. He knew bringing up Pops would make me think twice about things. Maybe I did have a small habit of being unreasonable and judgmental. But I loved Rebecca. I couldn't let her suffer because of my issues.

"Fine," I said, begrudgingly. "I'll try to be better."

"No more assholes?"

"Sure."

But my fingers were crossed the tiniest bit.

After all, I still had to meet the new neighbors.

Chapter Two

"So do ya'll want to have one of them sex parties at my house next week?" Zero to Sixty asked. Perched on the edge of my hot tub holding a glass of wine, her long red hair, wild and curly, the dim light of the citronella tiki torches made it look like she held a flute of crimson blood. Her face was shadowed, but if I squinted through the steam of the tub, I could tell she was already three sheets to the wind.

The warm bubbles tickled my water-logged skin as I draped one arm over the opposite side of the tub and glanced at the others. Submerged to her chin, Sophia rested the back of her head against the wall of the tub, her blue eyes glazed from the effects of too much wine. Jane had claimed a spot next to her on the underwater bench and she sat up straight, her face bright with interest at Alexis's question.

"A sex party?" Jane bent forward on the underwater bench of the tub, allowing the jets to gently pummel her back. "What does that mean? Is it like a key party or something?"

"A key party? Girl, please!" Zero to Sixty laughed. "That went out in the eighties. Nobody does that anymore. That was the kind of shit our parents went to."

"That's disgusting." Sophia shuddered. Lifting her head so she could sit up, she squeezed the water from her long blonde ponytail. "I don't even want to think about my parents having sex with each other, much less a different partner."

"So what are you talking about then, Alexis?" Jane asked, lifting her brunette hair and tying it effortlessly into a knot so the water wouldn't get it wet. The updo gave her an air of sophistication, causing envy to prick at me. My own blonde hair was also up, but it was lank and damp, most likely plastered to my skin. No sophistication there. "What's your definition of a sex party?"

I was curious, too.

And I was curious to see if Zero to Sixty could tell us without spilling every drop of her red wine in my hot tub. I hadn't really wanted to have them come over—after all, Zero was the hostess of the wine party I'd agreed to go to—but sometimes a drunk idea takes off. As soon as I'd mentioned how I couldn't wait to go home and relax with a vodka tonic in my hot tub, they'd interpreted it as an invitation to join me.

None of them had bothered to go home and get a swimsuit. Not even Zero whose house we'd been at. Instead, they'd run over with their booze and stripped down to bra and panties before sliding into my pristine tub. I'd have to clean it in the morning, but what was done was done.

Zero sipped from her drink and adjusted her yellow lacy bra so her nipple wasn't falling out. "I'm talking about the kind of party where you buy sex toys and lubricants."

"Oh yeah!" Sophia nodded, her ponytail bouncing along in agreement. "I went to a wedding expo last year, and they had people who were advertising that stuff for bridal showers and bachelorette parties. You can buy all kinds of dildos."

Did she say dildo? That sounded so odd coming out of her perfect mouth! I stifled a laugh.

"That's the kind all right," Zero said. "I'm going with a company called Lovely Lust."

"Really? Sounds like a bad porno," I said.

"Don't be a prude, Maisy. Lust *is* lovely, and we should nurture the passion within all of us!"

Drip, drip, drip. There went some wine into the tub just as the hot tub lights turned a pale green. The glow made the dark drops stand out, though no one seemed to notice it but me.

"I'm not a prude, Ze—uh, Alexis." I forced myself to remember her real name. "But I'm not sure I want everyone on the block to know which kind of lubricant I prefer or the name of my vibrator."

"I call mine Juan Carlos," Jane announced. "I dated a Latino boy once with a huge penis. My vibrator reminds me of him."

"What color is it?" Sophia asked.

"Juan Carlos? Purple. And it has little beads in the middle that you can make rotate for maximum oomph."

"I like my vibrator to have a little less oomph in the vagina and a little more pow on the clit," Zero said. "That's our sexual center, ladies."

"Who told you that?" I asked.

"The lady who signed me up for the Lovely Lust party. So what do you think? Ya'll want to do that next week?"

All the ladies chimed in with a chorus of "Yes!"

Zero narrowed her eyes at me and leaned forward so her nipple popped out again. Maybe she needed a better bra or something. My own large breasts never had as much trouble staying holstered as hers did.

"C'mon, Maisy," Zero said. "Don't tell me you couldn't use a little extra zing between the sheets. I don't know what your husband is packing in his pants, but it can't be that exciting. You never tell us anything about your love life. For all we know, you don't even have sex anymore."

"Yeah. Ya'll could be living together like…like…" Sophia couldn't find the words to finish the sentence.

"Like brother and sister?" I suggested.

It was hard to tell in the dim light, but I think she blushed.

"Well, let me tell you something, ladies," I said. "What goes on in my bedroom is none of your business. My husband and I have fantastic sex. Fantastic! We do it every Saturday and twice on Sundays. I have no complaints. None."

Of course, not one word of that was true.

"But regardless of how fantastic my love life is," I continued to lie, "I will attend the Lovely Lust party." I took a big sip of my vodka tonic.

"Well, thank you very much for agreeing to come down off your high horse and grace us with your presence." Zero smirked. "I'm sure you'll find something useful at the party."

"To Lovely Lust!" Jane held up her glass in a toast. "Cheers!"

We toasted and let the bubbles from the hot tub surround us in warm comfort. Zero started discussing the merits of sex toys, but I sort of zoned out of the conversation, thinking about Jensen and sex.

I wished we were having it. Sex, I mean. But we

hadn't ever done it. Not even on our wedding night.

Not that I wasn't interested. I just didn't want to force him.

I know what you're thinking. What about Rebecca? Where did she come from? Well, I can assure you it wasn't any kind of immaculate conception or anything. I did the deed with someone, and it resulted in my sweet girl.

Problem is, I can't quite remember who the father of my child is.

I don't sleep around or anything. It's just that one night in college a few years back, I attended a party and things got…interesting. Like fabulous sex interesting. Like fabulous sex interesting with a man whose face I can't quite remember.

It happens to us all, right?

I felt lucky Jensen had married me despite the fact I had no clue who the last person I'd had sex with was. Of course, it was all a bit of a business arrangement—the marriage, I mean—something to keep me safe. My paranoid guardian, Pops, who was being eaten alive by cancer faster than any of us had anticipated, had arranged my marriage to Jensen. And because Jensen is the kind of guy who is loyal to people he respects, he had agreed.

I was the one who balked at the arrangement. That's because I knew Pops had paid Jensen a lot of money to marry me. No woman wants to feel like she's being sold at auction, and I had told Pops that. After all, I was grown ass woman who could take care of herself and my child.

Still…it was Pops. I couldn't say no to him when he was dying—even though I knew Jensen only thought of me as a little sister. And deep down, I knew the truth. Pops hadn't wanted us to worry about money. He'd wanted us to have everything we needed when he was gone.

That was a year ago, and at the time, Rebecca was four and a half. Besides Pops, Jensen has been the only father figure she has ever known, having been there for her since she was born. They had bonded over the years and became almost inseparable as she grew. He never failed to bring her a small toy or have something special with her name on it every time he came over to Pops place.

How could I not marry someone who adored my child?

Throughout the year, we'd grown used to each other, become a family of sorts. But Jensen and I were never a couple. Friends, yes. After all, I'd known him since my teen years, and I trusted him implicitly. Sure, sometimes I caught him looking at me in a way that made me think he might be contemplating changing our status, but I couldn't be sure. I've had my fair share of dirty sex dreams. But Jensen has never laid a finger on me other than a chaste hug or kiss for Rebecca's benefit.

To be honest, I'm grateful Jensen took me on at all. So much of my life has been messy. Most men would have run in the opposite direction once they found out about my history.

But geez, Louise! If only I didn't have those sexual feelings about him! I'd die of embarrassment if I acted on them, and he rejected me.

Frowning, I slid lower into the hot tub, trying not to think about Jensen naked or the way his butt looked fantastic in tight jeans. And that laugh of his—how could a simple sound make me want to jump him?

The back porch lights of the Amityville house clicked on, taking my thoughts into a welcomed new direction.

All conversation stopped as we stared at the lights, curious. Several tall trees bordered the fence, but I'd cut them back that morning, telling Jensen they needed to be pruned. However, I think he knew cutting the trees here and there would allow me to see into the Amityville House, maybe even catch a glimpse of the new neighbors.

The interior lights remained off, but I sensed someone stood beyond the shadow of the French doors, watching us. Though the water hissed and steamed, a little chill ran through me.

Maybe Zero felt it, too, because she slid into the tub as if she didn't want to be seen. She nodded toward the house. "Have you met them yet?"

"Nope."

"I bet we were being too noisy." She giggled nervously. "Maybe they're coming out to yell at us."

One of the French doors opened. As it did, music trickled out, lifting into the breeze and raining down on us like a simple spell. *Moves Like Jagger.* I knew it instantly.

A man stepped onto the back porch, and we all gave a collective gasp—a mix of surprise, relief, and female appreciation—as we strained against the hot tub walls to get a better glimpse.

What a specimen of a man.

Tall—maybe six feet or so—with dark hair that kind of spiked a little on the top, the man's face was sharp and a bit pale, but his eyes…yowsers! They were magnetic, the kind that stare into your soul and know all your secrets, the kind of eyes that may or may not kiss and tell, but you just know the kiss will be worth any risk. From the distance we were at, I couldn't discern if they were green or purple, but it didn't matter. Something in the way he contemplated us made my nipples grow hard and my breath shorten.

And his torso…yum. At our angle, we couldn't see the lower half of his body, but it didn't matter. Shirtless, his toned abs were like something on the cover of a magazine, so perfect they must have been drawn on. Some sort of tattoo wove a little dance around his biceps and trailed across the hairless chest. I couldn't tell if they were pictures or symbols, though.

I was too busy salivating, too busy imagining myself running a hand along those sculpted muscles, riding their curves with my fingertips. Mmm…

And he kind of reminded me of someone. Someone famous.

The name surfaced in my subconscious, watery and distant at first, but then he looked straight at me. The music helped my head clear.

Adam Levine.

This man was the spitting image of the lead singer of Maroon Five, and as I thought that, their song swelled in the background, his recorded voice crooning he would kiss me till I was drunk and he had the moves like Jagger. I let out a slow breath, wondering what that would be like.

Adam—how could I think of him by any other name—smiled, and we all giggled like high school virgins. He looked at each of us, almost as if he was having a silent conversation with his eyes.

Did I imagine his eyes lingered longest on me?

Did I imagine the words I heard in my head as clearly as if he stood next to me?

You are the one, Maisy. The one I've been waiting for all this time.

I nodded my head, certain I was the one, that Jensen was some guy I used to know, that Rebecca was not even my child, that I could run off and—

Rebecca.

Thinking of her made me come back to reality.

My daughter was the most important thing. Why else would I have agreed to hang out with the neighborhood bitches? Didn't matter how much my neighbor was a doppelganger for Adam Levine, I would never run off and leave her. What on Earth had I been thinking?

I looked down, surprised to see my vodka tonic floating in the water. It had slipped unnoticed from my hands. A quick glance at the other ladies showed they hadn't seen my *faux pau*, so I scooped up the glass and put it on the stone table next to the hot tub. The lights in the water changed colors again, this time going to a dreamy, soft purple.

Adam smiled once more and nodded before retreating back inside the house. I have no idea why he came out in the first place, but the next thing we knew, the French doors closed, breaking the spell we were under.

"Oh my god," Zero said reverently. "Did I just die and go to heaven?"

"He was so…so…beautiful," Sophia whispered. "I wish I could paint him. Or better yet, sculpt him."

"I'm going to have to go home and rename my vibrator." Jane sighed. "I'm going to call it Brad."

"Brad?" I asked. "Why Brad?"

"Because that man was Brad Pitt."

Had we been salivating over the same guy?

"Brad Pitt has brownish-blond hair," I pointed out. "And he's shorter."

"What the hell are you talking about?" Zero asked. "He was not Brad Pitt."

Good. For a second there, I thought I'd gone crazy. There is no resemblance between Brad Pitt and Adam Levine. Jane needed to get a better education about Who's Who in the world of entertainment.

"He was Dylan McDermott." Zero's voice was dreamy. "He reminded me of that scene in the first season of *American Horror Story* where he comes downstairs with his shirt off."

Dylan McDermott? Well, at least he had dark hair. But I knew who I'd seen.

Adam Levine.

We argued about it for a while. Sophia had seen someone completely different, too. She'd thought he was more of a Channing Tatum type with broad shoulders and huge muscles.

The more we argued, the less defined his features stayed in my memory. And opening that bottle of cheap champagne didn't help at all. Soon, none of us could recall the exact details of our new neighbor.

Around two in the morning, they finally staggered home, but not before Jane and Zero tried to get frisky with each other in the hot tub. Sophia and I had been arguing about the neighbor when I'd heard Jane gasp. Looking over, I saw one of her breasts had been freed from the cup of her bra. Zero's lips were clamped firmly on top of the nipple.

"Oh sweet, Jesus," Jane moaned, not at all upset by it. "Oh my god, that feels so nice."

Uh-uh. No way. No drunken sex was happening in my hot tub.

"Alexis! Jane!" I barked, making them jump guiltily. "It's time to go home. Do that shit somewhere else."

Both women's eyes dilated a bit in the dim light of the hot tub, but they nodded and slid out of the water without another word. They balanced against each other unsteadily as they left through the back gate.

"What sluts," Sophia said before leaving too.

****

As I slipped into the bedroom, Jensen snored in greeting. Briefly, I thought about climbing under the covers and seeing if I could wake him up, maybe finally get rid of all my pent up sexual tension, but my stomach revolted on me. I dashed to the bathroom and worshipped the porcelain god for a few minutes.

It's hard to feel sexy after that. Not that I had the guts to really get naughty with Jensen. He'd probably push me away. The only reason we slept in the same bed was so Rebecca wouldn't ask questions.

The best I could do was brush my teeth, grab an old T-shirt, yank on some shorty shorts, and flop into bed. I lay on my back, listening to the even snores of my husband, lulled by them into a comfortable, hazy state. My last image was of the DVR and the red light shining on it, which indicated it was recording something. What had I programmed to record in the middle of the night?

The Phantom of the Opera.

Gerard Butler's version of *Past the Point of No Return* melts my butter every time.

"Christine shoulda ditched Raoul and run off with the Phantom," I muttered out loud, closing my eyes.

"Hmm…what?" Jensen asked, still sleeping. "Yes. Do that."

Sleep whispered into my brain, forcing my body to relax.

Then came the first of many strange dreams.

I opened my eyes, startled to find the curtains billowing inward from the open window like in an old romantic, black and white movie. I sat up, realizing I no longer wore the T-shirt. Instead, a long, silky white gown which clung to my boobs dripped of my curvy form. Jensen wasn't next to me, and the bed wasn't even mine. A silk canopy floated over the top of it with long drapes hanging down the sides which could be opened or closed for privacy.

It was the kind of bed I'd always wished for but could never afford, the kind in high school I had dreamed about losing my virginity in.

Adam Levine with his soulful eyes stood at the end of it.

Shirtless again, all the wonderful tight curves of his abs were on display. He wore a pair of worn jeans that hung low on his hips, hinting at the possibility of the delightful things the material might mask. Tattoos snaked around his skin like living creatures, encircling him from his biceps to his wrists where they interlocked like chains.

"I am a slave to you." He held out his arms. "I always have been."

He lowered his arms, and the tiniest swell of music could be heard in the room. As a music teacher, I pride myself on knowing a tune within the first few bars. This time, my musical theatre background kicked in, and I couldn't help but smile at the melody I heard.

It was the love song from Phantom of the Opera. *All I Ask of You.*

Adam sang the first verse to me. The sincerity in his eyes took my breath away. He sang the next verse, too, and then it was my turn to chime in. My voice is normally a little flat, something I agonize over as a teacher, but in this dream, it sounded like I'd been training in opera all my life. I fell to my knees on the bed and stretched my hands toward him, singing.

He took my hands in his, and a snap of electricity coursed between us as our skin made contact. Our voices swirled into a crescendo of tormented agony and unrequited love being discovered as we sang the next verse while staring deeply into each other's eyes.

At some point, he drew me from the bed, and we danced around the room as skilled as the celebrity dancers on *Dancing with the Stars.* And then, in a bold, dramatic, Broadway-styled routine, we faced each other, eyes locked by our passion, hands tightly grasped in between us as we sang the big moment of the song.

At the end of the line, Adam lowered his sensual lips to mine in a passionate kiss that involved tongue and left me breathless. He ran his fingers through my hair and then down my shoulder, causing goose bumps to break out on my skin.

He nuzzled my neck. The sensation of his lips brushing against my skin, his teeth cutting into my flesh, his tongue stroking the little sensitive area—it made me dizzy.

And a little orgasmic.

Adam lifted his head, giving me a knowing smile before scooping me up and carrying me to the bed, laying me down as if I were fragile flower. He drew back as the ending notes of our song sounded. Instead of singing the final line, he said it.

"Love me," he whispered and kissed me. His hand inched the nightgown up, and he brazenly stroked the damp cleft between my legs. I moaned softly. "That's all I want from you."

"Okay." My skin was on fire from his touch and an ache grew in me, all that pent up heat begging to be released. I would have agreed to anything at that point. I wanted more. So much more. "I can do that."

Greedy with need, I fumbled with the button on the top his jeans, desperate to see what lay beneath. Adam chuckled and took my hands in his, kissing the tips of my fingers.

"Sleep now," he whispered.

Sleep? Was he kidding? It was a dream. Where was my sexcapade?

His eyes locked onto mine again, and I got lost in those dreamy, hazel orbs. Exhaustion overwhelmed me, and because it seemed the easiest thing to do, I rolled over on my side, ready to comply.

Jensen's green eyes met mine, wide with wonder.

Where had he come from?

I woke up with a start and glanced around the room, sure Adam would still be there. But everything was quiet. The window was closed, and the blinds were tightly latched. Jensen still snored beside me.

Yet, there was a sense someone had just left the

room.

A light clicked off outside, and our bedroom was shrouded in darkness.

I settled back in the bed.

As I fell into sleep, I realized the light that clicked off outside had been the back porch light of my new neighbor. My Adam Levine.

What had he been doing up this late?

Had he been thinking about me, too?

Chapter Three

"So can I?" Rebecca's voice whined in my ear, a fly I couldn't easily swat away. "Please, Mom?"

I rolled over, wishing I had a glass of water to get the taste of "morning after" out of my mouth. Fuzzy tongue syndrome sucks, and because I'd slept with my mouth open, my throat now hurt. A drum line had taken up residency in my head overnight, and they pounded out a steady, throbbing beat which grew worse when I opened my eyes.

"What?" I muttered. Rebecca face was two inches from mine. Her blue eyes were wide with hope and anticipation. "Back up, please."

"Edgar asked if I could go to the pool with him and his family!" Impatient, Rebecca raised her voice. "So can I?"

"Sure. Uh-huh. Go." I hid my face in a pillow, banishing the sunlight and sight of the wild, brown tangles of hair all over Rebecca's head. "Put on…um…that stuff…"

Coherent thought fled as the darkness soothed my eyes.

"Sunscreen?" Rebecca's voice blasted from impatient to excited in two seconds. "No problem. Thanks, Mommy. You're the best."

"And brush that hair, kid. Looks like a bird's nest."

She scampered from the room before I could give

further instructions. Not that I wanted to. My body ached to go back to sleep.

"Really?" Jensen's amused voice disturbed my almost escape back to dreamland. "You're going to let her go swim with Seth and Sophia? After all your SOS shit?"

Wait. Was that what Rebecca had asked?

"Huh?" I rolled over, forcing one of my eyes open again. "Wha…what?"

"Edgar is Seth and Sophia's son."

"I know that. I know the names of all my daughter's friends."

I tried to sit up like a responsible parent as I mentally ticked through the list of kids Rebecca played with. Edgar. Which one of Sophia's kids was he?

"Wow." Jensen looked me up and down and quirked an eyebrow. "Wow. You must have been really drunk. You look…fantastic…this morning."

Which probably meant my own blonde hair was as tangled as Rebecca's, with last night's mascara caked under my eyes, and dried throw up stuck to my cheek.

Was it any wonder Jensen had never made a pass at me?

"I'm a little hung over."

"I'll bet." Jensen looked yummy in his tight jeans and blue, button-down shirt.

His new job believed in a relaxed dress code which I know he appreciated. For a moment, all I could think about was creeping over the bed and unbuttoning his shirt, maybe running one hand down his toned abs while the other hand mussed the soft, dirty blond hair he'd worked so hard to brush down.

He cocked his head. "You guys were pretty messed

up when I saw you."

"My head hurts."

"I figured that was why you let Rebecca go with the SOS family."

"Aw, hell." I got out of bed. "I need to go with her I guess."

"I'm sure she'll be fine, Maisy."

"You say that, but if I don't go, she'll be the kid who gets molested because I was too hung over to take her to the pool. I don't want to be a shitty parent."

"Too late." Laughing, Jensen dodged the pillow I tossed. "You're a great parent. I really think there is nothing to worry about. Let Rebecca have her fun."

I plopped back down in bed, letting out a long sigh. Jensen was probably right. Surely nothing would happen in broad daylight.

"Besides, Seth is not a sex offender because he molested anyone. He just likes to show off his wang," Jensen mocked. "I'm sure he'll be well-behaved at a swimming pool full of prepubescent girls."

And just like that, I was back on my feet.

"Take a shower before you go," Jensen called after me. "Maybe wash off some of the vomit I see in your hair."

Men.

I forced myself to shower and swallow two ibuprofen. Pulling my damp, blonde hair back into a ponytail, I grabbed a pair of old shorts, a Comic Con T-shirt, and my sunglasses. The granola bar I forced down wasn't near enough to stop the pitch and roll of my stomach. Even though it was wrong, I added a little leftover champagne we'd missed to my orange juice and packed it in a traveling cup before heading out the door.

Sipping on my hangover concoction, I managed to walk to the neighborhood pool.

The water shimmered in the hot morning sun. Kids of all ages were cannon balling in while their parents lounged in the white plastic pool chairs our HOA had bought last summer. Coconut-scented tanning oil had spilled by someone's towel, and thanks to my over-sensitive, alcohol-drenched stomach, the strong, sweet scent almost made me gag.

I closed my eyes, sipped my drink, and prayed I could keep everything down.

Exasperated with myself, I weaved my way through the neighborhood sunbathers to where the SOS family had set up their stuff. Seth and the kids were already bobbing up and down in the water, playing some diving game. To my tired eyes, it appeared his wang was still firmly tucked into his swim shorts. Rebecca waved at me, a happy grin on her plump little face.

"Maisy!" Sophia smiled. "Didn't know you would be joining us."

"Hey, girl," I greeted her. "You feel like hammered shit, too?"

"The worst," she moaned.

She didn't look like hammered shit though. Sophia reminded me of a sleek movie star in her white 1950's style swimsuit that was both classy and revealing. Her eyes were hidden behind a pair of white-rimmed glasses with tiny black polka dots. A matching scarf held back her long, golden tresses.

"Why did we drink so much?" Sophia waved me to the seat next to her. "Sit down. Let me sip from your cup. I can smell the alcohol radiating from it."

"Really?" I handed it to her. "I know it's wrong, but I needed a little something."

"Hair of the dog." She gulped the drink down, winced, and then passed it back. "My mother used to say that every Sunday as she sipped from her mimosa."

"My mother was not drinker." I sipped from my cup. "She had a whole other set of issues that would not have been helped by alcohol."

"Really? Like what?"

I thought about my mother, Elizabeth Harker. Self-proclaimed demon seer. She'd been in and out of mental institutions her whole life, had never been the nurturing type. Pops had referred to her as "Mommie Dearest."

I thought of her more as an Andrea Yates.

Both of them had heard voices that weren't there. Both of them had strong religious beliefs about the devil. Of course, Andrea had five kids, and my mother only had one.

More importantly, Andrea had been successful in her attempt to murder her children.

My mother had tried to kill me but failed.

An image of Momma surfaced in my memory. I remembered the last time she'd taken me to the pool. Her black swimsuit had complemented her fair skin and light hair, but she seemed unaware of how beautiful she was. The red lipstick she always wore had smudged a little, almost as if someone had just kissed her. An odd, dazed fog had clouded her eyes.

I wasn't sure what I'd said to upset her, but a few hours later, she'd tried to kill me. Momma had called me into the bedroom, her long, white silk robe swirling around her too thin body. Her hair was pinned up in a perfect ballerina bun, the blue in her eyes like ice chips.

Then she'd wrapped her cold hands around my neck and squeezed.

"Maisy?" Sophia's voice brought me back to the present. "You okay? You kind of spaced out there."

"I'm fine." I shook my head, trying to clear it even as rubbed at my neck. "Thinking about my mother always makes me feel…a little off."

"Mine, too. Let's not talk about them then." She shifted in her seat, silent for a moment. "So…did you happen to see our new neighbor again after we left? Good God, he was yummy looking."

"No. I went inside the house and passed out practically before my head hit the pillow."

Unless, of course, you counted the amazing sing along I had with Adam in my dreams…

"Well, I had the craziest dreams," Sophia confided, leaning closer to me. "And they all were about *him*."

"Really?"

A little twinge of jealously pricked at me. Adam was supposed to have only been in my dreams. He had no business in the nocturnal world of the incestuous creep next door.

"Uh-huh. Me and Brad Pitt totally got it on last night."

"I thought you said you were dreaming about the new neighbor."

"I was. He is a ringer for Mr. Pitt."

I sighed. Poor Sophia. She really needed to get her eyes checked, but I couldn't help feeling slightly relieved it wasn't my Adam she'd been with.

"He and I had all kinds of crazy monkey sex in my

dreams." Sophia glanced at Seth who still splashed in the pool. One hand fluttered nervously at the scarf holding back her hair. "I'm telling you it felt so...real. So amazing. I woke up feeling like I'd had the most erotic experience of my life."

"Interesting." I glanced at Seth. "Better than with your husband?"

She bit her lip. "Well, sex with Seth is always so...so..." She turned and lowered her glasses down her nose to make eye contact with me. "The dream sex I had with Brad Pitt trumped every sexual experience I've ever had. And then he did the kinkiest thing."

"Oh yeah? What?"

"He bit me." She blushed as if admitting it were some horrifying secret.

I tried not to laugh. "Bit you? Where?"

"On my inner thigh. I'm telling you, when his teeth sank into me, every fiber in my being came unglued. It was crazy."

"Did he draw blood? Or was it just an erotic nip?

"Just a nip. I think." She frowned. "I know you're going to think this is crazy, but...well, when I woke up this morning, look what I found." She peered around, scanning the area to be sure no one was paying attention to us. Satisfied, she sat up and then shifted her leg so I could see her inner thigh.

A set of bite marks stood out on the pale skin just below her bikini line.

Weird.

"Sophia, did it occur to you that Seth may have been messing with you while you were sleeping?" I asked. "Maybe he was totally feeling you up, getting his rocks off, and then he bit you or something."

Sophia stared, a strange little light in her eyes. Then she shoved her sunglasses back up and pulled her leg away so I could no longer see the bite. Her lips pursed.

"I guess you could be right," she said, looking out at her husband. "I suppose that's what happened."

"But that's a good thing. It means your husband can still make you feel a little bit wild and crazy. Isn't that what all married women hope for?"

She shrugged.

"You should ask him about it," I suggested. "He's probably wondering if you even remember."

"Yeah, maybe." I got the distinct impression Sophia was not happy with my thoughts on her dream.

Okay, I admit having dream sex with Brad Pitt does sound appealing, but no way was Brad really our neighbor. Sophia had drunk way too much if she was under the impression that he was. And to be dreaming about him? To be turned on by the thought of him biting her inner thigh? What kind of depraved world did Sophia live in?

Then again, I did sing songs from *Phantom of the Opera* with Adam Levine in my dreams. And I did feel very tingly in the vajayjay when he looked at me.

Who was I to judge?

"So…what do you think about Alexis's sex party idea?" I asked, deciding a change in subject might be good for both of us. "Think she'll really do it?"

"Are you kidding? I bet she's already been on the phone this morning setting it up." Sophia brightened. "Hey, we could invite the new neighbor."

"I guess so. I thought this kind of party was more for women."

But even as I said that, the idea of seeing him again in the flesh tantalized me. We all really needed another glimpse of the guy so we could agree on who he reminded us of.

"Oh, please. I'm sure it doesn't matter if men attend," Sophia said. "I'll text Alexis about it after while."

Sophia may have said it didn't matter, but I was willing to bet she wasn't going to have Seth come join us at the party.

We spent the rest of the morning lounging in the sun and watching the kids play. Jensen would have been proud. I'd managed to be social more than one day in a row with our neighbors.

This not being an asshole thing wasn't as hard as I thought it might be.

Chapter Four

I spent the rest of the day with sex on the brain.

Every time I tried to focus on something, my thoughts drifted to Adam and the wonderfully lush bed, imagining what could have happened if we hadn't stopped. In the span of one day, I'd turned into a horny housewife who needed to do the laundry and clean the house but couldn't think about anything but her dream lover.

It didn't help that later in the evening, I caught sight of Jensen naked.

He was getting out of the shower and hadn't shut the bathroom door all the way. Droplets of water covered him, sprinkling off his broad chest and down his firm tummy. My eyes swept down, glancing at his hard legs before traveling to the core of him.

I'd never seen him naked. Shirtless, yes. He liked to sleep in just pajama pants. I'd seen his strong arms on display, but viewing the full package was something I'd hadn't been privileged to. Looking at it now...damn.

My mouth watered at the sight of Jensen in all his glory.

Why had I been cursed to marry such a hottie? Why couldn't Pops have chosen someone a little less...delicious...to look at?

Fanning myself, I closed my eyes and forced

myself to make some noise in the bedroom.

"That you, Maisy?" he called.

"Who else would it be?" I tried to keep the mood light. "Your girlfriend?"

He didn't respond right away. Oh God. Did he have a girlfriend? It was possible. We'd never agreed to not see other people just because we were married. Still, I'd never thought about him seeing anyone else, and he'd never mentioned another woman. Not that he had to tell me anything.

And what did it matter? I may have been feeling a little hot in the britches, but it would pass. Jensen didn't care about me in a romantic way, and if he found someone he did care about...well, we'd have to negotiate another aspect of the marriage.

"What did you say?" He stepped outside the bathroom, a towel covering his lower body while he used another to dry his hair. "Something about a girlfriend?"

"I was teasing you." I smiled and subtly wiped at the drool on the side of my mouth. "You got a hot date or something? You took a shower early tonight."

"I might need to go out later. Work stuff. You know how it is."

"Yeah."

Jensen did some very specialized work. I'm not even sure what you would call it really. He's not a cop or a private detective, but if you want to find out someone's secrets, Jensen is your guy. Pops had always thought Jensen was one of his best employees because he could use not only his fists but his mind, too. Because of that, Pops had encouraged him to work for the small computer software firm called The Institute when they started sniffing around for new talent. The head of the company had seemed very eager to snatch Jensen up.

Software firm, my ass! No matter how Pops tried to dress it up, whatever Jensen was doing had nothing to do with writing software. I assumed he was some sort of hacker.

See, when someone runs an organization like Pops had, having brawns *and* brains were important. I had never been privy to the ins and outs of the "business" as Pops had liked to call it, but I knew not everything he did was legal.

Or safe.

To the outsider, Pops—Thomas King to the world—had appeared to run a mechanics shop. Used cars, new cars, classic cars—they all found their way to his place where he and the guys who had worked for him would fix them. Nothing odd about any of that.

But Pops' employees were the kind of men who could get information about all kinds of other things, information people would pay good money for. Want to know if your wife is cheating? Want to know the color of your neighbor's panties? Who really shot JFK? These guys could find out for you, and their methods weren't always friendly. So from time to time, people would get pissed at Pops about the information he sold and would try to retaliate.

Pops had tried to shield me from the worst of it, but when a gunfight is going on above your head as you hide in the cellar, it's hard to ignore that something is a little off in your home life. However, I learned early on not to ask too many questions.

When I was a teenager, Jensen would show up at

the house where Pops and I lived, covered with all sorts of cuts and bruises. When I asked Jensen how he got them, he only smiled while Pops would tell me to mind my business and go to my room. I used to fantasize Jensen was like an American James Bond, taking on the evils of the world while I slept safe in my bed.

And even back then, my fantasies often involved our bodies fused together in a steamy night of unbridled passion and soft, morning-after kisses.

Reality sucked. I slept with a hot man who wasn't interested in me.

Well, it was too late to turn back. Pops was gone, and Jensen's sense of loyalty to him would never allow him to divorce me. If he wanted a girlfriend, I should be willing to turn a blind eye to it. He'd given up enough for me already.

"You okay?" Jensen asked. I tried not to stare at the sight of him so scantily dressed. "You seem flustered."

"I'm fine. I was thinking about curling up in bed, maybe watching a movie."

"Sounds nice. You want me to get you a glass of wine, or are you done with alcohol for a while?"

"I'm good."

"Okay. I'm going to do a little work in my office for a few minutes. I'll lock up if I have to go to work."

I took a quick shower, trying not to think about how good Jensen looked naked or how the scent of the soap he used to wash himself lingered in the air, a constant reminder of what I couldn't have. I never thought I'd find myself wishing to be a bar soap. It certainly got more action than I did.

I got into bed, unable to shake off the small fire of

sexual energy humming beneath my skin. The soft, blue silk nightgown I wore reminded me of the one I'd been wearing in my dreams the evening before. As I slipped beneath the sheets, the delicate material rubbed against my nipples, making my overactive libido even more alert. My hands brushed over my breasts, sliding down my body to hover just above my waist. I'd worn no panties, and the urge to touch the softest part of my body grew strong.

But Jensen was just down the hall.

What if he walked in?

Just do it. So what if he catches you. Maybe you can convince him to join you. You can be pretty persuasive when you want to be…

Thinking of Jensen, I closed my eyes and slipped my hand over my skin, tingling with anticipation. I sighed as I found my clit, rubbing it gently, letting the feeling of being naughty intoxicate me.

Let yourself go. Let yourself feel.

The words were in my head but not in my voice.

Adam.

The sound of him bathed my senses in lust as I caressed myself. Pictures flooded my head, incoherent at first, but gradually my imagination took over, guiding me into a new fantasy.

I imagined myself with Adam.

In this fantasy, I lay spread-eagle and naked on a bed covered in black silk sheets and oversized pillows. A large mirror overhead reflected everything—the roundness of my full breasts, the slight tan of my skin, the curve of my hips, the way my finger worked over my clit.

My face didn't look like me. At least not normal

me. I looked pale, but my blue eyes were bright as was the brilliant red of my lipstick. I ran my free hand across my nipples, gently tugging at each of them while my hand continued to stroke and tease, slipping into the dampness between my legs.

Then something in the room changed.

Candles flared to life all around me, and the sweet scent of vanilla and lavender perfumed the air. I jerked my hand away, suddenly afraid. Darkness lay beyond the glow of the candles and someone stood at its edge, watching me.

"Don't stop," a male voice rumbled. "I like to see you enjoy yourself."

"Who are you?" Instinctively, I pulled one of the black sheets up, covering myself. "Come into the light."

There was no answer.

An invisible hand yanked the sheet away, revealing me to the stranger.

"I like to look you at," the voice soothed. "No need to be afraid."

Unseen hands stroked my ankles. "Lay back."

I hesitated.

"Please, Maisy."

The way he said "please" struck a sexual match inside me, and I knew the man now. *Adam.* His voice was the same timbre as the angel who'd sung with me in my dreams the evening before. My fear left. There was a rush of heat between my legs as something stroked my thigh. A finger? I wasn't sure, but pent up desire—wild and hard—coursed through me.

"Touch yourself," Adam commanded, raw lust in his voice. "Do as I bid."

My finger stroked the sensitive area between my

legs. He chuckled softly, and the sound made the fire in me grow. A mouth closed in on my breast, causing me to cry out. I stared at the mirror above, loving the feeling, but confused at what I saw reflected back.

There was no one on the bed but me.

I moaned as the invisible mouth sucked and bit at my breasts, switching from one to the other. As it did so, I thrust a finger inside myself, the gentle build of an orgasm rippling through my sex. But I didn't want it quite yet. I wanted my body burning with sexual fire, wanted to be devoured by my invisible lover, my Adam.

His mouth left my nipples, and he chuckled at the sigh of disappointment I made.

"Don't worry. We aren't done here." His tongue trailed down my stomach. "Put your hands above your head. Let me finish this for you."

Once again, I did as I was told.

A tongue lapped at the cleft between my legs.

"Oh god," I moaned. "That feels amazing."

Lips closed around the little mound of flesh, nibbling at it like a delicacy until I was in a frenzy. A tongue slid in and out of my wetness, allowing its owner's mouth to suck on my clit.

The mirror reflected a wanton woman, thrashing passionately alone on the bed. I could hardly believe it was me.

And then things got crazy.

Even as my invisible lover worked me over, two separate mouths closed on each of my nipples, tonguing them with expertise. Multiple hands stroked my skin, leaving trailing imprints of heat, building the fire ignited within me. Someone kissed me, their lips soft and tender. Overwhelmed, I kissed the invisible stranger back, loving the dizzy spell I was under even as the battering tongue against my clit drove me toward a climax.

Waves of pleasure rolled through me as I reached my peak.

That's when I felt the hardness of a cock slide deeply inside me. I gasped, still coming from the orgasm already started. The depths my invisible lover prodded were almost painful, but I'd never felt so full, so complete.

So at the mercy of someone else.

My hands were pinned to the bed, my legs spread. I saw no one and yet, I was being fucked hard and long, and I loved every minute of it. My lover kissed me, momentarily stifling my cries of pleasure before he nuzzled at my neck with soft butterfly kisses.

The pace of our union quickened. Stronger, deeper he plunged in and out of me. He shifted my legs so they were in the air and I could take all of his hard cock. That delicious spark of an orgasm built again, and his teeth sank into the soft skin of my neck.

"Oh god," I whispered, closing my eyes, wishing I could wrap my arms around this unseen man, wanting to feel the heat of all of him as he came inside me. "Yes!"

He sucked at my neck. I opened my eyes, desperate to catch a glimpse of him in the mirror above us. Perhaps his guard was down, because this time, I could clearly see him. His rounded and well-toned ass muscles contracted at the exertion of his amorous movements. The dark hair on his head confirmed for me who this invisible playmate was though I couldn't see his face.

Adam.

"Adam," I whispered, unable to help myself. "You're amazing. Please let me touch you."

He chuckled against my neck, and just like that my hands were free, the spell holding them hostage against the sheets broken. I ran my fingers along his back, loving the smooth skin before I gripped his ass, wrapping my legs around him, and using my inner muscles to milk his cock with everything I had.

This time, he moaned. Adam jerked back, his eyes dilated with so much lust they almost appeared to be shadowed with red.

"You are special," he whispered. "This time, I know it will be you."

I glanced in the mirror. Blood dripped from my neck and onto the black sheets. Where had it come from? Dazed, I could do nothing but enjoy the bliss of my second orgasm as it shot through me. Adam's cock surged, and he cried out, finding his release, too. Breathless, I closed my eyes, unaware of anything else for a while as I fell into a light sleep.

When I awoke, darkness shrouded my own bedroom except by the window. The blinds were rolled up, the glass slightly open. How had that happened? Had Jensen come in?

And how had my imagination conjured up to such a vivid fantasy?

A shadow flitted to life in the room, coming toward the bed. A man—but it wasn't Jensen or even Adam.

I couldn't hold back a squeal of surprise. Actually, it may have been more like a scream because Jensen came running down the hall.

"Maisy?" Jensen's face was serious as he stepped in the room, snapping on the overhead light. He looked around, ready to clobber anything that moved or shoot it with the gun clutched in his right hand. "Where is he?"

No one was there. The bright light flooding the area proved that.

"I just...just dozed off and had a weird dream." I tried to calm down, to think rationally. "No big deal. I didn't mean to scream."

Jensen stared, his expression unreadable.

"Really, I'm fine, Jensen. Go back to whatever you were working on." I eyed the gun and then looked back, composing myself as if I had everything under control. I stared at him. "Go on. And be careful with that thing. Make sure you put it where Rebecca can't reach it."

Almost against his will, he left the room, the muscle in his right jaw twitching. That little movement told me a lot. Anytime Jensen was worried, I would see that twitch. I'd scared him with my scream.

I'd scared myself. And to be honest, no matter how cool I tried to be about it to Jensen, my nerves were on edge. I knew what I'd seen. A shadow of a man. And the blinds...they'd been up with the window slightly open.

They were closed tight now. How was that even possible?

Oh god. Was I starting to lose my mind? Was I turning into my mother, seeing things that weren't there?

I touched my neck, reminded of my dream and of one of the paintings my mother had once created. It had depicted a naked woman lying on a swooning couch.

Her face had been twisted in a mask of pleasure as if she'd been ravished. Blood dripped from a gaping wound in her neck, creating a dark puddle on the floor. In the window just behind the couch, Momma had painted the shadow a man peering into the room.

I half way expected to feel blood on my own neck.

But there was nothing there.

Taking several deep breaths, I forced myself to calm down. That's when I became aware of a new sound. Faintly, I could hear something being scraped—metal on metal.

I sat up, thinking it came from the window, but as I listened, it seemed to be coming from somewhere else in the house. What the hell was that? With one last look at the closed blinds, I got out of bed, pulling the blanket along, too. Wrapping it around me, I opened the bedroom door and peered out into the dark hall.

A sliver of light escaped from beneath the door of Jensen's office.

Clink. There it was again.

What was Jensen doing? I could have easily knocked on the door and found out, but for some reason, my instinct was to stay quiet, to not let him know I was there. Cracking the door, I peered in.

Jensen sat at his desk, his Bluetooth headset on. He talked to someone and was turned so he didn't see me. He held a wicked-looking knife with a curved blade attached to an old and worn handle. Jensen sharpened it with a grinding stone, running the blade along it with practiced precision as he spoke in low tones.

The sound gave me chills, filling me with dread.

That's when I saw the chest on the floor.

Wooden and about the size of a small beer cooler,

its lid was open, displaying the weapons inside it. Many of them appeared to be antiques. A few had strange markings and symbols. All were some sort of knife or sword.

I closed the door and crept back to the bedroom, feeling ill. The sight of all that hardware so obviously meant to cause pain upset me, reminding me of the past, of my childhood with Momma, of scary times with Pops.

I slid under the covers, rearranging the blankets. As I did, I thought about Jared Ramos, my mother's last boyfriend before she was locked in the mental ward. Six foot two with a massive frame and long, braided black hair, Jared had adored my mother. He'd followed her around like a love-sick puppy.

She'd always had the power to make even the strongest of men do her bidding.

But seeing Jensen with the knife collection reminded me of a memory of Jared, the last one I have of him. Jared also had a cache of weapons similar to what I'd just seen and had spent considerable time taking care of them.

One of them ended up planted deep in his chest, the handle stained with blood.

My mother had put it there.

I shuddered. In the end, Jared hadn't been able to protect himself, even with all of those knives. Death in the form of my mother had come for him.

What did Jensen need protection from?

Chapter Five

Five minutes in to her sex toy party, Zero to Sixty was already drunk as a skunk.

Bloodshot eyes and smeared mascara accented her mane of red hair and made her look like a bizarre clown as she clutched the large red vibrator, a big grin on her face. Her black painted nails reminding me of talons.

"Damn! This thing is huge!" she proclaimed. "I could do some damage with this."

Everyone laughed.

"Don't forget your lube," Jane called. "It's Pina Colada flavored."

"Oh, I don't need lube." Zero rolled her eyes. "I'm always ready."

The ladies giggled, including the hostess of the sex party. She was a short, voluptuous woman with bobbed black hair who Zero had introduced as Bianca Rivera, the Lovely Lust associate. Zero had gathered a mix of neighborhood women and other friends for her party, so I figured Bianca would have her hands full with orders later on. With the air of a worldly woman, Bianca gazed at us shrewdly, assessing who would most likely be a customer.

"Ladies, are you ready to see the next product? This one is my personal favorite." Bianca picked up a new toy. "It's called the Love Buzz."

She displayed a mechanical blue egg. A cord on it

led to an oblong-shaped controller with a button at the top. Bianca held the egg in one hand and tapped the controller button, causing the whole thing to buzz.

"Put this on your special spot, and you'll be in sexual heaven in thirty seconds," Bianca said.

"Thirty seconds?" Jane complained. "I like to work up to the big O."

"I thought you might say that." Smug and superior, Bianca hit the controller again. The egg buzzed in a different tempo. "The Love Buzz has several rhythms you can choose from so you can prolong your satisfaction."

"Ahhhhh." All the ladies breathed out the sound together, anticipating the feel of such a marvel.

All except Sophia.

She sat in the corner, her eyes bright and alert, but there were dark hollows beneath them as if she hadn't slept much. Though an early summer storm wreaked havoc outside, she'd chosen to wear jeans and long-sleeved shirt which seemed a bit hot for June. Occasionally, she would run her finger along her inner thigh almost as if she didn't realize she was doing it.

I hadn't talked to her since I'd seen her at the pool last week. Was she still having dreams about my neighbor?

I sure was.

For the last few nights, hot dream sex with Adam had invaded my sleep. Each encounter left me breathless and longing for more—though he'd never bitten me again. I'd even considered totally embarrassment by throwing myself at Jensen to relieve some of the sexual tension.

The crazy part was that I hadn't seen any sign of

my new neighbor since the hot tub night. He wasn't active during the day, and when I peered through the hole in the back fence, I could see nothing to give me any more clues about who he really was. Logically, I understood there was no way a rock star lived in the house behind me, and I had no business being such a snoop.

And yet because of those dreams, I felt like I knew him. Intimately.

Someone knocked on Zero's door, interrupting my reflections.

Sophia perked up, a little smile on her face. "I'll get that!" she announced, moving to the door and flinging it open. The warm night air trickled in along with a soft spray of rain and the most delicious scent—it was like vanilla and chocolate all rolled into one—the perfect catnip for women buying sex toys. "I've been waiting for you!"

The room fell silent when *he* walked in.

Adam Levine. My neighbor. Horny woman catnip.

He filled the doorframe, heat and merriment radiating from him like an aphrodisiac. A broad smile showed off his white teeth. The summer rain had drenched the blue T-shirt he wore, and it clung to his well-toned abs, inviting us to rip it off and see what lay beneath.

"Ladies, I hope I'm not intruding." He ran a hand through his black hair. "Alexis invited me over."

"You're…you're not intruding," Jane slinked toward him. "Come in. You can sit by me."

He grinned at her easy invitation and stepped into the room, shutting the door behind him.

"You must be Jane." Adam touched her arm, and I

felt a stab of jealousy. "Alexis told me all about you."

"She did?" Jane blushed. "I hope it was only the good stuff."

"But it's the bad stuff which intrigues me."

He turned back to Sophia, who practically salivated at the sight of him.

"Sophia, we meet again." He lifted her hand to his lips, but at the last moment, he turned it so he kissed her wrist instead. She shivered, and like two headlights turning on, her nipples got hard enough to poke at the fabric of her shirt for all of us to see. "A pleasure to see you."

She giggled.

Adam gazed at Zero next.

"And my sweet Alexis, the lovely hostess," he purred. "Thank you for inviting me. I would have been bored at home on a night like this."

"You invited him?" Jane asked.

"Well, sure." Zero shrugged casually with a mischievous gleam in her eye. "I went over yesterday evening and welcomed him to the neighborhood."

Welcomed my ass. She probably threw herself at him.

"It was a fine welcome. Now I feel properly...at home." He chuckled. Damn, but the sound was sexy. "I hope the rest of you don't mind that I'm here."

The other ladies all made appreciative noises, but I stayed silent as he greeted them.

He hadn't even noticed me.

Was I so hideous, so unworthy? I mean, I'd only taken the time to dream about him every night. We'd done totally mind-blowing things together. Never mind that he didn't know about them. The least he could do was glance at me, give me a nod, or something.

Adam turned to Bianca. "And you are?" His back stiffened, and while his words to her were friendly, there was a trace of coolness in them.

"Bianca." She tilted her head to the side, studying him with none of the lust on her face that the rest of us felt at seeing him. "You look familiar. Have we met before?"

"I don't think so," Adam said. "I've traveled quite a bit, though."

With a dismissive nod, he turned from her, and at last his gaze settled on me.

"Hello." His lazy smile made my heart do flip flops. "You're the neighbor who lives behind me, right? I've seen you from time to time in the back yard."

Oh god. I hope he didn't see me spying through the hole in the fence.

"Yes." I managed to stay composed despite the heat radiating around us. "I'm Maisy Harker." I extended my hand.

He took it gently, his thumb caressing the inside of my palm. "Harker?"

"Yes. You've probably seen my husband around, too. His name is Jensen."

He released my hand. "Where is Mr. Harker tonight?"

"Oh, he's not Mr. Harker," Zero broke in. "Maisy and Jensen are modern newlyweds. She didn't take his last name when they got married."

"So Harker is your maiden name." Adam seemed amused by this information. "Interesting."

"It's a family name," Zero continued as if we were best friends or something, but I think she wanted the attention back on herself. "All the women in her family keep their maiden name."

"Thank you so much for sharing personal information with a stranger," I snapped. "I'm so glad I made the decision to tell you about it in confidence. Why don't you go sit down and sniff the lubricants again?"

Zero blinked, unsure if I was being sarcastic or was really mad. Hell, I wasn't sure myself. I only knew Adam had been talking to me. Not her. *Me.*

The funny thing was that Zero did exactly as I asked. She sat down and picked up the nearest lubricating oil, sniffing it.

"Maisy, your secrets are safe with me." Adam's eyes darkened a bit. "Anything you share would be safe with me."

Like my body? My soul? My heart?

Little adulterous leaves of dirty thoughts drifted through my mind.

Adam turned away, and I couldn't help the disappointment at losing his attention.

"So what's been going on?" he asked. "What naughty things have you girls been up to so far?"

The women gathered around, thrusting different vibrators and lubes at him in their quest to be the one he favored with a comment. I hung back, hurt at being dismissed without a second thought while the little voice of my conscience tried to soothe me.

You are so silly. It's not like he knows you've built a dream relationship with him.

That didn't make it any easier.

Something about Adam radiated familiarity as if I'd always known him. The way he moved, the sound

51

of his laugh, the curve of his ass in his tight jeans—I'd seen it all before.

Or at least, it felt that way.

"Would you like some wine, Maisy?" Bianca hovered nearby, watching the women fawn over Adam. "I know I could use another glass."

"Then let's go to the kitchen and get one." It hurt to leave Adam, but since he was obviously not paying attention to me, I figured I might as well top off my drink. "C'mon."

In the kitchen, a rush of cool air spilled over me. The jealousy dissipated so quickly I felt off balance. I hadn't experienced a quick change of emotion like that since the first time I started my period and became insanely hormonal. Pops had nicknamed me Maisy KaBoom because of my ever changing mood swings back then.

What the hell had just happened?

Bianca refilled our glasses. The woodsy aroma of the cabernet we drank soothed me, bringing me back to reality.

"Who is that man in the living room?" she asked. "Everyone seems very taken by him."

"The new neighbor. He moved in a few days ago."

"Oh? He looks so familiar to me. What's his name?"

It was on the tip of my tongue to say Adam, but I realized I didn't know for sure. He'd come in and greeted us, but never introduced himself. Sure, he looked like Adam Levine, but come to think of it, I'd not heard him say his name. Maybe he was such a big star there was no need for an introduction.

"You know, I don't know for sure, but I think it's

Adam."

Bianca narrowed her eyes. "Adam? "Why would you think that?"

"He reminds me of the singer from Maroon Five."

"Adam Levine?"

"Yeah. Do you know who I'm talking about?" I sipped from the wine. "Those other girls tried to tell me he was Brad Pitt or Dylan McDermott."

"Maybe that's who they see when they look at him."

"Um...Bianca, Brad Pitt and Adam Levine don't look anything alike."

"True." Bianca smiled. "But this man in the living room has never actually told you his name. Don't you think that's odd?"

"That is kind of weird." I frowned and picked up a piece cheese from a nearby platter. "I mean, who saunters into someone's house for the first time and doesn't give out the basics, right?"

"A man with secrets."

Secrets. I didn't like those. It's one thing to gossip or know things about others, but some secrets were dangerous.

If Bianca was right about Adam, then he was someone to be careful around. No matter how good looking he was. Or how hot he looked in a wet T-shirt. Or how much his smile made me feel weak in the knees.

"You are attracted to this man," Bianca mused. "I can see that."

"Well, duh. Aren't you?"

"No. He's not my type."

"What are you? A lesbian?"

"I am not a lesbian." Bianca grinned. "Though I do have sex with women. I'm bisexual."

"No wonder Zero was so anxious to have you host a party," I muttered.

"Tell me, do you feel as attracted to him now that he's out of your sight?"

"Well…" I paused, thinking about it. In the other room, my body had been gripped with sexual tension and jealousy, but the minute I'd stepped away, that heat had disappeared. "I—I don't know."

"I think you do know." Bianca gave me a stern look. "Hold out your hand."

"Why?"

"I won't hurt you. Just let me see it."

Instead of waiting for me to give it to her, Bianca grabbed my hand, studying the palm intently, her nose wrinkling at whatever she saw there.

"You are special, Maisy," she said. "You have a swerving lifeline. It's all over the place."

"You read palms? Are you a gypsy and a sex addict?"

"How ever did you guess?" Her eyes met mine, amused. "Actually, I do have a bit of gypsy blood in me. Palmistry is my specialty."

"That's so cool. What do you mean I have a swerving lifeline? I thought life lines were supposed to be straight?"

"Your life is full of adventure. Many adventures it would seem. Frankly, I'm surprised by it." Bianca's eyes were dark and calculating. The sudden intensity of her gaze chilled me almost as if she were seeing past me and into my soul. "But you have to get around this first destiny."

"First destiny?" I tried to laugh, but she was so serious that the sound got caught in my throat. "Can there be more than one?"

"Not for most in your line. You will be special."

The temperature in the kitchen changed. The cool air whisked away, replaced by the same sexual heat I'd felt only moments before.

"There you two are. We were wondering if you were going to come back and finish the party, Bianca."

I knew without turning who had entered the room and so did my nipples. Like Sophia's had, they perked up, hardening at the sound of Adam's voice, begging to be touched. I pulled my hand away from Bianca, fanning myself.

"I guess I should get back to Alexis and the others," she said.

"I think Alexis is eyeing something called 'Nip Tips'," Adam said.

"And what have you been eyeing?" Bianca asked.

For a second, Adam looked annoyed. "Not a thing." He turned slightly and spoke directly to me. "I have no need for sex toys."

"Are you coming, Maisy?" Bianca called over her shoulder. "Looks like your glass is plenty full now."

"Sure." I brushed past Adam, my arm feeling the coolness of his skin. Such a contrast to the heat he gave off. "Excuse me."

Before I knew what happened, his hand snaked out and stopped me from leaving. "Wait a moment." He smiled. "I'd like to talk to you."

"About what?" My face flushed and I had that high school feeling, the one where you find yourself by the lockers with the cutest boy in school, but then you don't know what to say. You just pray you don't start babbling. "Is something wrong?"

"Wrong?" He shook his head. "No. It's just that I've been a bad neighbor. I should have introduced myself that night when I saw you and the others in the hot tub."

"Oh, well, it's probably just as well you didn't. We were all a little relaxed."

"Relaxed? Don't you mean drunk?" He cocked his head to the side, a charming smirk on his face.

We laughed.

"That, too." I sipped from my wine. "I'm not sure we would have made the best impression."

"You could never make a bad one."

He stepped closer, and the scent of his vanilla spice cologne wrapped around me.

"Well, I think I need to get back out there," I said, trying to ignore the flush of pleasure winding through me at his compliment and at his scent. "Sex toys don't hang around forever, you know."

"I'm sure we'll talk again."

I headed back into the living room where the ladies were cackling over something Zero had said. There was a moment of blissful cool air, but it was immediately smothered by the heat Adam seemed to carry with him.

The rest of the evening ticked by as I tried to maintain control over my feelings.

Adam's deep rumbling laughter mixed with the high-pitched, delighted squeals of my neighbors. All the women jostled each other from time to time, trying to get closer to Adam. I thought Sophia and Jane might even duke it out at one point when Jane slid into the open spot next to him on the couch and subtly sniffed his neck. The anger in Sophia's eyes was unmistakable. Luckily, Adam scooted over and created a spot for Sophia on the other side of him.

Then it was time to order our Lovely Lust products. I was torn. So many choices. I thought of the glimpse of Jensen's cock I'd seen the other day. Which one of these vibrators would be a close match to the thing I wanted most of all? Dream sex was nice, but real sex was better.

"Can't decide?" Adam's breath was warm in my ear as I studied the catalog. "That one looks interesting." He pointed to the Love Buzz. "I think it's supposed to provide extra stimulation." He put a hand on my shoulder, squeezing gently. "Extra stimulation can be a good thing."

Oh boy. Thoughts of all the things he'd done to me in my dreams flashed in my head.

"You know what?" I tried to sound calm and collected, tried to shove my own dirty thoughts to the back of my mind. "I just realized I don't know your name."

The room stilled. For the first time, Adam looked uncomfortable. His suave, self -assuredness melted away, and he glanced around, noting the anticipation from the other women. Narrow eyed, Bianca leaned forward.

"My name is…" A strange energy pulsed in the room, followed by a loud hum. I shook my head. Through a thick curtain of white noise, I heard him say his name. "Adam."

I knew it. He was Adam Levine.

Yet as I prepared to gloat my triumph, the other ladies looked equally triumphant, as if they'd been right all along, too.

Bianca was the only one who didn't look happy. Her eyes widened, and a beaded line of sweat broke out on her forehead. One hand flew up to her mouth as if she were trying to keep back a scream.

"You all right?" I went to her. "Bianca?"

"Yes…" She stammered, looking down at the floor. Her body swayed, and I steadied her by taking her elbow. "Yes, I'm fine, but I need to be going. I don't…I don't feel well."

She wobbled over to Zero.

"Alexis," Bianca said, touching a hand to her head. "I'm not feeling well. I've got a pounding headache and need to go. It's a migraine. Once they get started…oh…" She shivered and swayed again.

"But what about our orders? I need at least two of these vibrators." Zero could have cared less about Bianca's health. "I'm going to spend a lot of money."

"I'll come back and collect them tomorrow."

"You're leaving your inventory, too?" Zero asked.

"Yes. I'll come back tomorrow." Bianca practically ran for the front door, her face pale.

"Bianca?" I followed her outside where she slid easily into her car, oblivious to the falling rain. "Do you need me to give you a ride? If you're that sick, maybe you shouldn't be driving."

"No. No…I can handle it." She wiped at her forehead. "You be careful."

"Of what?"

"What did you hear when he said his name?"

"Adam. Just like I thought. Why? What did you hear?"

Instead of answering, Bianca fumbled in her glove

box for something before pulling out a business card. She pressed it in my hand. "Call if things get bad," she whispered. "I can help." She slammed the car door.

"With what?" I called, watching her through the window fumble with getting her car keys out of her purse. "What should I be careful with?"

She gave me a half wave as she roared out of the driveway, her taillights lighting up the wet night as she drove off.

"What a strange woman." Adam stood a few yards away, having crept up without me knowing. The rain drenched him, but it only made him sexier. I found myself vaguely wondering what it would be like to screw him right there in the front lawn as the water fell around us. "I wonder what's wrong with her."

Her? What was wrong with me? Screw my neighbor on the lawn? What was going on with my head these days? I shook my head, trying to clear it. I forced myself to give him an apologetic smile.

"I don't know, but you know what? I don't feel so well, either. I'd better head on home."

"So soon?"

"It's kind of late actually. And it's raining. I'm getting soaked."

"A little rain is good for the soul."

"Ya'll coming back in?" Zero stood in the doorway, frowning at us. "Rain is coming in my foyer."

"Alexis," I called over Adam's shoulder. "I've got to go. I'll see you tomorrow."

"I'll walk you home," Adam said.

"I live across the street, so that's not necessary."

"A lot can happen between here and there." He grinned. "Better safe than sorry."

"I'm good, but thanks for the offer."

"When will I see you again?" Was that desperation in his voice? "I really want to talk to you somewhere less…crowded."

"Why?" I couldn't help but be incredulous. Me? Adam Levine wanted to talk to me? "I'm nobody."

"Nobody?" He shook his head and then touched my chin so he could look into my eyes. His own were a deep, intense mix of green and brown I found captivating. "Oh, Maisy Harker, you are so wrong about that. You have no idea who you really are, what kind of power you actually hold. I look forward to helping you discover it."

Chills went through me. Maybe he meant to be flirtatious, but his words…. I'd heard them before. I couldn't quite recall where. An image of Adam leaning over me flitted through my mind. Maybe it was during one of my dreams?

"We'll talk soon," I said, trying to keep things light. "I'm sure we can shout at each other through the back fence or something. I've got to go now."

As I looked across the street, the porch light of my house snapped on.

Jensen opened the front door and stepped out. He frowned and crossed his arms when he saw Adam.

"Who is that?" Adam asked.

"Jensen. My husband."

I darted away from Adam, letting the summer mist drench me as I went home. Once I reached the safety of my porch, I turned back.

But I didn't see Adam Levine.

Instead, something horrific and frightening replaced his handsome features, reminding me of my mother's description of a creature she always claimed to see around her. I'd personally never seen one, but my mother had been a good artist. There had been a time when our house had been littered with pictures of this same thing. Elongated, pale face with red eyes and deadly sharp teeth—her work had haunted my imagination.

Yep, I knew exactly what I'd seen.

A demon.

Even in the dim light, I could see its face distorted by anger.

Panicked, I couldn't hold back a gasp of fear.

"What is it?" Jensen asked.

I looked again, but Adam was gone.

"Nothing. I have a headache."

But foreboding filled me.

This was how my mother started to go crazy.

Chapter Six

I made an excuse to Jensen that night about needing to go to bed early. The image of the demon wouldn't leave my mind, but the niggle of fear that settled in my stomach bothered me more. Turning into a paranoid freak who saw things that weren't really there wasn't on my bucket list, and the last thing I needed was for Jensen to see how unbalanced I was.

This is what happened when one doesn't have real sex for years.

I closed my eyes, hoping sleep would come quickly with no dreams, but it wasn't meant to be. I dreamt of my mother.

We were seated on the small porch of the little house at the beach that Momma had rented one summer. Screened in to protect from the elements, the porch was like a second living room. From the sofa, we could look out at the roll of the waves against the sand or glimpse the occasional sunbather. I loved sitting there at mid-afternoon with the salty scent of the ocean in the air, watching the clouds float by, daydreaming about so many things.

But in this dream, the child version of me had been replaced by the cynical adult I'd become.

"Look at that water." Momma sat next to me on *the blue-and-white striped sofa, her bony and gnarled hands idly picking at a piece of string. "You don't see*

that back home. So much sun."

"It's peaceful here," I said. "I wish we'd moved here instead of going back to Texas."

"I was still young back then, still silly enough to think I could control my instincts." Momma chuckled and tucked a strand of her blonde and gray hair behind one ear. "I thought I was stronger than him and the curse."

"Stronger than who?"

Momma quirked an eyebrow at me. "You know who. You've always known."

"You always think I know more than I do." My gaze fell to the carving knife lying on the coffee table next to Momma's art pad. Its blade glimmered in the light. Why was it there? Was she going to stab me this time?

Nervous, I got up and grabbed the art book. Studying the familiar and gruesome drawings in it, I tried to keep the tone of our conversation light. "Your art work is still horrific even after all this time. I see you're still crazy as ever."

So much for light.

"That's an easy excuse to hide behind." Momma stood. "I never talked crazy a day in my life. And my art tells the truth."

"So I guess you weren't crazy the day you tried to kill me? You did that in a completely sane frame of mind?"

Her eyes closed and she turned her head away. "What I did...it was to help you. To protect you."

"Is that why you killed Jared?"

Her eyes snapped open, filled with a cold fury. "I did not kill Jared. He was...was the love of my life after your father." She grabbed my arm, her fingers pinching my skin, catching me off guard so that I dropped the art pad.

Desperation clouded the worn lines of her sharp, angular face. "Maisy, we don't have time for all this. I need to tell you something. Something that could save your life."

"Now you want to save it?" I yanked away. "That's a change."

"You can't trust him."

"Who?" I shook my head, confused. "Are you talking about Jensen? 'Cause he's completely trustworthy. I know everything about him."

"Oh, darling. Don't be silly. You know nothing about Jensen. Not really." Her condescending laugh pissed me off. "But he's not who I mean, and you know it."

Adam. She means Adam.

"Adam?" I asked.

"Is that what he's calling himself now?" Momma's laughter turned derisive. "Probably decided to name himself after Adam from the Bible. He always did think he was the first of his kind to make a name for himself."

"What do you mean?"

"Are you really so simpleminded? Don't make me say what he is. Saying it is like inviting him into the damn house. And by the way, that's exactly what you did when you were a kid. All that 'Stranger Danger' crap they taught in school flew out the window for you. If it weren't for you, I might not ever have had to deal with him or the consequences."

Momma stared out the screen door. "He killed your father. I'm convinced of it. And Jared...poor

Jared. He was only trying to protect us both."

She still knew how to hurt me. Even in a dream, Momma could stab me with words.

I looked away, trying to keep the sting of tears at bay. "I don't know what you are talking about."

"Yes, you do. He's made you forget. He thralled you all those years ago," she shrieked, a crazed look in her eyes. "That thing you invited into our home, that thing that you are still in contact with, that thing which you allow to touch you intimately—it's evil. It wants the women of our line. If it can't have you, it will kill you and go after your child. I tried to stop it, tried to kill it, but you saved me from death. Somehow, you did it."

She didn't sound grateful that I'd saved her. If I had to label her feelings, I'd say she was pissed. Once again, I'd messed up some delusional plan she'd had— though I had no idea how I had saved her life. All I remembered was that she'd tried to take mine.

"Adam is not evil." I argued. "And he's too young to have killed Daddy or Jared."

"Adam is hundreds of years old. He has stalked us for over a century."

"How?"

"Because he's a creature of the night. One of the undead."

"A creature of—" I tried to comprehend what she was saying. My hand went to my neck, to the spot where Adam had bit me in my dream. Playing dumb, I asked, "You mean…he's a zombie?"

"A zombie? Really? Do zombies look as good as your Adam?"

A creature of the night? Shit. *Did she mean vampire? That was crazy.*

65

And yet hadn't my mother always claimed they existed? Hadn't her drawings of demons included fangs? I shivered, trying to block out those horrific images.

Sharp teeth. Cruel eyes. Pale faces distorted by evil. Hair that flowed in an unseen breeze. Blood dripping from the body of a victim. Wide, sightless eyes caught in the grip and agony of Death. Momma's drawings painted a gruesome picture of a demon that preyed on human blood.

"You know," Momma whispered, nodding her head, her gaze flickering to my neck where I still had my hand. "You know what he is. He's tasted you. Tell me, is it still confined to your dreams? Or has he bit you for real?"

"Are you trying to tell me that Adam is a…a…vampire?"

Thunder rolled deep and long, and the sky outside of our cottage changed from bright and sunny to overcast with churning black clouds. Choppy waves crashed against the shore, and a rank, rotting garbage smell overwhelmed the small house, causing us both to fan the air.

"Now you've done it." Momma looked around, anxious. "I told you not to say what it was out loud."

"This is a dream. I can do what I want."

"This is not a dream. This was a meeting I arranged through a gypsy." She picked up the carving knife from the coffee table and pointed the blade's tip at me. "You have to protect yourself. They let you live in ignorance. It's time for the truth. I wanted to warn you."

"About what?" I backed away, scared of the knife

and what she might do. "What are you warning me about?"

"The vampire who has stalked our family is after you now. He's waited longer for you than the others. Maybe it's because your mutation, your little defect, scares him. But be prepared. Once you let him into your dreams, once he gets his hands on your skin, the curse will do the rest."

Fearless, she grabbed the blade of the knife with her other hand and then offered it to me, handle first. I gripped it, unable to keep from flinching at the dark blood dripping from her palm. "You have to fight him with every breath."

I jerked awake. A cold sweat had turned my nightgown damp. The knife my mother had given me was heavy in my hand, but when I looked, there was nothing there. Both of my hands were clenched into fists.

Once you let him into your dreams, once he gets his hands on your skin, the curse will do the rest...

He'd already been in my dreams. What curse was she talking about? And she said I had a mutation. What was that?

"You all right, darlin'?" Warm and soothing, I mentally fought my way to the calm of Jensen's voice. "Maisy?"

I snapped on the bedside light. For a split second, I thought the demon I'd seen earlier was lying next to me.

A scream caught in my throat. But then the moment was gone.

"Darlin', what's wrong?" Shirtless and in only his pajama bottoms, Jensen slid out of bed and came to my side, putting an arm around me. "Are you okay?"

So many thoughts rushed through my head followed by memories of the past I had shoved into a dark corner of my mind.

"Talk to me," Jensen urged, brushing a strand of my hair away from face, his hands gentle and warm. "Was it a bad dream?"

"Yes," I managed to get out. "About Momma."

His green eyes filled with sympathy. "Everything's okay. Your mother is locked up. Remember? She can't hurt you. It was just a dream," he soothed, kissing my head. "I'm here, baby."

I leaned against his shoulder, overwhelmed by the reassurance in his voice. And I loved that he called me "baby." That wasn't something you called a friend. Was it? Maybe he cared about me more than I'd imagined.

Even as I thought that, a dark little voice in my head piped up.

But why does he a have a trunk full of weapons?

"Jensen," I asked quietly, hoping he couldn't hear how loud my heart pounded. "Why…?"

"Why what?"

"Why…why are you so good to me?" I buried my face in his shoulder. "I don't deserve you. I know I'm a burden."

"What are you talking about? You're not a burden. I wouldn't have married you if I felt like that."

"Pops made you marry me. You could be out there right now with some beautiful model living the good life."

"Who says this isn't the good life?" He kissed my head again and ran a soothing hand down my back.

My heart melted. Damn, this man made me so

crazy. Maybe...maybe...this was the moment I'd been waiting for...maybe I could make a small move.

"You're sweet." I kissed his neck, breathing in the citrus scent of the soap he liked to use. Good Lord, he smelled good. I nipped at him lightly. "Too sweet."

His body tensed, and he caught his breath.

I shifted my head to gaze up at him. Was he affected in anyway by holding me this close? His eyes were wary, but interest glimmered there. He stroked back another strand of my hair and then tilted my chin so he could plant a soft kiss on my lips.

Heaven. Pure heaven.

Little shocks of electricity sizzled between us as he lingered. Mmm...he was a great kisser. Not too rough. Not too eager. Just sort of taking his time. I pressed closer, hoping for more. The short, form-fitting, T-shirt night gown I had on would be easy enough to take off or even put his hand under.

But he pulled away, not meeting my gaze.

"I think you should lie down." Jensen released me quickly as if repulsed. "It's late."

Damn. He might as well have thrown a bucket of ice on me.

All business, he stood and hurriedly tucked me back into bed.

"Aren't you going to lie back down?" I asked when he headed toward the door.

"I'm going to grab a drink of water first."

Disappointed, I fought the tears welling in my eyes. This was the rejection I'd expected all along, but it hurt more than I'd anticipated. He didn't want me. Not really. Oh sure, he may have thought about it a second, but in the end he'd realized he didn't think about me like that. I must not be good enough or something.

I closed my eyes, refusing to cry.

When he came back five minutes later, he held a glass of water in one hand. I pretended to sleep but watched him through half-slitted eyes. Jensen put the drink on the end table on his side of the bed. Then he glanced at me. Very carefully, he brushed back the hair from my neck and stared at the bare flesh—almost as if he were studying it.

What on Earth was he looking at?

His examination only lasted a few seconds. Satisfied by whatever he saw there, Jensen slid beneath the covers. Soon, I heard his steady breathing.

I couldn't turn my mind off. Between the staggering rejection I'd just received and the awful dream about Momma, sleep was not in the cards. Jensen's efforts at comfort had distracted me from what my mother had said Adam was supposed to be for a little while. But like a one track train, it all rushed back.

A vampire.

Undead. A bloodsucker.

All my life, I'd heard the word tossed about—especially when Momma was in the asylum. She'd developed a deep obsession with vampires in there, always claiming she saw one following her. Was I about to start thinking crazy like that, too?

Her hands around my neck. So tight.

I couldn't remember much about the months leading up to her trying to kill me nor the months after. Pops had once told me that was because I'd blocked it all out to help my mind heal from the trauma. That made sense to me. To be honest, I'd never wanted to delve too deeply into that event. I mean, who really wants to know why their mother would prefer death over being with them? After a half hour of trying, I gave up on sleep.

I left the bedroom, tiptoeing down the hallway to Rebecca's door. Pressing my ear to the hard wood, her soft snores put my mind at ease. My baby was okay.

I stopped outside Jensen's office. Normally, I didn't go in there without his permission. There was never any need to, but I kept thinking about the box that reminded me so much of Momma's last boyfriend, Jared. What was Jensen doing with that thing?

Only one way to find out.

Nervous, I pushed open the door and stepped inside.

The screen saver on his computer—something from *Star Wars*—illuminated the room enough for me to see without turning on the overhead light. Bookshelves, computer, desk, a television, pictures of me and Rebecca, a few posters advertising games he liked to play online—it looked like pretty normal stuff for an office.

I peeked in the closet but saw only cardboard boxes neatly labeled as things like tax returns or medical records. A collection of comic books I didn't recognize sat on the top shelf. Next to that lay an old Atari and a nineties Nintendo, reminders of Jensen's more nerdy hobbies.

No wooden box.

I shut the closet door and leaned against it.

The Star Wars screensaver changed. A message popped up. Curious, I stepped closer to read it.

Helser Eight, what is your current status?

Helser Eight? Must be part of one of those live action games Jensen was always playing on the computer. It was kind of close to his last name though—Helsing. Unable to resist, I typed a message back.

Helser Eight is snoozing.

There was a slight pause, and the screen flickered:

Report to Institute tomorrow. Need update on your wife.

Um…why would a gamer need to know about me? I'd never heard of Helser Eight before. I backed away from the screen, uncertain what it all meant. Tomorrow, I'd ask Jensen.

Still restless, I went downstairs. The summer rain storm from earlier had left things stifling in the house, causing me to wonder if the AC was working. Outside, darkness had fallen like a thick curtain with no moon to part it. Unable to help myself, I stared through the window of our back door at the fence separating Adam's backyard from mine.

Or as my mother said, the creature that has been stalking us for over a century.

Cue the spooky music.

Now that I'd had time to calm down, I could see how silly the dream really was. Momma was in the crazy house for a reason, and my dream had been just that: a dream. There was no reason to think my neighbor was a vampire. My eyes must have been playing a trick on me earlier when I'd thought I'd seen a demon.

Still, you should be careful, Momma's voice echoed in my head.

Unwilling to listen to it, I opened the French doors

and stepped out into the warm night air. It felt a bit naughty to be outside in only my T-shirt nightie with no panties underneath. Knowing there was no one to see how unladylike I was, I plopped down on the wicker chair on the back porch and sighed. When would I be old enough for Momma's tales to stop affecting me?

The mental health facility she lived in was in San Antonio—about two hours away. I visited her from time to time, but I always felt so drained, so depressed afterward. Her thoughts were a jumbled mess, and she never could articulate what she wanted to say very well. Jensen also wanted to know why I even still bothered to see a woman who'd tried to hurt me.

No matter what she'd done to me, Elizabeth Harker was still my mother.

"You all right, neighbor?"

Little prickles ran up my spine, and I made sure my nightie was smoothed down. I knew that voice.

As I peered across the lawn, the moon decided to come out from behind the clouds. The dim light was enough to make out Adam looking over the fence at me. His eyes glittered in the moonlight.

"Adam?" I asked.

"Hi." I heard the noise of him shifting his weight on the slat of the fence, allowing him to be high enough to see me. "Didn't mean to scare you."

"What are you doing up this late? It's like…three in the morning or something."

"I'm a night owl. I do a lot of business at night. What about you?" He tilted his head, studying me. "Why are you up? Don't you have work in the morning?"

"I'm a teacher. This is my summer break."

"Ah…a teacher. I'd wondered what you did for a living."

"Yeah, I teach music at the local elementary school."

"Are you a singer or a musician?"

"Neither, really. I just like music."

"I see."

A little silence fell between us.

"You said you do a lot of business at night. That's because you're a singer, right?" I asked, watching his reaction. "For a well-known band? You must have a lot of late night gigs."

"Is that what you see?" Adam grinned. "Then it must be true."

"Well, aren't you?"

"Perhaps."

Perhaps? Was this guy playing with me or what? As I was thinking those things, he started to hum a slow Maroon Five song.

"*Lost Stars.*" I recognized it instantly. "I love that song."

As if I'd asked, Adam started to sing. What was strange is that while his singing was good, mesmerizing almost, it didn't really sound like the Adam Levine on the album. I'd noticed that at our *Phantom of the Opera* sing along, too. This Adam's voice was much deeper, more resonating. Strange.

"You better sing softer or you'll wake up the SOS house." I nodded my head toward Sophia's place. "Not that Sophia would mind."

"SOS?"

"Sex Offender Siblings."

"Ah. I sense there is story behind that label."

"Oh yeah. You see…" I paused, thinking better of telling him my idea about Sophia and Seth. After all, I didn't really know Adam. He might think I was just a rude gossip if I told him my crazy neighbor theories. "Well, it doesn't matter. It's a silly idea I'd had. I shouldn't spread gossip."

"I'm intrigued now. Do you mind if I come over the fence and join you? Just for a bit?"

Don't invite him in!

A flash of my mother's face came to me. The words echoed in my head, a long forgotten memory trying to resurface. I couldn't quite grab on to it.

Adam only wanted to come into the yard. That wasn't the same as the house. Besides, vampires weren't real. He could come into the damn yard if he wanted to.

"Um…I'm not exactly dressed for company," I said, gesturing to my skimpy apparel. "What if someone saw us?"

"We're just talking. Besides, I like your outfit." Adam tilted his head to the side, charming me with a smile. "C'mon. Invite me over."

"Sure. Okay. You think you can climb over without hurting yourself?"

Adam hauled himself to the top of the fence one leg at a time, before hopping down into our yard in a long, graceful leap.

"Tell me everything, Maisy." He eyed my nightie, and suddenly I felt I might as well have been naked. The slow grin spreading across his face when he sat down was lecherous and sexy. His long fingers gently drummed against the patio table. "Leave nothing out."

And somehow I found myself sharing with him my

theory about the neighbors. Adam laughed as I explained my *Flowers in the Attic* idea.

"You are the most creative of them all," he said when I was done with my tale. "You really are the one."

"The one what?"

"You're the one I've been waiting for," he whispered. "And I've waited a long time."

I was unable to fight being aroused by this sexy man with the fierce, dark eyes. His lips were a pale red, and as I looked at them, my mind instantly pictured us in a heated lip lock, our tongues ravishing each other. All my senses jumped to high alert.

"I don't know what you mean," I whispered back, unable to keep the shake out of my voice. "You don't know me. And…and I'm a married woman."

"Married?" he scoffed and grabbed my hand, kissing it lightly. "That doesn't matter when it comes to destiny."

Damn. The feel of his lips on my skin set my heart skipping. I started to feel a little tingle between my legs.

"Destiny?" I asked, shifting slightly.

"Don't play dumb with me, my sweet Maisy." Adam smiled and then stood in front of me so quickly I didn't see the actual movement. "I know you were in communications with your mother recently."

"My mother? No. I haven't seen in her in months."

Except for an hour ago in my dreams.

"You can't deny the passion you feel for me," he said, going to his knees. "I've been in your dreams. I know your desires."

He put a hand on my bare leg, sliding it up to my thigh as light as a feather.

"That's not possible." I shivered, wondering if he would slip that hand higher and discover how vulnerable I was without panties. "You're teasing me."

"Am I?" He smiled, massaging my thighs as he sang softly our *Phantom of the Opera* song.

"Whoa. Wait a second. How could you know about that?" I tried to twist away from his devilish hands.

He was determined to get as close to the core of me as he could. I tried to scoot my chair back, but it wouldn't budge. Adam leaned in to kiss me while his hands slid the bottom of my nightie up so he could grip my hips. Cool air brushed against my bare skin, enhancing the delicious tickle of desire.

"Who are you?" I demanded.

"You know the answer. You know the word. All you have to do is say it."

I stared into his eyes, trying not to get lost in them as he nudged my legs apart and gently stroked my clit with the pad of his thumb. I sighed with pleasure even as I warred with my conscience.

Vampire. He wanted me to say it out loud. But if I did that, I'd be admitting my mother wasn't crazy. Or worse, I'd be admitting that I was.

No. I couldn't do that.

"I can't," I said.

He continued to stroke me, making me wet with need, ignoring my words. I forced myself to meet his gaze, to not break away, feeling a slight shift in power.

"You should go." My words came out almost like a command.

Adam drew back, blinking in confusion. His hands left me, and I felt the loss of them. This was no dream. This was the real deal. And yet the rational part of me argued with my horny side, pointing out that this man wasn't a man at all, but a creature. A thing.

"No. Don't use your dark gift to make me go." He shook his head as if trying to clear it. "It's one thing to be with you in a dream, but when I saw you at Alexis's tonight, it was like finding my heart's beat again."

His heart's beat. So romantic.

So ridiculous if he was really a vampire. They were dead.

"You're crazy. I don't have any dark gifts." Confused by my feelings, I broke eye contact and put a hand on his hard chest, trying to keep him back.

Suddenly, he was in control again, and I may as well have been pushing a steel wall. Adam leaned in closer, his hands back at my thighs and clit, stroking the sensitive mound. I gasped at the pleasure of it.

"Please, don't do something we'll both regret," he begged.

Oh god. Adam lowered his lips to mine and slipped a finger inside the wetness he'd created, making me moan against his mouth and wish it was his cock. His clever lips nibbled down my neck, sucking the flesh before he removed his finger and sat back.

"I have something for you." He reached into his pocket and removed a little silk pouch. "I saw you eyeing this at the party tonight."

He opened the drawstring of the bag, and an egg-shaped vibrator slipped into his hand. The Love Buzz. The one we'd been ooing and ahhing over before he'd arrived.

I knew what he meant to do with it. My mind tried to resist while my body desperately wanted to feel it against me.

"I thought you said you didn't need vibrators," I said, remembering his earlier comments.

"I don't." His soft laughed was slightly sinister. "But you like them."

He pressed against the controller button and the egg buzzed with life. Was I really going to let him do this to me? In the back yard?

"Be still," he said with another deep, penetrating look. Again, I felt powerless to do anything else. "Spread your legs farther apart and lean back in the chair."

Obedient, I did as he asked.

He placed the pulsating egg against my clit, and I moaned softly at the immediate jolt of pleasure. Adam smiled and slipped his finger back inside my wet warmth as the amazing little egg did its job.

"How does that feel, my darling?" he asked. "Does it make you long for me?"

"Oh god." I knew it was wrong to let him do this to me, but I couldn't seem to snap out of it. The pulse of the vibration ran through my body, touching every nerve and ramping up my desire. "Don't stop."

"I don't intend to, but I want to see you writhing in that chair, dripping with need, begging me to fill you," he whispered. "I won't be satisfied with anything less."

His forceful manner, his confidence—it was a turn on. To be wanted by this stranger after such a long dry spell and after being rejected by Jensen kept me from doing the right thing, from saying no.

His finger slipped away, and I gave a whimper of disappointment.

"Relax, my sweet," he whispered. "I'm just changing the tempo."

The egg buzzed harder, the whirring noise a sexual song of need, making my heart race and my body quiver with heat. Adam's sly smile clued me into the fact that whatever was going to happen next would be more intense than everything up to this point. I braced myself, still warring with my conscience.

He inserted the egg so it was about halfway into my wet core, threatening to slide in and provide all sorts of delights. I shuddered at this new penetration, already feeling the build of an orgasm. The pad of his thumb stroked my swollen clit while his tongue and teeth danced along my thighs, nibbling and licking. I gripped the sides of my chair, undone by the multiple sensations.

He touched the controller again, and the Love Buzz took it up another notch.

Adam pushed the egg so it penetrated me, revving and hitting a spot I'd never known existed. I cried out, unable to contain the ecstasy of being aroused like this. The orgasm ripped through my body, taking my breath and all rational thought.

Again and again, the little egg's vibrations shuddered through my body, rendering me helpless, unable to focus on anything but the pleasure and sound of Adam's knowing laugh.

You love this, don't you? I can give you so much more. I'm your vampire, sweet Maisy. That's what I am.

Some of the fog cleared in my brain.

What was I doing out here? Why was I letting this beautiful stranger do this to me? How was it I could hear his words in his head? Maybe I truly was crazy. There was certainly something wrong with me.

I'd practically given myself without a second thought to this man. I looked down to see his head in my lap. A sharp pain flared at my thigh, followed by pressure as Adam kissed the area.

Wait. He wasn't kissing. He was...he was biting me, taking my blood, and God help me, I could feel the tiniest bit of pleasure from his actions. If I let this go any further, I would end up letting him do whatever else he wanted.

He lifted his head slightly, a tiny trail of blood leaking from his mouth while he looked into my eyes.

No. *No.* This couldn't be. I would not turn into my mother.

"Go." I broke whatever weird psychic connection we were sharing with my demand.

He frowned, blinking in confusion. Pushing myself back, the chair flipped over so I landed with my body against the ground and my legs in the air. All my charms were on display for the world to see.

Quickly, I scrambled up.

But Adam was gone.

He wasn't in the yard. He wasn't standing behind me. He wasn't perched on the fence. Adam had vanished. Had I been dreaming? Did I imagine it? How had I managed to make him go?

But my lips were still warm from where he'd touched them. The ache between my legs was real. The need he'd built in me with the Love Buzz had been enough to cause me to want to abandon everything. He'd been there. I was sure of it. I hadn't imagined a whole five-minute conversation with him.

The Love Buzz. I spotted it on the ground, still vibrating. Snatching it up, I turned it off before hurrying in the house, locking the doors behind me. Taking deep breaths, I climbed the stairs to my bedroom. I tucked the vibrator into my dresser drawer and sat on the edge of the bed, listening to Jensen's snores, debating about what to do. Maybe I should wake him up?

What would I tell him? That I'd let our neighbor get a little too friendly with me in the back yard? That I'd allowed a vampire to pleasure me with a vibrating egg? Hmm...not sure that even my sweet husband of convenience would think that was okay.

He'd think I was losing my mind, and I didn't need him thinking I was crazy yet.

But I did have proof. I rubbed the spot where Adam had bit me on my thigh. The bite mark would be enough to convince him something had happened.

What would Jensen do when he saw that? I just didn't know.

I settled into bed and tried to force sleep to come.

Chapter Seven

The next morning, I was up bright and early.

I had to get some answers to the millions of questions raging through my head. I wasn't exactly sure what was going on, but I knew no matter how ridiculous it seemed, I needed to know if my sexy neighbor really was a vampire.

An examination of my thigh this morning had revealed nothing. Unlike Sophia, I had no lingering bite marks on my skin, no proof of what I'd seen the evening before other than the Love Buzz. I'd made sure that was still tucked deep in my dresser.

Was I going crazy like my mother, seeing things that weren't there?

I didn't think so, but I wasn't going to wait until dark fell to find out.

If the lore was true, my vampire friend should be totally conked out during the day, and that meant I could do a little snooping around his house. Maybe I'd dig around in Jensen's office one more time and look for that box, too. Some of those weapons might come in handy if I had to face the undead.

Oh my god. Could this really be happening? Was I suddenly embracing everything I'd promised myself I would never believe in?

"What are you doing up?" Jensen plopped down into a kitchen chair, his face still soft and groggy from sleep. Boyish. A tuft of his hair stuck up. "I thought you never got up until ten during the summer."

"Couldn't sleep." I flipped the bacon I'd been frying, trying not to look at him. Guilt over my secret dalliance in the backyard assuaged me, but I couldn't forget about the way Jensen had rejected me. "Restless."

"You feeling okay?"

"Yeah. I….couldn't sleep. I decided to get an early start today."

Jensen studied me as I flicked a piece of bacon onto a plate. "Want to tell me about the bad dream you had last night?"

"No."

"You said it was about your mom."

"It was nothing. Just a dream. I didn't mean to wake you."

Jensen rose. He leaned against the counter, forcing me to acknowledge him.

"What's up?" I asked, risking a glance. Damn. He was so handsome, so yummy to look at in the morning with his tousled hair and bedroom eyes. "Did you sleep okay? You seem antsy."

"This is the second time this week you've had a dream that woke you up, screaming. I'm worried about you. Is something on your mind?"

Hmm…sex, vampires, and you.

"Nope," I said. "There's nothing to worry about."

"You haven't— You haven't been experiencing any…well, hallucination type things?" Jensen frowned. "Like what your mother used to get?"

"No!" I shook my head. "No! I'm not seeing…demons."

Jensen nodded but kept his eyes on me.

"Hey, have you met the neighbor behind us yet?" I asked, looking for anything to change the subject.

"No. Have you?"

"Yes. He was at Zero's party last night. I was talking to him when you opened the door."

"I didn't get a good look. Describe him."

"I think he looks a lot like Adam Levine. Dark hair, thin face, muscular."

"I didn't know you were into Maroon Five." Jensen opened the fridge and took out the milk, giving the jug a light shake. "Thought you were more of a Michael Jackson kind of person."

"Um, Jensen, how long have we been married?"

"A year."

"And how long did you know me before that?"

"Six years or so?"

"When have you ever heard me sing a Michael Jackson song?"

"When have I ever heard you sing a Maroon Five song? You're always into that musical theatre crap."

"First of all, mister, musical theatre is not crap." I handed him a glass. "It's a reflection of our life and times. And secondly, it is impossible not to be a Maroon Five fan. The radio stations around here have them on a steady rotation."

"And what did you and this Adam Levine lookalike talk about?"

Which time? The time he was in my dreams singing? The time he was my invisible lover? The time he climbed the back fence and told me he was a vampire and almost had his way with me?

"Nothing."

85

"Uh-huh." Jensen downed the milk. "Nothing at all?"

"Nothing that I remember."

"Well, be careful."

"Of what?"

"I don't know. I thought he looked at you kind of funny last night. Made me wonder if he was one of Pop's guys."

That hadn't even crossed my mind. In the year we'd been married, there had been no trouble from any of Pops shady associates.

"I'm sure Adam isn't one of those. He's a rock star. Not an assassin."

"Probably not, Maisy. Just be careful. That's all I'm saying." He munched on a piece of bacon. "Sometimes, you are too trusting and other times, not trusting enough. Wouldn't want some bad guy to sweep you off your feet and steal you away."

The last time someone swept me off my feet, I'd ended up pregnant. Since then, there had been only one person I wanted to sweep me off my feet, and so far, it hadn't happened. After last night, it looked like it never would.

"Men have never been banging down my door to carry me away, Jensen."

"You always act like you're not beautiful," he said, looking into my eyes, his gaze intense. "But you are. I remember the first time Pops introduced us."

"Yeah, I do, too. You didn't say three words to me."

"Only because you were so pretty, I didn't know what to say."

"You're talking crazy now." My heart skipped a

beat. If I didn't know better, I would think…he was…attracted to me. Wait…was there still hope?

And while I was thinking about that, Jensen leaned in close and kissed me, catching me off guard. Unable to hold back a little moan of surprise, I stepped into his space, and his arms slid around my waist. My hands went to his hard chest, caressing the muscles beneath the thin shirt he had on. Something pressed against my lower abdomen, and I tried not to gasp in shock. It was Jensen's cock.

My thoughts started sliding two steps ahead of what we were actually doing. The kitchen table was right behind me. Maybe if I didn't give him time to change his mind, maybe he'd take me right there and at last we could consummate this damn marriage. And if that happened, maybe this whole vampire thing would just disappear. I could think about sex with Jensen versus sex with a dead guy who probably just wanted my blood.

But once again, Jensen pulled away, dashing my hopes.

"Maisy, last night…I—" He didn't quite meet my eye. "I didn't mean to—"

"Ew. Gross." Rebecca's voice caused us to jerk apart. She stood in the doorway, her face in a grimace. "Kissing is disgusting."

Jensen stepped back, letting me go. *Didn't mean to…what?* He didn't mean to kiss me, or he didn't mean to stop? Oh god, I hoped it was the second one.

I leaned against the cabinet, catching my breath.

Jensen turned to Rebecca as if nothing had happened, as if he wasn't in the least bit as affected by me as I was by him. Shit. Maybe it was a pity kiss, the kind you give when you feel sorry for someone or think they're a pathetic loser.

But I know what I'd felt, brushing against my lower abs. *That* wasn't pity.

"So what's on the agenda of my favorite five-year-old today?" he asked.

"I'm going swimming at Mother's Day Out, and then I'm going to have a tea party with Mr. Bear," Rebecca announced before sliding into one of the chairs at the table. She played with a tendril of her brunette hair thoughtfully. "Then I'm going to paint my toenails."

"Sounds exciting. I think you should consider brushing your hair, too." Jensen kissed the top of her head. "I'm going to get ready for work." He left the room without even looking at me.

"You want bacon?" I asked, still trying to figure out what had just happened.

"You bet, Momma," she said. "Give me some bacon with a side of the undead."

"What?" I almost dropped the plate I'd been about to hand her. "What did you say?"

"Um…" She looked flustered for a moment. "I said give me some bacon with a side of the undead."

"Undead? What does that mean?"

Was my mother talking to Rebecca in her dreams?

"Undead means you're not quite dead. Duh. Everybody knows that." Rebecca shook her head. "You know, like a zombie."

"A zombie? Have you been watching those movies again?" I narrowed my eyes. "You know they give you nightmares."

"I haven't been watching anything," Rebecca said,

her little face solemn. "I can't help it if they pop in my dreams."

Oh boy.

"What else is popping up in your dreams?"

"Nothing." She frowned. "Why?"

"Just curious."

"Momma, were you walking around on the roof last night?"

"Not to my knowledge," I said, sitting next to her. "Why do you ask?"

"Just heard weird noises. Like someone walking around."

"Probably just a squirrel."

I hoped it was true, but I had a sneaking suspicion something else could have been on top of our house. In the bright morning light, the idea of vampires seemed crazy. Yet I knew if I didn't do a little investigating, I'd keep on wondering.

My mother had said *I'd* invited the vampire in when I was kid. What if this vamp was trying to get in my daughter's head? The thought made me even more impatient to find out the truth.

"Hurry up and eat, so we can get you over to Mother's Day Out."

"I just got up. Give me a chance, Momma."

An hour later, I dropped Rebecca off at Mother's Day Out and formulated my steps for spying on my new neighbor. Even though it was still morning, the day had already turned humid. By this afternoon, the temperature would skyrocket, baking the Earth and causing an overflow of steaming bodies at the neighborhood pool.

I pulled into the driveway, deciding to go for a

walk after parking the car. No sense in putting this off. A good walk around the neighborhood was the perfect excuse to drop by Adam's house.

Or break in.

Jane was outside, digging around in the shrubs along her front porch. She looked up. "Hey."

"Hey, Jane," I called back, hoping that would be the end of our conversation. "See you later."

"Where you going?"

"Just for a walk."

"Mind if I join you?" She stood, wiping at her forehead. "I could use a break."

"Sure," I said, not bothering to hide my reluctance.

"Great."

We started down the street.

"So you missed a good time last night," Jane said. "After you left, things got wild."

"What do you mean?"

"Alexis and Sophia were all over Channing."

"Channing? Who's he?"

"Channing? The guy that lives behind you. You were talking to him right before you left."

Adam. She meant Adam. Only she'd heard a different name when he'd given it. I remembered how Jane had argued that he looked like Channing Tatum.

"Oh yeah. Him." I nodded my head. "So how did he react to them throwing themselves at him?"

"He didn't seem to mind. In fact, he kind of encouraged it."

"And you? Why weren't you part of that?"

"I'm a married woman." The picture of innocence, Jane shook her head. "I have some standards that even a movie star can't tear apart."

Hmm…not sure I believed that. After all, I'd seen her and Zero about to get it on in my hot tub the other night.

"So did he eventually leave?" I asked.

"I don't know. I left. I was frustrated at the way those two were acting." Jane shrugged, but when I glanced over, I saw a hint of jealousy on her face. "As if Channing could ever really feel anything for those two bitches."

"You know, Jane," I said as we rounded the corner and walked down the sidewalk which led to the street running behind my house. "Maybe we should drop in on Adam—I mean, Channing, and see if he's recovered."

Her face brightened. "We could apologize for the actions of our friends."

"All right. That sounds good."

But I was really thinking there was strength in numbers.

If Jane saw a demon, it would mean there was nothing wrong with me. We couldn't both be crazy. We turned down the Adam's street, and a tickle of anticipation ran through me.

Yet I hesitated at the foot of the driveway.

"Well, c'mon," Jane urged. "What are you waiting for?"

We were going into the lion's den, unarmed. If Adam was truly a vampire, what would stop him from killing us? I'd watched enough *Buffy the Vampire Slayer* to know you never entered into the nest of evil without a plan.

And what exactly was my plan?

Ask Adam if he was a bloodsucker? Ask him what

he'd done to my mother? Why was he after me now? What the hell had I done to get the attention of a sexual creature like him? Was I supposed to kill him or something?

Maybe if you had weapons like the ones in Jensen's trunk...

Wait. A little light bulb flickered uncertainly in my head. Was that what those weapons were for? Killing vampires?

Jared had kept a trunk like that, and odds were good he knew what my mother thought was following her. Had he been trying to protect Momma? And if Jared knew about them....well, hell.

Did Jensen know about vampires?

No. Surely not. That was...crazy. Right? Then again, he'd seemed very interested in inspecting my neck last night. Maybe he was looking for bite marks?

"Maisy, are you coming or not?" Jane tapped her foot, eager to go in. "It's hot. I don't want to stand out here all day. Someone might see us."

"Sure." But I hesitated. "You know, it's kind of early for a social call."

"What's he going to do? Shake his finger at us and tell us we're naughty?"

"No..."

But he might drain us of all life.

Jane knocked. The door swung open. We looked at each other.

"Um, did you see that?" Jane asked. "This door opened on its own."

"I noticed. Kinda creepy."

"Maybe he didn't shut it last night. What if someone broke in?"

"What are we? Charlie's Angels?" I stepped back. "If someone broke in, we should call the police."

"But we don't know for sure. Maybe the door is accidentally unlocked."

We peered into the dark hall of Adam's home, trying to make out objects, but with the sun shining behind us, it was hard to see.

"Well? Should we go in?" I asked.

Jane frowned and nodded.

Together, we stepped into the house.

The door swung shut behind us, a clichéd and bad movie omen.

I expected to see all sorts of wild and unusual objects in the house—coffins, cemetery dirt, strange amulets, maybe a map of Transylvania on the wall. After all, a vampire who was as old as my mother indicated had to travel with a cadre of antique magical items, right? In his centuries of stalking the women in my family, surely he'd picked up a few instruments of torture.

But the walls of the short hallway leading into the living room were bare, and the living room itself looked normal. A couch, end tables, an overstuffed recliner situated directly in front of a massive television—it wasn't exactly what I expected a vampire's lair to look like. And he wasn't even a tidy vampire. There were soda cans all over the coffee table as well as, two large, empty bottles of cabernet and a half-full bottle of vanilla vodka.

Hmm….that brand of cabernet… If I wasn't mistaken, it was Zero's favorite kind. I looked closer at the soda cans. Yep, that was the kind Sophia liked to drink, too. She liked to add a little vanilla vodka to her drinks to give them more flavor. Had those two women been here last night?

Jane's frown grew deeper as she looked at the trash, but she gestured toward the stairs. Together, we left the living room behind. I expected the stairs would lead into another hallway, but that wasn't the case at all.

The entire top floor had been gutted and turned into one ginormous room. Positioned in the middle of it sat the largest bed I'd ever seen. Black silk draped the strong, wooden headboard. The sheets were a luxurious silky white. Matching, oversized pillows were tossed all over.

A mirror on the ceiling clearly reflected what else was strewn there.

Zero, Sophia, and Adam.

All intertwined with legs and arms wrapped around each other in lewd ways, Zero's large breasts hung out for all the world to see as did Sophia's smaller ones. A thin silk sheet covered the rest of them, but nestled in between the redhead and the blonde with a satisfied smile and closed eyes lay Adam. He looked like the damn Cheshire cat, a little too pleased with himself even in sleep.

Anger—red and raw—rose in me.

Hadn't he said just last night that I was the one? The most creative of them all? Hadn't he been kissing me on my back porch at three in the morning? Wasn't it his finger that had ignited a fire in me so hot that I'd let him almost do whatever he pleased with me? Did that mean these two sluts had been in the house the whole time, and he'd returned to them the moment I'd gone inside?

Mother fucker.

Wait. *Wait.*

Why was I getting so upset? According to my mother, Adam was a vampire. He'd admitted as much to me last night, too. Hell, I should be lighting the torches and grabbing the pitchforks. I should be finding the garlic and the wooden stakes. I should be telling Jensen to get out his little trunk—it's head chopping time.

But no. All I felt was irrationally jealous and outraged that Adam Fucking Levine dared to sleep with my neighbors.

"Those sluts!" Jane hissed. "Those evil sluts. They told me they were going home."

"Well, I guess they were a little confused about where home is."

Sophia's eyes shot open. Bleary eyed, she looked at us while pulling the covers up over her boobs. "Wh—what time is it?" She sat up and winced. "Oh, god, do I have a headache."

"I'll bet," I said. "How much did you have to drink?"

"Not that much." She looked down at Adam, who continued to sleep peacefully. "Oh Lord, tell me I didn't do what I think I did."

"You did." Zero sat up. Unlike Jane, she didn't bother to cover herself. She stretched and yawned, letting her breasts fall forward while her red hair rippled down her back. Her pink nipples jutted out, and I couldn't help but admire the lovely picture she made. "We had a great time, and don't you go denying it, Sophia."

"But...but you're both married," Jane sputtered, stomping her foot. "Don't you think your husbands might have missed you?"

Zero and Sophia looked at each other.

"Brad said he'd take care of it." Sophia shrugged.

"Brad? You mean, Dylan?" Zero frowned. "Dylan said he'd smooth things over with your husband. Mine is out of town."

"Brad? Dylan? Don't you mean Channing?" Jane pointed at my Adam. "His name is Channing. How can you sleep with someone and not know their name?"

Zero and Sophia looked at Jane as if she'd grown a second head.

"Look, ladies, it really doesn't matter what he calls himself. How on Earth could he possibly explain to your husband that you slept with him in a way Seth would be okay with?" I asked. "Have you lost your minds?"

Not in the least bit ashamed by my words, Zero rubbed her head and slid out of bed, grabbing at her clothes which were on the floor. Sophia stared wistfully down at Adam.

"He drugged us," Zero announced with a nod. "That's what happened. He drugged our wine and then lured us here."

"Lured? Really?" I didn't bother to hide my sarcasm. "I don't think it would take much to lure you into anyone's bed."

"You're just jealous." Zero's eyes flashed with anger. "He didn't pick you."

"You weren't drugged, Alexis. If anything, you were under his thrall."

"His what?"

"His thrall. C'mon. Haven't you figured it out yet?" I looked at all three of them, frustrated. I mean, the answer was so obvious! "Adam Levine is a vampire."

Silent, they stared at me.

"What the hell does Adam Levine have to do with anything?" Zero crossed her arms. "What's wrong with you?"

"No! That man on the bed over there, that thing, is not what you think he is," I explained, recalling how my mother had described him in my dream. "He is a vampire. And vampires can use a thrall to sort of take over the mind of the person they are fixated on. He can make us see whatever we want to see. I see Adam Levine when I look at him. Jane sees Channing Tatum. You see Dylan McDermott."

"Brad?" Sophia poked at his shoulder. "I think you need to wake up now."

"And dumb ass over there sees freakin' Brad Pitt."

Zero and Jane turned to study the man lying motionless in the bed.

"Brad?" Sophia shook him and then looked at us. "I don't think he's breathing."

We looked at Adam, each of us seeing him in our own way. With an impatient sigh, Zero checked his pulse. Her hand dropped away, shock coloring her face.

"Holy shit," she whispered, backing up. "We killed him, Sophia."

Sophia squealed and hopped out of bed, dragging the sheet with her. "What?"

"He's not breathing," Zero said. "But look at that…"

When Sophia removed the sheet, she'd left Adam naked. For a dead guy, he sure was one beautiful package. Sculpted abs, muscular legs, and one hard cock sticking straight up—drool worthy even in death. Both Sophia and Zero sighed, no doubt remembering the escapades of the evening before.

"He's alive." I tried not to be stirred by the beautiful specimen of a man before me. "Trust me. He's very much alive. No one's cock can be that hard in death."

Jane walked toward the bed.

"What were you saying, Maisy?" she asked, staring at Adam's erection. "That he's a vampire?"

"Yep. And he's been trying to get us all under his thrall."

"Why?"

"Why not?" I countered.

"How do you know he's a vampire?" Jane asked. "Did he bite you? Show you his fangs?"

"No," I said, hesitantly, but Sophia and Zero exchanged meaningful looks. "He didn't bite me."

"Then how do you know?" Jane sat on the edge of the bed, her eyes never straying from Adam's naked body.

"A little birdie told me." Impatient, I walked over to Jane. "Just trust me. This guy only wants to suck your blood and run away with me."

"Run away with you?" Jane laughed. "I think you're making this whole vampire stuff up because you want him for yourself."

"Um, Jane. Do you hear yourself," I asked. "You're a married woman. You shouldn't even be thinking about him in the way you are."

"You're married, too."

She ran a finger down his stomach, unafraid.

Behind me, Zero and Sophia breathed a little

heavier. Even in sleep, this vampire clearly held some kind of power over them. And now, Jane was starting to feel his spell. This was crazy.

"He's a vampire," I insisted.

"It would explain all the biting he did last night." Zero sat back on the bed. "He definitely likes to nibble." She ran one of her nails up and down his cock.

"I know!" Sophia said. "He bit my wrist. Where did he get you?"

"Not on the wrist." Zero rubbed her inner thigh. "He was a bit more demanding with me."

"Oh, whatever," Sophia scoffed. "He did that to me last week."

Zero grasped Adam's cock, stroking it up and down. We all sucked in our breaths as a little drop of pre-cum appeared at the head. Sophia leaned down and licked it up before placing a gentle kiss on the foreskin.

Oh god. Things were about to get out of hand. I just knew it. There had to be a way to get these bitches back to reality.

"You both let him drink from you?" I asked, trying to block out thoughts of his mouth sucking against my thigh. "That is fucked up."

As if he heard me, his eyes fluttered open, and he gave them a slow smile. My neighbors sighed, and any hint of sanity slipped away. Sexual tension clouded the room. It didn't matter if he'd been the devil himself. These horny women were going to do whatever he wanted.

And so would I, if I didn't get out of there fast.

"Jane, dear." Adam guided her down next to him on the bed. One of his hands cupped her breast through the thin blouse she wore. "So glad you dropped by. I was dreaming of you."

"Of me?" Jane giggled. "Oh, Channing."

He looked around the room, but when he spotted me, he looked slightly perturbed. I raised my eyebrow. Adam glanced at the other women and then back at me as if unsure how to explain the situation.

"And Maisy," he shifted, uncomfortable. "I didn't see you there."

"Well, I certainly see you." I looked at his hard cock. "All of you."

The discomfort turned to amusement. "I hope you enjoy the view." He raised an eyebrow suggestively. "Perhaps you should come closer."

Oh, I wanted to. I wanted to do more than look, but I fought the lure of what he offered. "I've seen enough."

Zero began taking her clothes back off, and Sophia let the sheet drop to the ground, her eyes fixed on Adam.

Jane sighed and wiggled closer to him. He continued to stare at me even while his hands squeezed and tweaked her breasts.

I heard his voice in my head.

Maisy, it's not what you think. These women are distractions. A means to an end.

"Do they know that?" I asked out loud. "Do they understand how indifferent you are?"

Indifferent? On the contrary, I love watching them play.

Sliding into bed behind Jane, Sophia took Jane's shirt off. Her yellow bra framed her large breasts perfectly, but Sophia unhitched the clasp of it, releasing Jane's generous mounds and tossing the fabric away with a flick of her wrist. Cupping the soft, bulbous flesh gently from behind the other woman, Sophia offered them to Adam while Zero kissed his neck. He licked each of Jane's nipples, flicking his tongue across them until they hardened into two twin peaks and mewling sounds of pleasure erupted from her.

He dared look at me again.

What is so wrong about providing them a little pleasure if you won't give in to me?

"Give in to you? I don't even know you."

But you do. You know me. I've been with you the last few weeks. I've tasted your flesh, kissed the softest part of you.

"Only in my dreams. It's not the same as this," I pointed out.

A technicality I hope you'll let me remedy soon. And you can't deny the pleasure I brought you last night.

I blushed.

Zero worked her way down his body, her tongue probing at his abs, nipping at his skin before her lips wrapped around his cock. He flinched a little at her mouth sucking on him, but he never broke eye contact with me.

You've always known me. My heart wants only you. Your blood is mixed with mine. Come on. Join us. Give yourself to me and enjoy our short time together before everything changes.

Longing nipped at my libido. As I watched the women become more passionate, more adventurous with each other, a part of me wanted to join them, to strip naked and let whatever was going to happen just happen.

"No," I struggled to get the word out. "I can't."

Adam's lazy look of desire disappeared, replaced by a glare of frustration.

"Let me help you then," he said out loud and raised his hand. A wave of power surged around the room. "Sit down. You will stay."

A chair slid up behind me, knocking me in the legs so I was forced to sit. I was going to watch the sex show before me whether I wanted to or not.

Adam laughed when I struggled against his powers and gently stroked Zero's head as she bobbed up and down on his cock. On the other side of him, Sophia tugged at the shorts Jane wore. Once they were off and Jane was completely bared, she licked her lips catlike and set her tongue against Jane's clit. Her tongue flicked the sensitive spot slowly, tantalizing me and driving Jane wild.

"Oh god," she moaned. "That feels so amazing. I've never been with a woman before."

"Do you like that, sweet Jane?" Adam purred. "My Sophia has many talents."

Jane's cries of pleasure echoed in the room as she lay against the silk pillows, spread eagle, letting Sophia have her way.

"Sophia, you two should try out the product you purchased last night at Alexis's party," Adam suggested, running a finger across one of Jane's nipples as Sophia tongued her sex. His other hand still massaged Zero's head as she sucked his cock. "Maybe you can pleasure each other at the same time. You put it in the drawer over there. I know Maisy has a fondness for these things, too, so I'm sure she'll enjoy this little show."

Sophia sucked on Jane's clit one last time before lifting her head. With a mischievous smile, she reached into the drawer of the end table and produced a vibrator that appeared to have two large phalluses on it.

Jane's eyes widened. "Oh god, how did you get a double Juan Carlos?" she asked, sitting up. "How does that work?"

"It was way down deep at the bottom of all the boxes that Bianca lady left. I'll show you how it works." Sophia stroked one of the phalluses and then went to her knees on the bed. "You're gonna love this."

A mechanical whir came from the double vibrator. One of the heads shimmied at a quick pace, and Sophia lowered herself onto it.

"Ah." Sophia gasped, her eyes closed. She pinched her nipples, letting the vibration tease her clit.

"I want to try that, too," Jane said.

"Come on." Sophia stroked the other phallus. "Let's fuck each other."

Jane needed no more urging. She clicked the button on the base of the thing and murmured in anticipation as it whirred to life. Putting her hands on Sophia's shoulders for support, Jane took the fake cock inside her. Sophia's arms wrapped around Jane, and the two women kissed, each lifting their hips in a different pace, grinding against each other, nipple to nipple.

I liked to see you like that, Maisy. Like to see you take and give pleasure.

The whole thing was a huge turn on. The two women pressed closer to each other so that it did indeed look like they were fucking each other. Sophia succeeded in maneuvering Jane onto her back, riding the cock as her own pressure forced the one in Jane deeper. My panties were soaked with my own juices, my nipples hard, and the need to be a part of the scene made all rational thought flee. Subtly, I rubbed my clit against the chair, looking for even the smallest bit of relief.

The problem with having a tool like the one Jane and Sophia shared was that it apparently brought about a quick climax. On the other hand, what a delicious problem to have. Their cries circled in the air as they came hard and fast, collapsing with their arms around each other. Neither removed the vibrator, letting their bodies writhe together in the throes of their orgasm.

Zero paused in her blowjob to glance at the other women. Adam took this small break to guide her away from his swollen cock. He kissed her a moment before maneuvering Zero into a new position. Her upper body lowered to the bed and hips in the air with Zero's ass displayed for him. He took advantage of that by running his fingers from her ass to her damp cleft. Lazily, he played with her soft flesh, causing her to thrust her ass higher.

"Oh god, Dylan," Zero moaned. "Please tell me you're going to fuck me like this. I love being taken from behind."

"So you showed me last night," he said, slapping her ass. "But today I want to take you here." He touched the tight hole of her ass.

Her eyes widened.

"Don't worry. I won't take you there without making sure you're good and ready." Adam opened the drawer of the end table by his side and produced a bottle of lube "We brought this over for a reason, remember?"

As the lotion was rubbed into her ass, Zero shuddered at the invasion by his fingers but did not protest. He played with her there, one hand slipping around to touch her clit, smiling at her soft moans. His eyes met mine.

She's so tight. Fucking her like this is going to be so hot. You'll see.

Adam tapped his hard cock on her ass before inching the head in little by little. She cried out, but there was no mistaking the lust on her face. If there was pain, it was edged with pleasure. With a slight smirk, Adam rode her hard, his eyes never leaving mine.

This could be you. I could be fucking you like this, filling you like this, driving you beyond all reason.

My throat went dry as his words bounced in my head. That hard cock, the deep measured thrusts as his hands gripped soft flesh, the thought of him stripping away my soul and doing all those decadent and slightly depraved things to me.

I couldn't resist any longer. I nodded, wanting to let him have his way with me. His eyes lit up in triumph, and the power holding me down in the chair slipped way. Standing, I unbuttoned my blouse.

"Alexis, my sweet," Adam whispered, running a hand down her back. "I want you to help me pleasure Maisy."

"Whatever you say," she gasped as he fucked her harder. "Just don't stop. Please. You're so hard."

My blouse, followed by my bra, dropped to the floor.

"Come here," Adam commanded though he never stopped what he was doing to Zero. "Cup your breasts for Alexis. Let her have a little taste."

I couldn't have disobeyed if I wanted to, and I lifted my large breasts so Zero could suck both nipples at once. Her tongue swirled around them, sending hot shivers down my back and straight to the wet body between my legs. Adam leaned over her back to kiss me, his tongue mirroring the things she did to my breasts. I think that position allowed him to penetrate her more deeply, because she moaned and sucked even harder.

I'm going to take you next. Give you the greatest pleasure you've ever known. Your silly husband could never give you this.

Jensen. Bringing him up caused me to pull out of the moment. What was I doing? An orgy with my neighbors? How would I ever face them again if things went any further?

I'll send them away if you'll come to my bed. You almost gave yourself to me once before. And then there was last night. You were so close.

I wanted to give in. I wanted to feel him inside me, wanted his hands to caress my body, his lips on my breasts—not in some dream, but for real.

Jensen can never love you as I do.

Jensen. He shouldn't have said my husband's name. All the delicious heat was smothered in an instant, replaced by a cold reality. What the hell was I thinking? I shook my head, trying to clear it.

"I have to go," I said, backing away. I clasped my shirt and bra to me. "You all should come, too, before he turns you into a vampire."

"Oh, they'll be coming soon." Adam's eyes twinkled, but disappointment rang in his voice as he watched me dress. "They always come with me."

You will, too. It's a matter of time. I will have you. We are bound to each other.

I shook his voice out of my head and turned to go. At the stairs, I looked back in time to see his eyes shut with pleasure as he vigorously fucked Zero.

Bastard. Fucking vampire.

I was going to have to get rid of him for my neighbors' sake.

Who was I kidding? There was no way I would be able to resist him forever. I had to get rid of him for my own sanity, too. Having sex with vampires isn't something sane people do.

And I couldn't say no to him for much longer. I had lusted over Jensen for a long, long time, but when someone doesn't want you back, it's hard to ignore sexual heat from somewhere else. I didn't fully understand my mother's warning about Adam, but the more time I spent around him, the more rational thought left me.

If I wasn't careful, sooner or later I was going to end up in that vampire's bed.

Something told me there would be no coming back from that.

Chapter Eight

Back home, I'd taken a cold shower and then hopped online and researched vampires. Billions of sites popped up.

I avoided all the ones which talked about vampires sparkling.

Adam didn't sparkle. But he could create something called a thrall. I didn't know what that meant really, but one website explained it really well:

A vampire thrall is how the vampire keeps his victims in line. He uses it as a means of control, and once a victim is under his thrall, it is all too easy to then bite them or use them for other means. Sex is often a part of the thrall and the way that most vampires are able to entrap their victims for long periods of time.

Hmm….that made sense. Look at my skanky neighbors. Then again, I doubted Adam needed to use much of a thrall on them. They were sluts to begin with.

Getting rid of a thrall is difficult. Breaking a vampire's spell is never simple, and it is easier to remove the vampire itself than to break the thrall.

Remove the vampire? Kill it?

My cell phone rang. Jensen's number flashed on the screen.

"Hey," I answered. "What are you doing?"

"Nothing much. Just takin' a break," Jensen said. "Thought I'd see how you were doing."

He was calling to check on me? He never did that. How sweet.

"I'm fine."

Just been dealing with the vampire living behind us. Maybe even considering sleeping with him. No big deal...

"Good." he said. "So I was wondering...you want to go to dinner tonight?"

"Sure. Should I get a sitter for Rebecca?"

"Yeah. Maybe you should call my mom. I think she wanted to keep Rebecca for a few days."

Ugh. I hated talking with my mother in law, Gertrude Helsing. An old- school German lady who'd immigrated to Texas, she'd been divorced from Jensen's dad a long time and refused to ever speak of him. Every time I visited her house, her beady eyes watched me like a hawk. Jensen said I was imagining things, but I knew I wasn't.

Gertrude and Jensen had been estranged for a long time, but right after we had got married and Pops had died, the older woman started making an effort to stay in touch with her son. To her credit, Gertrude loved Rebecca and vice versa, but everything about me seemed to irritate her, from the way I dressed to the way I breathed.

Still, it probably wouldn't be such a bad idea to get my child away from the house now that I knew a vampire lived behind us.

"Maisy? You still there?"

"Sure. I'll call your mom in a little bit." Thinking about Gertrude Helsing made me remember something. "Hey, I forgot to ask you something this morning. What is Helser Eight? Some kind of game?"

"Where did you see that?" His voice carried a sharp undertone I didn't like.

"On your computer. I was..." *Think fast. What were you doing in his office?* "I was cleaning a little and saw it pop up on your screen."

Long pause.

"Yeah, it's part of a game I've been playing on line," he said. "You don't have to clean in my office."

"It's no problem," I said, but I couldn't help the funny little feeling inside me. Jensen wasn't being truthful. "Why would it want to know about your wife?"

Another long pause.

"It's one of those games where you create a fake family," he finally said. "Sort of like the SIMS people."

"I see."

"Listen, I gotta go. I'll be home by five-thirty to take you out to dinner. Call my mom about taking Rebecca."

Jensen hung up. What was he hiding? Again, I wondered about that box of weapons. Did he know about vampires?

And then it hit me. *We were going out to dinner. Like a couple on a date.* Thoughts of our morning kiss made me tingly in all the right places, and I couldn't help but let my imagination run with other possibilities of what the night might bring. Don't get me wrong— having a vampire next door was a big problem, but if I could change my lack of sex status, that would be very helpful in combating Adam's advances.

Part of the reason I'd stopped myself from getting involved with the orgy next door was Jensen. When Adam had said his name, I couldn't help but think of my feelings for my husband. It's true that I lust after him, but I have known him a long time. I do love him for being willing to marry me. He may not really be in love with me, but I owed it to him to be respectful of our vows—fake or not—and at least try not to turn into a vengeful slut who slept with vampires.

Oh god. Jensen deserved so much better than me.

An ugly thought occurred. What if this was like a break- up dinner? What if Jensen was going to try and let me down gently by plying me with food and alcohol? What if he was going to say, "Hey, I know we're married and all, but we can only be friends."

Or worse yet, what if he wanted a divorce? What if I was wrong about his loyalty to Pops?

Were things ever going to be easy in my life? Somehow I doubted it.

Focus. One problem at a time.

I glanced out the window, the roof of Adam's house peeking over the fence line. Were they still up there?

Didn't matter, I told myself.

But it does matter, a little voice insisted. *What if he turns your neighbors into vampires? Then the whole neighborhood is in trouble. And how dare he claim that you were special and then turn around and sleep with those women?*

And then there were the things he had said. We are bound by blood or something? That I'd given in to him before? Surely, he meant the naughty dreams.

I really needed to talk to someone who knew about these things.

My mother.

It was a two-hour drive to visit her, which wasn't

terrible, but Jensen would ask questions if I took off to see Momma. I'd never make it there and back in time for our dinner tonight. Besides, this wasn't the sort of thing I wanted to discuss on the phone

How had she gotten in touch with me, if I weren't going crazy? A gypsy?

I knew one of those. Bianca Rivera, my favorite, Lovely Lust sales associate.

Bianca had even told me to contact her, and I would know why. I fished her card out of the pocket of the pants I'd been wearing last night. Her name and phone number were printed in neat little comic sans letters. I ran my fingers lightly over the words, wondering if she could help me.

Might as well give it a try.

She picked up on the second ring.

"Bianca?" I asked. "This is Maisy Harker. We met last night at Alexis's party."

"I've been expecting your call."

"Really?" I asked.

"Most certainly. When that vampire walked in, I understood you were going to need my help."

"Vampire? So I'm not crazy?" Relieved she'd brought up the "V" word first, I could have cried. "I thought for sure I was losing my mind."

"On no, my dear." Her voice thickened with emotion. "You are not crazy. But you will be if you don't do something about your current situation. Vampires make terrible neighbors."

"I would imagine so," I said.

"I'm surprised your husband hasn't done something already."

"Jensen?" What was he supposed to do? Computer

code the vampire to death? How did she even know about Jensen? "What would he do? Do you know my husband?"

There was a pause.

"Um...you do know about your family history, correct?" Bianca asked, caution in her voice. "You understand things?"

"No. What history?"

"Your last name is Harker?"

"Well, yeah. It's a family name."

"You are descendant of Mina Harker?"

Mina Harker? Now why did that name sound familiar? I'd heard it before.

"I'm not sure," I said slowly. "Who is that?"

Another long pause.

"I think you should discuss the matter further with your husband," Bianca said. "You need to be enlightened about your family curse."

"Curse? What curse?" Frustrated, I tapped my fingers on the desk of my computer. "Look, what I need is answers, but my mother holds them. I need to get in touch with her through you. My husband would think I'm going crazy."

"You're wrong. Your husband knows more than you think."

"I'm not sure what's really going on, Bianca, but I'm starting to freak out."

I thought about telling her how I'd compulsively checked over every inch of my body for bite marks while I was in the shower, and then I had erased *The Phantom of the Opera* from my DVR. In fact, I'd almost thrown out my entire Andrew Lloyd Webber collection based on an irrational fear that Adam would start singing the libretto to *Cats* as a way to entice me into his bed. For all I knew, his rendition of *Jellicle Cats* would make me orgasm on the spot.

"Can you please come over?" I begged. "Or I can even meet you somewhere if you prefer."

She didn't say anything right away, leaving me to speculate about what secrets Jensen might be keeping me in the dark about.

"All right. How about this afternoon? We can talk more about...well, about what's going on," Bianca finally said. "What time does your husband get home?"

"He's home at five thirty today."

"All right....that should be enough time," she mused. "As long as I don't get caught."

"Get caught? What do you mean?"

"What we are doing is a violation of the Helser Institute. I don't know why no one has told you any of this." Bianca paused. "Does two o' clock work for you?"

Helser. There was that name again.

"Sure. I'm in the house across from Alexis's."

We hung up, but I was more curious than ever. What did Bianca know? More importantly, what did my husband know? The Helser Institute didn't sound like part of some online computer game.

And how come no one had told me anything about vampires being real?

****

"It's good to see you again." Bianca's friendly smile turned to a frown when I opened my front door farther. "You look pale."

"My mother-in-law was just here," I said. "She picked up my daughter for a little vacation at her house, but the woman always makes me crazy."

"I've heard Gertrude Helsing can be quite intimidating," Bianca commented. The filmy blue skirt swished around her legs as she strolled in. The white, tailored blouse was open at the top, showing off her cleavage. Her perfectly plucked eyebrows furrowed. "Of course, I've never actually met her."

How did she even know about my mother-in-law?

"Oh, this is going to be fun." Bianca smiled at the look of confusion on my face. Her short, black bobbed hair swung to the left as she tilted her head. "Tell me, do you have any vodka?"

"Sure. Would you like some?"

"Oh no. It's for you. You're going to need a drink."

Oh boy.

"Look, Bianca," I said, leading her into the living room. "I don't know what the hell is going on exactly, but it's about time someone started explaining. I'm either crazy like my mother, or I'm not. I need answers."

"And I'm going to give them to you. But first, you must promise that when you confront the Helser Institute, you leave my name out of it. And this is especially important—do not mention it to the creature stalking you." Bianca shuddered. "I have a long history with the Institute and with vampires. I don't want any more to do with them than I have to. It was hard enough hearing his true name last night."

"You heard something different when I asked him for his name, didn't you?" Understanding flooded me as she nodded. "That's why you left. You got scared."

"True enough. I've heard whispered stories about your vampire, Maisy. I never thought I'd meet him. I was taught it is better to run away than confront the creature who slaughtered my ancestors."

"Then why would you help me?"

"You are special." She gestured to my hand. "I saw your life line. You can fight a lot of things in this world, but destiny is not one of them."

With that, I went to the liquor cabinet and found the vodka. Grabbing two glasses, I set it all down on the coffee table.

"All right," I said. "Tell me everything. I'm ready."

Bianca laughed softly. "No. You're not. But then, no one can ever be ready to hear their destiny lies with an old vampire who is obsessed with her family." Bianca closed her eyes and took a deep breath. "Let me open the pathway to the past."

Open the pathway to the past? That sounded cryptic.

To my surprise, she filled one of the glasses I'd put on the coffee table with vodka.

"This must be a really shitty tale if you think I'm going to need that much to drink," I said.

She smiled, but said nothing. Reaching into her purse, she pulled out a little silk bag. Loosening the drawstrings to it, she dipped her fingers inside and sprinkled a fine, white powder into the vodka. For a few seconds, it floated on top of the liquid. Then it started to fizz and bubble.

Bianca waited a bit longer before waving her hand over the vodka. "You ready?" she asked.

"Sure." I had no idea what she was doing. It looked to me like she was wasting alcohol. "I hope you don't expect me to drink that."

She grinned and then snapped her fingers above the

glass. A purple flame sparked to life.

"How did you—"

She shushed me. "Look into the flame," she instructed and took several deep breaths.

I did as she asked and became conscious of the energy in my house shifting. A dark shadow fell on the living room. The candles above the mantle of the fireplace suddenly burst with bright flames as did the two long candlesticks I kept on the coffee table for decoration. The heavy curtains tied back at each of the windows slipped free of their restraints and closed, leaving the room in darkness save for the candles. The scent of patchouli filled the room.

It reminded me of Jared. He'd liked patchouli and insisted on burning it all the time in little incense burners my mother kept around the house. Later, I figured out he used it to mask the skunky smell of pot.

"Patchouli is a heavy scent." Bianca opened her eyes. "It's strong enough to create a curtain, blocking the sound of our voices from prying ears. It keeps those who seek to harm us in the dark. Give me your hand, Maisy Harker. It's time to begin your journey."

Our hands sparked when we touched, and she gripped tightly when I would have pulled away. Her eyes glowed with a light amber shine as she leaned forward. "Look at me. See me," she whispered. "Only me."

Bianca lifted her free hand and blew. More of powder from the little silk bag flew into my eyes, stinging and irritating. I blinked as my vision blurred, but even though I couldn't see clearly, the world around me was changing. The living room walls faded, and black space surrounded us. Wind rushed around, lifting my hair, chilling me to the bone.

Everything stopped.

The deep silence hurt my ears. My body felt stretched, yanked in all directions. I wanted to scream, to cry out, but there wasn't air to do that.

There was a loud pop and a rush of motion surrounded me.

I'd been dropped into an old Victorian photograph. Or at least, that's what it looked like.

I stood in the middle of a crowded street. People pushed and shoved to get to their destinations, avoiding horse poop and carriages. Women with high collars, slim waists, and long skirts walked past me. Their faces were devoid of makeup and their hair was piled up high. The men were equally fashionable in their dark suits and derby hats. One of them studied a pocket watch as he passed, but I sensed he didn't see me. In fact, no one appeared to notice that a stranger from the future, clad in shorts and a T-shirt, had been dropped into their midst.

I didn't have time to look for long. A woman exiting a nearby building with the word "Theatre" on it caught my eye. Starkly blonde and wearing a beautiful, blue silk dress which brought out her eyes, I saw traces of my mother in her. Clutched in her hand were two white gloves.

"Mina, my dear." A tall man dressed in a black suit coat with a matching top hat followed her. His brown beard was meticulously trimmed, and his green eyes flashed before he stopped Mina, standing with his back to me. "You simply must stay and see Irving's new show. I'll save a seat for you in my box."

"Bram, I would love to, but you know how

Jonathan is." Mina's grin was full of mischief as she glanced at the old building behind him. "He doesn't approve of the theatre or of my old friends. He fears you mean to corrupt me."

"And who says I haven't done that already?" The man's throaty chuckle brought a smile to her face. "I take it your Jonathan Harker does not know about your aspirations as an actress."

"No. He wouldn't approve." Mina's gaze grew stern. "And you are not to tell him. That life is over for me."

"Shame. You were a skilled Ophelia. Everyone mourned your death."

"I doubt that. I seem to recall overhearing someone in the audience say I couldn't have died soon enough."

"Everyone's a critic. I should know."

"I must go now, Bram, darling." She pulled on the white gloves and brushed at her skirt. "Jonathan will be wondering where I am."

"Please give him my best." Bram tipped his top hat at Mina. "I shall call on you soon. I want to hear all about your married life."

"I fear it would bore you," Mina smiled. "Still it would be nice to see you again."

Bram turned from her, and I could see he was a very handsome man. His high cheekbones gave way to a sensual mouth. Something dark and dangerous lurked in his green eyes, something deliciously sexy despite the stiff Victorian setting. Mina felt it, too. She sighed as he walked away. Then she turned and set out in the opposite direction.

I followed her. Judging from the accents I heard on the street, I figured we must be in England. Soon, we turned up the walkway to a large, white Victorian mansion surrounded by well-kept bushes and trees.

Mina opened the door, and I slipped inside before she shut it. She took off her hat and gloves, calling, "Jonathan, I'm home."

There was a noise from the room to our right. After a moment, a tall thin man appeared at the doorway. Handsome, though not in the same way Bram had been, he had dark hair and wore small, wire-rimmed glasses.

"Where were you, Mina?" he asked, smoothing down his vest. "I was worried."

"Just took a walk, darling." Mina kissed him. "I had to get out of this house."

"I wish you would take one of the maids with you. The streets are not safe for a woman alone. I've been reading the papers and there is another madman on the loose. They're likening him to a second Jack the Ripper." Jonathan pushed her away so he could look into her eyes. "He preys on women."

"He preys on prostitutes," Mina said. "I'm not his type at all. And everyone knows Jack the Ripper— whoever he was—is long dead."

"We don't know that for sure. They never caught him. You mustn't believe every piece of idle gossip your friends ply you with." Jonathan frowned. "And you do frequent...well, I know you still frequent the theatre district. Such a seedy part of the city. A man like the Ripper or even one impersonating him would be drawn to a low class area like that. I'm aware you enjoy attending performances at Henry Irving's theatre."

Her eyes darkened with anger. "Have you been spying on me?"

"I'm simply concerned for your safety."

"Is that it? Or is it something more?"

"What else could it be?" Jonathan turned from her, entering the room he'd just come from.

Mina followed him into a sumptuous study filled with books and heavy, dark furniture.

"I'm your husband," he said, standing at a large window framed by green velvet curtains, which complemented the masculine Victorian couch against the wall. "It's my duty to take care of you, to make decisions for you."

Both Mina and I bristled at that.

"You are not my lord and master," Mina spat. "You are not my father."

`Jonathan turned to her, on the defensive. "Then don't act like a child. Don't be secretive. Tell me if you are going to see that...that man who works for Irving. What is he again? Some sort of assistant who occasionally plays at being a writer?"

"I assume you mean Bram." Mina narrowed her eyes. "And for your information, Bram Stoker does not play at anything. He is quite accomplished."

"I guess you must know all about his accomplishments in other areas, too?" Jonathan's face flushed with anger. "Do you imagine I do not know about your affair with Stoker before we were married?"

Mina grew pale, but her voice quavered with indignant shock. "Well, I am certainly not having an affair with him now!"

"But you did once. Do you deny he was your lover?"

"I deny nothing. It was over long before I met you." Mina stamped her foot. "Long before you married

121

me."

Jonathan studied her, his expression softening. "I know, darling." He put his hands on her shoulders. "I know. It's just…he still considers you his muse."

"I don't know about that," Mina whispered, allowing him to wrap her into an embrace. "I'm nothing to him."

"You are everything to me," Jonathan whispered into her hair. "My wife. My love. My heart. You are mine."

"As you are mine."

And just like that, their squabble dissolved, and they passionately kissed. With gentle hands, he removed the pins in her hair, letting her golden locks fall free. She gave a little sigh of contentment as he nuzzled her neck, wrapping his arms around her, pinning her to the desk, but there was nothing threatening in his manner. This was the picture of a sexual encounter built on love.

The raw lust and heat I'd experienced lately had been eye-opening…but this…this is what I wanted for myself someday. This is what I'd imagined being with Jensen would be like.

I looked away, embarrassed, and my eye was drawn to a figure standing outside the window. Pale with a sharp jawline both beautiful and cruel, his high cheekbones gave him the look of one of those old paintings where the people in it were too perfect to be real. Glossy, black hair curled becomingly at the edge of his pale cheek. His dark cloak hid the rest of his clothing.

He gazed intently at the couple, unashamed to be watching them as they grew more and more intimate, more heated. Jealousy and hatred blazed in his eyes as Jonathan stripped off Mina's clothes.

Without regard for anyone else, the couple made love on the desk.

So much for Victorian primness.

However, the man outside the window continued to watch, his face twisting and contorting with undisguised need and hate. And his eyes…they turned a blood red. Chilled, I was glad he was unaware of my presence, though he looked incredibly familiar.

The animal lust I sensed in him was disturbing.

And a turn on.

Whatever little time bubble Bianca had created decided it was time to shift forward. The room dissolved and cold air rushed around me again. I squeezed my eyes shut, hoping this would end soon.

Everything stilled.

I took a cautious peek through one eyelid.

A bedroom. Mina's. The windows were open, and the curtains fluttered in the breeze. The bed in the middle of the room was like the one I'd dreamed about when I encountered my invisible lover. In fact, I was pretty sure it was the same bed.

Mina lay in the center of it, a blue, silk night gown pooling around her. Her head was turned to the side, lips slightly parted while she moaned in ecstasy. She writhed on the bed, enjoying the attentions of some invisible lover as I had.

The he appeared—the man I'd seen outside the window. Naked and bold, he slid his thick cock in and out of her with ease, deepening his thrusts enough to get her to cry out. The man pinned her arms so she was unable to stop him. Not that she wanted to.

This wasn't making love like I'd seen Mina do with her husband. This was more primal, more passionate. Her lover was claiming her in a way Jonathan couldn't, and I could tell by the way she arched toward him, by the way she cried out in joy, that she wanted this man in an entirely different way.

The man's mouth found her neck. Mina moaned again as he thrust deeply inside her. He chuckled and turned his head enough so I could see the blood dripping from his lips.

He'd been drinking from her.

The room fell away, and the windstorm swept me back into the dark.

In the distance, I could hear someone speaking.

"Mina, you must let me help you." Bram's strong voice grew clearer before he came into view.

I now stood on the dim stage of a theatre opposite a grim faced Bram whose brown hair was tousled as if he'd been worrying at it with his hand. His wrinkled shirt was open at the collar and the unkemptness of his appearance made me wonder when he'd last found time to change clothes. There was no mistaking the worry in his voice when he spoke to Mina.

"This is no joke," he said. "Dark forces are trying to take you from this world. You must fight."

"Bram, darling." Clad in a long, black dress, Mina stood center stage, her weary voice matching the dark circles beneath her eyes. "You are so dramatic. It's—it's not what you think."

"It *is* what I think."

"A vampire? Don't be ridiculous. There is no such thing."

"But there is. My father told me about them. He

even fought a few in his lifetime. I know the signs." Bram pushed back her hair, revealing two bite marks on her neck. Mina jerked away. "You must not let him do this to you anymore."

"And how am I to stop him?" Mina flicked her hair back down, covering the bites. "I am powerless when I'm around him."

"Do you...have feelings for him?"

"No. Of course not." Mina laughed, a shrill, nervous sound. "I could never love a— Well, whatever he is."

"A vampire. This creature is a vampire. They kill without thought. The fact that he has taken such an interest in you is worrisome."

"What do you mean?"

"Tell me the truth, Mina. Have you drank any of his blood?"

The guilt in her eyes was unmistakable.

"I see." Bram's face became lined with sadness. "He wants you for his bride. For his companion. If you have taken his blood, then you would become one of the undead should you die. You must stop drinking from him now and remove yourself from his company. Doing so will weaken his influence, and over time, you will be normal again. Otherwise, I fear this creature will arrange an accident to occur, one that will result in your mortal death. Darkness will consume your soul."

"Oh, Bram, I didn't know what to do at first," she whispered. "But he made me feel...so many things... I had no choice but to drink. And the truth of it is that I wanted to. I would pledge my very soul to his. I'm ready to die."

"You were always a passionate woman." Bram

patted her shoulder, an odd look on his face. "A creature such as this would naturally be attracted to you."

"What am I to do? I do have…feelings for him, Bram. I can't be without him." She sobbed.

Before I could hear Bram's answer, I was once more whisked away. The hollow sound of her crying swirled in the cold air around me as I waited to see where I would end up next.

But this time, I was deposited back in my living room. The candles whooshed out. Bianca sat across from me, pale and out of breath.

With shaking hands, I poured vodka into the empty glass. I took a few sips, trying to get my hands to stop shaking.

"So let me get this straight," I said after getting some semblance of control. "Mina Harker was a real person."

"Yes."

"Okay, I'm not completely stupid you know," I said. "I've read *Dracula*. Seen the movie a bunch of times. Totally thought Winona Ryder should have dumped Keanu Reeves for Gary Oldman. But am I to understand that it's a true story?"

Even saying it aloud sounded ridiculous.

"Not entirely. Bram Stoker wrote it down as a tribute to his Mina. But he changed certain details to protect himself."

"But my ancestor is Mina Harker?"

"Yes. She is the start of this wicked curse on the women of your family. She drank the vampire blood and bonded with him, was even willing to become his undead bride."

"That's…crazy. You're telling me this is where fiction and real life collide?" I fanned myself, struggling to take it all in, and yet wanting to know more. "So things didn't work out for them?"

"A gypsy curse was placed on them, one that has been passed down through the generations." Bianca sat back. "It lingers like a poison on your bloodline, waiting for Dracula to suck it out."

Considering the time I'd spent with him already, the thought of Dracula sucking anything was both revolting and thrilling.

"So that guy next door is not Adam Levine, but he's Dracula in disguise or something?" I shook my head. "You've got to be fucking kidding me."

"Do I look like a woman who jokes around?" She sniffed disdainfully. "Oh, and the reason he looks like Adam Levine is because that's Dracula's big thing. He can tap into your subconscious and learn about the kind of man you desire. Then he projects your wishes so that when you talk to him, it's like your fantasy guy is right there. This helps him get whatever he wants."

"And now he wants…me?"

Unbelievable. In my wildest dreams, I'd never expected to be the object of a vampire's desire. Hell, I couldn't even get my fake husband interested in me. How was I supposed to believe the real Dracula wanted to turn me into some kind of vampire bride?

"Yes. He can't help but be drawn to you," Bianca said.

"Why?"

Bianca shifted, uncomfortable. "The curse. It calls to him to you just as it will call you to him."

"I don't understand. What is the curse exactly?"

"Mina was pregnant at the time the curse was placed, and the blood from the vampire marked the unborn child. The curse decreed that all women in Mina's line would feel attraction for him. But it could never turn to love," Bianca said. "Dracula feels it, too.

"According to what the Institute has recorded about your family, the vampire wants to find the one woman in your family tree, the one closest to Mina's soul, the one who will choose him over all others. She's the one who can break the curse. But it never happens. He is called by your blood, obsessive with his feelings, but when the love is not returned, it never ends well for the Harker women."

"None of the other ladies in my family have...succumbed to his charms?" I asked. Surely, at least one of them must have slipped up. "None have fallen in love with him?"

"Oh, I wouldn't say that. They've all had dalliances with him, sexual encounters." Bianca looked at me knowingly, and I couldn't help but squirm with guilt. "A few have even claimed to have loved him, but none have given him what he truly desires, what he wants most of all. He kills when he doesn't get it—their heart."

Killed? I took a breath, ignoring the slight shake in my voice. "I don't understand. How have the other women managed to stop him?"

"Stop him?" Bianca shook her head. "Most have died at his hands due to his uncontrollable anger, leaving behind a daughter of their own to carry on the curse. However, they've also had the help of the guardians."

"Uh...who?"

Bianca grinned. "All the Harker women are assigned a guardian by the Helser Institute. You see, the Institute was started by Bram Stoker." Bianca sipped from her drink. "It was a private group meant to study and protect humans from the supernatural. It's funded by a German family who had been plagued by all sorts of supernatural beings. One of the men in the Helsing family was the inspiration for the character of Abraham von Helsing in Bram Stoker's book."

Helsing? Jensen's last name. My heart beat faster with worry, but I couldn't quite go there yet.

"Momma's guardian…was that Jared?"

Even as I asked, I knew the answer. Of course, he'd been her guardian. The box of weapons Jared had carted around had been for her protection. It made much more sense to me now.

"Yes…but I believe his feelings for her were much deeper. Just as your guardian's feelings run strong for you."

Who could possibly care about me enough to protect me from a vampire? Taking on a task like that—one that meant possibly dying to protect your ward—I couldn't imagine a man doing that for me. Surely, Bianca was confused.

"I have a guardian?" But the answer came on its own.

Jensen.

My emotions twisted up, taking my breath away, making my head swim with appreciation and anxiety. Jensen was my guardian, the person who had taken on the task of protecting me.

How sweet.

How romantic.

How...weird.

"Jensen asked to be assigned to you six years ago," Bianca said, slowly. "His father was very against it. You see, Jensen was being groomed to take over as the head of the Institute one day, but even Thomas King knew he wouldn't be able to change his son's mind. Jensen was dead set on being your guardian."

"Wait a minute. Thomas King? You mean Pops? Pops was part of the Institute?" I asked before leaning back as what else she said hit me. Deep down, I'd always believed Pops might be a distant relative of *mine*. It would explain his kindness to me, the way he'd taken me in. To find out he was Jensen's dad...I couldn't tell if I was disappointed or elated to get the truth. "Jensen is his son? I thought—I thought he was someone he'd taken under his wing."

"Oh no. Jensen is his child and your guardian."

Well, that explained the money Pops had given us. It wasn't payment to Jensen. It was inheritance. Some of the guilt I'd felt about shackling my husband in this crazy marriage lifted. Maybe he had been freer to make the choice than I'd thought.

"This is a lot to process." I poured another drink, feeling the buzz of alcohol starting to ease some of my disbelief. "*A lot* to process."

"True. It's not every day you find out that your husband's real job is to kick vampire ass."

"Considering Jensen has trouble with basic things like running the dishwasher or the washing machine, I'd say finding out he is supposedly capable of kicking vampire ass, as you put it, is pretty much in the sphere of unbelievable."

"You should see the footage they have of Jensen in

the field in the Institute archives."

Footage? There was film of Jensen in action? I tried to picture that in my mind but kept coming up with an image of Buffy the Vampire Slayer. Did he spout witty catch phrases as he staked vampires? Knowing Jensen, he probably apologized as he killed them, flashing that charming smile I knew so well.

"Was Pops a guardian? Is that why he took me in?"

"No. His brother, Jared, was one."

Jared had been Pops' brother? What the fuck? Could this get any weirder? Why had I been kept in the dark? And of course, all the people who could have enlightened me further on that relationship were either dead, in a mental institution, or bent on keeping me ignorant.

"And how would I get a hold of something like the archives?" I asked. "Apparently, I'm not even supposed to know they exist. What's with that anyway? I mean, Momma obviously knew something. She was in the loop on this whole curse. Why did no one tell me?"

Bianca frowned. "The current head of the Institute thought it better you were told nothing."

"Well, that's stupid. If every female in my line has suffered from Draculaitis, then it seems to me that a little heads up about it would have been appropriate."

"I don't always agree with the Institute." Bianca's eyes flashed in anger. "They have a way of keeping too much to themselves until it's too late. I know this first hand."

"Oh yeah?"

"Let's just say that like yours, my family also has a long history with the Institute. However, I prefer to take control of my destiny. That's why I stole their files and learned how to hack into their systems undetected," Bianca said.

"And here I thought you just specialized in dildos and lubricants."

Obviously, this woman had mad skills that went far beyond the sexy persona she put out there. Why would a big company like the Institute let her go? Bianca was a woman I wanted on *my* team, not the enemy's. It didn't take a genius to see that whatever the Institute had done to her, they'd screwed up badly.

"Well, dildos and lubricants often pay the bills, but hacking is a commodity which people pay much more for." Bianca smiled. "That's why if you are interested in seeing Jensen in action or you want to peek at the rest of your family tree, I'm willing to help."

"And what do you get in return?"

She gave a throaty laugh. "I get to fuck with the asshole running the Institute."

"You sure you want to make an enemy like that? I would think someone who runs a secret group might be someone you don't want to cross."

"*I'm* someone you don't want to cross," she said. "Unfortunately, he did."

Hmmm....sounded like there was a great story there, but since I'm shallow and was too overwhelmed with all the info she had given me about my heritage to ask more about her own, I decided to let it be.

"Bring on the secret info," I said. "I still have plenty of time before I need to get ready to meet Jensen, and I want to go to dinner knowing what I'm up against."

"Does he have an office here at the house?" she asked.

"Yep."

"Then that will make this even easier. Take me to it."

We gathered our drinks and headed into Jensen's office.

****

"Wow. Did you see him cut that thing's head off?" I turned to Bianca.

The computer screen was frozen on the decapitated body of a female vampire in a retro nightclub. The vamp's gold dress caught the flashing lights in the club, making bright sparkles on the screen. Her head lay nearby. Mercifully, it had landed so that the eyes were covered by her long red hair.

Bianca smiled and nodded.

"Does he do that all the time?"

"This is old footage." Bianca leaned across me and clicked on another video. "This one is more recent."

"Recent? Like how recent?"

"About a month or so old."

I watched as a grainy video of a parking garage played on the computer.

A woman walked into the eye line of the camera. Her head was down as she searched in her bag for something. Probably her keys. Sure enough, she pulled them out, but while she'd been searching, a man dressed in a dark suit crept up behind her.

"How can she not know he's right there?" I muttered. "He's literally breathing down her neck."

"Vamps are very good at stalking their prey. They're light on their feet and very bendy."

"Bendy?"

Bianca didn't say anything. Her eyes were trained

on the screen, and I couldn't help but follow her gaze. Mr. Bendy was still stalking the woman. She stopped next to the passenger door of a blue car her hands gliding the key into the lock. Just as she was about to open it, Mr. Bendy lunged.

He shoved her against the door, knocking the keys out of her hand. In one swift motion, he ripped the purse off her shoulder and tossed it away. Tilting her head to the side, he opened his mouth and prepared to sink his fangs into the woman's soft flesh.

And that's when my husband appeared.

I don't even know exactly how he got there, but the next thing I knew, he grabbed the vampire and pinned its arms to the side. His mouth opened as if he might be shouting at the woman. She took off, scrambling to grab her purse on her way.

Then Jensen went to work.

He slipped out a sharp dagger from his boot which glittered on the computer monitor despite the grainy footage of the security camera. The vampire jerked back, head butting Jensen. It whirled around, its pale face a storm of fury and hate as it lunged. Jensen easily sidestepped out of the way and managed to jab the creature before it recovered and rushed him.

The knife slid into Mr. Bendy as if he were butter.

The vamp's eyes widened, and his lips moved. There was no telling what it told Jensen before it burst into a ball of flame. Jensen stared at the burn left behind on the ground and then turned toward the camera.

His face was blank, emotionless.

"Your boy is a bad ass," Bianca said. "Helser Eight—that's Jensen's code name—is a legend at the Institute."

I got up and went to the window. The afternoon sun was shifting, as was my world. Vampires were real and my husband killed them for a living. My mother wasn't as crazy as I'd always thought, and now, due to some crazy family curse, I was the object of the real Dracula's lusty desire. The Kardashian family had nothing on me when it came to reality. "This is all so....so...wild."

"That's one way to look at it." Bianca clicked the mouse of the computer. "But at least you aren't in the dark any longer. Now you can take steps to protect yourself."

"I can?" I laughed bitterly. "How? Where do I start? Do I go to dinner with Jensen and say 'Hi, honey, how was your day as a vampire slayer?'"

"It's not the way I would go about it."

I turned to Bianca. "And what would you do?"

"I'd ask him how the curse got started in the first place. The Institute has detailed files on their version of it."

Their version of it? Was there more than one?

"And I'd start figuring out how to kill my neighbors," she added.

"Wait. Do you mean I have to kill my neighbor, Dracula? Or am I going to have to kill those horny bitches who appear to have fallen for him? Are they vamps?"

"Fledglings. They still have a chance to be normal, but you gotta get rid of Dracula."

"And if I don't?"

"Then they become vampires."

Oh, shit. Vampires in my neighborhood. If that happened, technically, it would be my fault. I mean,

I'm the one with vampire magnet in my DNA. I'm the reason Dracula moved in behind us, the reason my neighbors were having the greatest sex of their lives right now. Of course, that didn't mean they deserved to be transformed into creatures of the night. And what about their families? Would the ladies eventually turn them into vampires, too? Would we have a little vampire colony living on our street?

"This is a lot of pressure."

"Maybe you should have some more vodka." Bianca patted my shoulder. "It's going to be okay. I've gotta go, though. Check out the stuff I left you, talk to Jensen, and then call me tomorrow. If you want to get in touch with your mother still, I can make that happen, too. She probably used my cousin, Belinda, to make it happen on her end."

I'd completely forgotten about getting in touch with my mother. All the other information had swamped my original plan to get her help. Still, she was the sole surviving Harker woman who'd ever dealt with Dracula even if it did make her crazy. There had to be some advice she could give me.

"What if I don't make it through the night?" I grabbed her arm before she could leave. "What if Dracula comes over and tries to put the moves on me?"

"Jensen will protect you, and you're not as helpless as you think." Bianca patted my hand before gently shaking free. "You've got a gift for persuading others to do your bidding."

"A gift? You know, Adam mentioned something like that to me. And Momma had said I had some sort of mutation. What is she talking about?" I asked.

Bianca bit her lip, trying to decide something. She

shook her head. "You must ask Jensen," she finally said. "He'll tell you, guide you from now on."

She sounded so sure, but I wasn't. Realistically, shouldn't this Helser Institute have been able to stop Dracula in the last hundred years? My husband looked like a badass on screen, but could he really handle Dracula?

Could I?

Chapter Nine

"Are you okay?" Jensen studied me over the top of his menu. "You look...nervous."

Considering that we rarely went out to dinner as a couple, I normally would have been beyond excited to be seated opposite the man I'd been fantasizing about. But now that I knew the truth of things, that excitement had edged into full on anxiety, bordering on hysteria.

"Um...well, there is something I want to talk to you about." I put the menu down and picked up my wine glass.

Somehow, I had managed to keep from bombarding Jensen with questions the minute he'd walked in the door. Getting dressed in my favorite blue dress, doing my hair—I made it look as natural as I could. But my nerves had been humming with anticipation. When I'd seen him all dressed up and so handsome in a maroon dress shirt and dark pants, I'd almost lost my nerve to confront him at all.

Now that we were at the restaurant, I couldn't contain myself any longer. Jensen had pulled my chair out for me before sliding into his own, ever the gentleman. But I couldn't be a proper lady. Word vomit tumbled out. "I had an interesting conversation today with the lady I met last night who sells the dildos."

The waiter sidled up to our table at the precise moment I had said *dildo*. He blinked and managed not to laugh. "Are you two ready to order?"

Embarrassed, I kept my eyes averted and let Jensen order for both of us. The steak knife laid out with all the other silverware got me thinking about what I'd watched him do that day. If a vampire attacked us right now, would he gut it in one swift slash of the knife and then calmly cut his meat?

"So, what were you saying about dildos?" Jensen grinned as the waiter left.

"I was saying—I was saying—" I took a deep breath and decided to go for it. The direct approach was always best with him. "I know you kill vampires in your spare time."

Startled, he knocked over his water glass. He caught it before too much could spill, but his expression changed to the one I'd seen on the video. Blank. Emotionless.

"What I'm trying to say is…well…" I tried again. "I saw some footage of you at work. I was cleaning in your office upstairs and I…I snooped a little, discovered a few files. I know about Mina Harker and what happened to my ancestors."

I had decided this would be a better story than bringing Bianca into the equation. She'd been pretty adamant about wanting to keep her name out of it.

He studied me. Would he even tell me the truth? Would he deny the entire thing? Try to make me feel as if I were crazy? He probably wouldn't have to try too hard on that one. Crazy seemed to be the order of the day.

"So you finally found out." He gave a small nod. "You must have questions."

No denial? No pretending I'd lost my mind? No

anger at me snooping in files? For some reason, that made the reality of it even worse. I mean, I knew the truth, but still…I hadn't expected him to come clean with me so easily. The last bit of hope that this was an elaborate prank came crashing down, leaving me slightly nauseous.

"Um…questions…yeah, I have a few," I said.

"I'm not sure we should discuss this here. Maybe we should eat and then talk."

"You eat. I'll talk." I took a breath, promising myself I would take it slow. Instead, a mass of rushed thoughts poured out. "I want to know about my mother, and I want to know why you didn't ever tell me Pops was your dad. I want to know why no one told me about Mina Harker, and that I would be stalked by Dracula, or that I'm cursed. Those seem like kind of important details, you know?"

Finally, I saw some sort of emotion on his face. Regret.

"Maisy, believe me, I've wanted to tell you so many times. There was no way you wouldn't find out about all of this one day. I can't tell you what a relief it is to finally get it out there in the open. I was never an advocate for not telling you the truth."

"But you didn't. Start talking. Tell me about this curse."

Jensen sighed and drummed his fingers on the table. "I've always believed you are the first Harker woman to have a chance at ending it once and for all. You are the first woman in the line to grow up with almost no knowledge about your heritage or the curse. That means you can't be influenced by it as some have. I didn't agree with the decision to keep silent about the past, but a part of me does believe it will be the key to finally ending this, the key to protecting our daughter."

"You mean *my* daughter." It was a low blow, but how dare these people, these strangers make decisions about my life? I leaned forward and practically hissed at him. "She is not your child."

A shadow crossed his face.

"*Our* daughter." He shifted in his seat. "Rebecca is my biological child."

"Um, Jensen, I don't think so. You weren't there the night of her conception. I admit, I don't remember much about it, but I'm pretty sure I would have remembered you."

He tugged at his shirt collar, not quite meeting my eye. "I must have come up with a thousand different ways to tell you the truth over the years, but I never could. Pops told me it should be kept a secret, that what happened was due to your genetic bond with the vampire, but I've never felt right about it," he said. "I never meant to hurt you."

Genetic bond? I didn't like the sound of that.

He took a quick sip of water, still avoiding my gaze. "I'd been following you. It was your first semester of college, and Pops thought the vampire might show himself. Normally, a Harker woman already has several interactions with him by the time she's eighteen, but that wasn't the case with you. It worried Pops. He didn't want you to go off to school, remember? He was really proud of your scholarships, but he didn't want you to leave."

I remembered. Pops had taken me in when I was fourteen. He'd saved me from another hellacious foster home and told me I could stay with him as long as I did three things—get good grades in school, keep my room clean, and stay out of his business affairs. Compared to what I'd been living with, those rules seemed easy enough. But something had always bothered Pops about me going off to school although he would never say what the problem was.

"I wanted to make sure you were okay, too," Jensen said. "You didn't know it, but I moved into an apartment close by. I never could find a good reason to bump into you. I followed you to a party one night, thinking maybe I could run into you there and make it look like an accidental meeting. I mean, I'd only had a thing for you since the first time I'd ever seen you."

Normally, the words would have made me jump for joy, but right now, all I felt was a dark fear that Jensen was about to tell me something which would change all my feelings about him.

"It took me a long time that night to work up the courage to talk to you," he continued. "When I did, you'd disappeared. I finally saw you walking away from the party toward the lake with some stranger."

Yes. What he was saying jived with what I could remember. The party had been by Inks Lake. The breeze from the water had been soothing, tempting almost. And there had been a man with a magnetic voice and soulful eyes. I had gotten lost in those eyes, so lost…

"I followed you, but by the time I got there, the vampire already had you under his thrall." Jensen looked down at his plate. "You were naked, kissing him on the shore."

I blushed, mortified to think I'd been that easy.

"I called out, ran toward him. He whispered

something to you, or at least I thought he did, but he was gone before I got there. You were wide-eyed and didn't recognize me at first." Jensen swallowed hard. "I took off my shirt to cover you. I don't know where your clothes were, but something changed.

"Suddenly, you were calling my name and touching me, coming on pretty strong. I—I tried to calm you down. I don't know what kind of thrall you were under, but it was powerful. Sexually powerful. I'd wanted to be with you for so long…wanted you so badly…when you told me to love you, to *make* love to you, I lost my head."

Short bursts of memories from that night came back. Someone was on top of me, kissing me, making love to me, and I had enjoyed it, wanted it badly. Had that really been Jensen? The mere memory of it was enough to make my skin tingle and my breath catch even though a part of me was shocked it had happened at all.

"So you took advantage of me while I was under a thrall?" It came out sounding more accusatory then I'd meant.

I suspected the situation wasn't that simple. My gift of persuasion. The dark genetic mutation. I had a bad feeling that's what had influenced Jensen to have sex with me—not any romantic feelings he'd thought he had.

"I wish I could say I was a better person than that, and I had more strength, but you were the woman I had fallen in love with. I knew something wasn't quite right—how many times had Pops warned me not to stare into your eyes too long—but I was weak." Shame rolled off Jensen in waves.

Closing my eyes, I did battle with the revulsion in my stomach.

"I didn't even realize you were under the thrall when we made love until the next day when I saw you. Remember? You acted like it was the first time you'd seen me since you'd left Pops. You didn't remember our night together, which made me feel like the worst possible kind of man."

Have your fun with this boy. Weave your own thrall and make him love you. Allow him your body if that's what you desire. But don't lose your heart. You'll forget this all in the morning.

The words whispered in my head, another long forgotten memory from that night. It hit me that Adam, or Dracula, had made me forget my night with Jensen. He'd thralled me, creating a blank spot in my mind, but now the pieces were slowly coming back.

Weave your own thrall? Make him love you? Oh my god. Had I done that to Jensen?

"I know you can't forgive me for what I did. I should have been stronger for the both of us." Sadness underlined his words, but Jensen never took his sincere gaze away me. "I've loved you this whole time. I vowed to keep you safe, to never let you fall in harm's way again. To protect our daughter at all costs."

I didn't know what to say. Everything in my life was out of whack. He loved me? He'd vowed to protect me? He'd fathered my child during a weird party, and I could barely remember the details? All I could think was that it was a true lie—yes, it had all happened, but the feelings he'd experienced were not of his own choosing. Not really.

"Say something," he pleaded. "Ask me anything. I

won't keep anything back anymore."

"Was it Dracula?" I managed to get the words out, surprised by how normal my tone was. "The vampire that was with me that night?"

"Yeah. I don't know why he didn't stick around, start a fight." Jensen glanced around, worried. "And let's not say that name too loudly. Some Harker women have been able to summon him by just saying it."

"Sorry." I sipped from my water, clutching the glass tightly to keep my hand from shaking. "I didn't know until today that's who he was. I thought he was Adam Levine. Remember? We talked about him this morning."

"You thought Adam Levine actually moved into the house behind us?" He laughed, but the sound came out hollow and mirthless. "Into our neighborhood?"

"Hey, maybe Adam wants to live a private life. A small suburb in Texas isn't the worse place for him to end up."

"Okay." Jensen shook his head in disbelief. He leaned in, lowering his voice, his expression serious. "So what kind of things has he said to you? He must be about to make a move, or he wouldn't have showed himself to you."

"Oh. Well…" Embarrassed heat turned my face a lovely shade of red. "Well, he…uh…we…"

How could I tell him about the sex dreams? While I was horribly confused, even a little angry about what had happened at the party, I didn't want to hurt him.

But he knew.

"I see," he said slowly, disappointment crossing his face. "Is it still confined to nocturnal dreams or…have you slept with him for real."

How did he know about the dreams? Was that part of the curse? And how *dare* he look disappointed in me. I'm the one who'd been kept in the dark about everything.

"All Harker women are influenced by the dream thrall. It always starts that way," Jensen said, almost as if he'd heard some my thoughts. "But after a while... Well, he takes it to the next level. He starts to become more aggressive."

"I have been dreaming about him," I snapped, too flustered to think straight. "I thought it was just crazy dream stuff. Sorry to keep you out of the loop. Now you know what it feels like."

"It's fine." Jensen's brusque tone kept him from acknowledging my sarcasm. "Of course, you would dream about him. You're a Harker. It's simple genetics."

"What do you mean?"

"Ever since the curse started, the women in your family have been linked to the vampire. Your bloodline mixed with his thanks to Mina Harker."

"I have vampire DNA?"

"Yes, and each woman inherits some sort of defect because of it. They're also in tune to his thoughts and desires. Hence the dreams and other...fantasies...you may have experienced."

"What is my defect?"

"Persuasion," he said with a weak smile. "You can thrall almost like a vampire."

My heart sank. So it was true. I'd forced Jensen to fall in love with me, to sleep with me whether he realized it or not. What would he think of me when he figured that out?

"How is the Institute trying to break this curse?" I asked.

"They've had guardians try to kill him, and they've never been successful. The Harker woman either dies in the process or the guardian does." Jensen leaned forward. "But you...you are not as emotionally involved with the idea of him. These other women had known since birth, since the moment they were old enough to understand what their mother was telling them, that Dracula was their legacy, their fate. Living with that hanging over your head can't be easy."

"You'd always be looking over your shoulder. Never enjoy life," I agreed.

"Unless you were trained to deal with Dracula. I'm glad you didn't have the threat of him looming over you all this time, but I wish the Institute would have let you at least be trained." Anger blazed in Jensen's eyes. "Then you'd have been more capable of dealing with things...like what happened in college."

My throat ached from the lump growing there. Did he realize what I'd done to him?

"So why didn't you train me?" I asked, softly.

"I had to make a choice. I was supposed to take over the Institute, not be a guardian. It's part of my own family legacy, but I couldn't do it. I wanted to be in the field with you. In order to do that, the current Head of the Institute forbid me from teaching you anything. When your mother was committed all those years ago, the Head and the rest of the council came up with a plan for you. I had to agree to abide by it in order to be your guardian."

A plan for me? A plan I knew nothing about? This was my life. It didn't belong to some faceless council of the Institute.

"So I'm supposed to let Dracula mess with me? Just go along with some plan I know nothing about?" I sat back and crossed my arms in a huff. "What the hell is wrong with these people?"

"The Institute has changed its philosophy a bit over the last ten years or so." Jensen ran a hand through his hair. His jaw tightened and twitched. "They like to observe things, analyze. Many men have died, trying to kill Dracula. Though the Institute was founded with your family's case in mind, I think they want to see what happens if they stop fighting."

"Then why not train me to fight so none of their people has to die? I kind of get the keeping me in the dark thing—although it doesn't make me happy—but to leave me with nothing to protect myself…that's cold."

I thought about all those innocent guardians who lost their lives on what appeared to be a hopeless quest. Why would the Institute not teach a few of us to fight? Okay, maybe the women in my family hadn't always demonstrated the best self-control around Dracula and that could have held us back from using defensive skills against him. But that didn't mean the Institute should just give up…unless…this was part of a new plan to rid themselves of the curse *and* the Harker women.

If one of us broke the curse and turned into the vampire's companion, there would be no need for guardians, no need for Institute members to lose their lives over Harker women. Unless there were other creatures in the world for them to hunt. I couldn't even begin to think about that.

"They want me to give in to Dracula?" Shocked, I sat back. "They want me to become one of the undead?"

Jensen studied me a moment before nodding. "They say the choice should be yours. All the other women have known about the curse and had preconceived ideas in their head about their destiny. Even the ones who claimed to love him have turned away at the last minute. Who knows why? Maybe the thought of becoming a vampire is just too much for them. The Institute thought keeping you in the dark would allow you the chance to choose without their influence. They hope to close the door on this." Jensen frowned. "They have bigger fish to fry. Dracula isn't the only vampire out there, you know, and vampires aren't the only supernatural threat in existence."

Too much information. I couldn't process anything but the one thought that popped up when he said the Institute didn't want to fight anymore. "But if I give in, I'll become a vampire."

"Honestly, I don't think the curse will let you give in. Here's the thing. I've studied this very closely, and I think I see what the Institute has somehow missed all along. They don't understand that Dracula doesn't kill the Harker women because they won't give in to him. In fact, we have documented at least two times where the women in your family have proclaimed to be in love with him. But I think that's the catch. A large part of the curse is that you feel attracted to him, you want to give in, but then the lust stops right before—"

"Then they would have to kill me, too." My breath caught as the realization dawned on me. "I would be a vampire."

Jensen looked away, grim.

"Oh god." I gasped. "Would you have to kill me?"

Still he said nothing.

"Am I going to become one of your jobs?" I demanded. "Are you going to chop my head off?"

"Maisy, I would never—"

I stood, my anger blocking out all rationales.

"I can't believe I trusted you. All you want to do is…is…drive a stake through my heart or something." I snarled when he stood, and I pointed a finger at him. "Sit down. Don't get up on my account."

His eyes dilated, and he sat back down.

I stomped away, uncertain where I was going.

Chapter Ten

Outside, I strode down the sidewalk. I had keys to the car. It would be easy enough to head to the parking garage and take it. Jensen could call his Institute friends and one of them could pick him up. Hell, who knew? With his super crazy double life, maybe he had a Batmobile lined up nearby in case of emergency.

However, I bypassed the parking garage and continued walking down the street. There were a couple of nightclubs open, and each serenaded me with a blast of music as I passed. I let the music carry me down the street, trying to sort out my thoughts which were jumbled and spiraling out of control. They mixed with scent of the barbecue and sugary funnel cakes from the street vending trucks boarding the area, reminding me I hadn't actually gotten to eat dinner on my failed date with Jensen.

But then again, I was too angry to eat.

I thought about my mother and how she'd tried to kill me, understanding suddenly why she'd done it. She was trying to end the madness the Harker women carried with them. If I was dead, then she would have been the last.

But what would she have done?

Lived as the undead?

Kill Dracula?

Kill herself?

The last one was the most likely. Momma had lived a hard life. She'd always told me her mother had been a mess, and she'd had to grow up fast. Momma had been stubborn, determined. And her moral compass was black and white. No in between.

She would have killed herself before becoming a vampire.

And me? What would I do? The Institute wanted me turned. The curse would end. Dracula would have what he'd wanted. The creature who murdered so many women in my family, who'd driven my mother to madness would have his greatest wish granted when so many others had suffered to give it to him. It wasn't fair. Not by a long shot.

And then what? Was I destined to live as a vampire, always on the run from the Institute? Always on the run from the father of my child, the man who claimed to be in love with me?

But two things bothered me. Not only had I thralled Jensen into having sex with me, but I think I'd thralled him into loving me. His feelings were due to my suggestion all those years ago, not because he really felt them. They'd even led him to alter his career path from next in line to run the Institute to a mere guardian.

He didn't really love me. Hot tears blinded me, and I covered my mouth, choking back sobs.

"Maisy."

Someone whispered my name, and the wind carried it to me. I looked around. My walk had taken me to the bridge overlooking the small creek running through town. During the summer months, it was typically dry, but due to the rain from the evening before, water bubbled and gurgled across the smooth pebbles lining the creek bed.

"Maisy."

This time, I knew who it was.

"My darling, are you all right?" Dracula stood next to me. He still looked like Adam Levine, dressed in his tight black T-shirt and jeans, but now that I knew the truth, I couldn't call him that anymore. "I sensed you were in pain."

"Did you?" I turned to see him better. "Do you sense every time I'm in pain, Dracula?"

His eyes widened in surprise.

"So you know," he whispered. "It begins again. Our time together is short. Things will happen quickly now." He looked a little sad.

"What begins again?" I asked.

"The hate, the denial, the attempts to kill me," he said. "All I ever wanted was for you and your kin to love me, to help me break the curse. But no. The fates all bring hate."

"Well, you do have a nasty habit of sucking the life right out of the situation."

He grinned. "Ah...a sense of humor. All the Harker women have been beautiful. All have had souls that call to my blood. But very few have had the ability to make me laugh, too." Dracula chuckled. "You are so different."

"So look, what's the plan here? Are you going to attack me? Am I supposed to run? Do I fight back? Just give me a basic run down on the scenario. I'm so confused I can barely wrap my mind around it all."

"Why are you confused?" Surprised, he cocked his head to the side. "Don't tell me the Institute hasn't given you strict instructions to stay away from me? I knew of their plans all along, how they planned to keep you in the dark about your family curse. A waste of time, really."

He lifted my chin and smiled. "What they don't know about this curse is what really happens in the end. You can't fight destiny."

"Actually, I found out the truth about you today." I jerked away. "So this is all new to me. Vampires are supposed to be in movies and books. Not real life."

"But your mother..." He lifted an eyebrow. "Didn't she tell you about me?"

"Nope. She said demons followed her around, and her boyfriend liked to play with sharp knives. Other than that, your name never came up. Demons, yes. Vampires, yes. But I don't think I ever heard her mention your name. I guess you were her demon, though." I eyed him as he stood, all broody and darkly sexy, on the bridge. And damned if I didn't feel that heat, that marvelous sensation of lust and libido mixing together. "Did you kill my real father? And Jared?"

"Both of them attacked me first." He waved his hand as if brushing those deaths away as if they weren't important. "I was merely defending myself."

So callous. How could I be attracted to someone like that? And yet I was. Maybe it was because I knew the truth now, but the heat between us was driving me crazy, stirring thoughts of jumping his bones even when I knew I should be running in the opposite direction.

"I see." I took a step back, trying to keep it together. "Look, I can't deal with all this. I have to go."

"Wait, Maisy. Let me show you my side of the story. The Institute may have done me a favor by keeping you in the dark. Perhaps your mind won't be as tainted as all the others. They were closed off to me, closed off to the truth of my tale. Let me explain how the curse got started," Dracula said. "Mina Harker was not as innocent as the Bram Stoker would have the world believe."

"Really?"

I thought about what Bianca had shown me of the past. Mina had been beautiful and devoted to Jonathan, but I couldn't quite forget the way she'd looked at Bram with such an appreciative eye.

Not that I could judge that. After all, I'm a firm believer that just because you're on a diet doesn't mean you can't look at the menu. There's no harm in admiring a healthy specimen of the opposite sex, but I'd only really seen a snippet of Mina's life. Who knew what kind of person she'd really been? What if she had "admired" a lot of men?

"All right. Tell me about Mina." I said. "I got so pissed at Jensen just now that I didn't even get an explanation about how this damn curse got started. Give me your version of the story."

His eyes lit up with hope. "Take my hand." Dracula grinned when I hesitated. "I promise not to harm you."

"I'm sure that's what…that's what…" I searched for an evil bad guy he would be familiar with. One from his own time period popped in my head. "I'm sure that's what Jack the Ripper said right before he killed his victims."

"Don't be silly. Jack the Ripper always told the truth."

"You knew him?"

"I took him under my wing for a while, and we

were quite close. Until he started getting out of control. But that's a story for another time." He stood, hand outstretched, a pleading look in his eyes.

Taking a deep breath, I placed my hand in his and took control of my destiny. At least, that's what I told myself I was doing.

"Look into my eyes. That's our connection, that's the gift my blood has passed down to you," he whispered. "See past all that surrounds you."

Oh, wow. His eyes…so magnetic. I wanted to get lost in them. But something was happening in my head.

The modern world slipped away, and once again, I was back in the late 1800s. Or at least in Dracula's memories of the time.

We stood in a small garden located behind a huge, Victorian mansion. I couldn't be sure it was the same home I'd seen Jonathan and Mina in earlier, but I suspected as much. All the lights in the house were out, but the moon shone down bright enough to illuminate the area.

A small fountain sat before us with a stone bench next to it. Tall bushes surrounded the area, creating a private spot shielded from prying eyes and perfumed by the heavy scent of honeysuckle and roses. I could see the top floor of the house from where I was and wondered if one could see into the garden from up there.

Mina Harker sat on the bench.

She wore a white, lacy robe, trimmed with blue ribbon, which made her both sexy and virginal. Her long hair was loose and free, her feet bare. She looked up as if she saw us, but then I realized she was looking through us to someone who stood at the edge of the garden.

Past Dracula stood there, gazing back with a mixture of lust and love in his eyes. He was beautiful with his pale face and dark curling hair, a mirror image of the creature I'd seen in the past that Bianca had shown me.

"Mina," he said, softly. "I am here."

"I am ready," she said.

Like a lithe cat he went to her, swirling off the dark cape covering his shoulders.

"Are you sure this is what you want?" he asked. "To be bound to me?"

"Yes. I want you."

He sank gracefully down on the bench and stroked her hair.

"You must be sure, Mina," he said. "Once we share the blood gift, it cannot be undone."

Mina lifted her finger to his lips, silencing his warnings. "I've decided. I know others won't approve of our union. But it's my choice. I want to be with you."

"Then it will be so."

The bushes rustled. Alarmed, Mina stiffened, but Dracula remained calm. His fingers stroked the ribbons of her robe.

"This is Armand. I've told you how good he is at satisfying my needs," Dracula said, untying the ribbons free with a suggestive wink. "He is going to perform the binding ritual for us."

A young man with hair a deep, chocolate brown stepped into the garden. Slung on his shoulder was a burlap bag. The long, filmy white shirt he wore was open at the throat and tucked into snug fitting trousers showing off hard, lean legs. The naughty smile on his face made it clear to me that he and Dracula were more than colleagues. I had a feeling how Armand chose to satisfy the vampire's "needs."

"Anything you want to share with me?" I asked the Present Dracula. "Seems you have all kinds of taste."

"I'm a vampire. I get around." He shrugged and stared at Armand. "This one was a clever man."

"Why do we need him?" Mina's tone of distaste made me think she knew what kind of needs Armand handled, too. Jealously flickered across her face. "I thought this involved the two of us, the sharing of our blood again before you take all of mine in order to truly turn me."

"I've made mistakes before, Mina. I've tried to create other companions, but it's never worked. It's easy enough to turn you to a vampire, but I don't want someone whose soul is changed after the union. Armand is a gypsy. He will work ancient magic that binds us through eternity."

Silently, the gypsy slipped off his bag and rummaged through it, laying out a small, silver bowl and one wickedly sharp knife.

Mina didn't notice. Dracula distracted her.

He opened her robe, sliding his hands beneath it to the soft and sheer nightgown she wore. He pinched her nipples through the fabric, and she gasped, putting her hands on his shoulders to steady herself. His mouth tickled her neck, kissing her tenderly.

Mina's eyes closed, but her hands roamed to the front of his shirt. In one deft move, she ripped it open, the buttons flying everywhere. Her hands caressed his abs, running over the flat edges of hard muscles.

"Mina," he breathed into her hair. "Your touch sets me on fire."

He stood, taking her up with him as he lifted the nightgown over her head. She stood naked and beautiful in the moonlight. Her pink nipples were hard little stones, and she breathed heavily. He gazed at her, love and lust on his chiseled face.

His hand slid to the soft spot between her legs, rubbing the flesh that was no doubt aching for attention. She moaned and spread her legs slightly in her stance to make it easier for his hands to work their magic as he kissed her.

"Lay on the bench," he said.

Mina did as she was told. Her upper body fit just fine, but her ass was right at the edge with a leg resting on each side. In this position, she was deliciously vulnerable, displayed so her damp folds could be seen. Wet and ready for the taking, she gazed up at him longingly.

"Do not rut with her," Armand suddenly said. "I am not ready."

"Don't be vulgar, Armand." Dracula dropped to his knees. "And it is I who is not ready. I want my Mina writhing with passion, certain that many lifetimes with me are what she desires."

Mina gasped with pleasure as the vampire slowly flicked his tongue over her clit.

Armand stopped to watch, a bulge growing rapidly in his pants as Mina begged her lover to go further. Dracula obliged, licking the wet seam between her legs before allowing his tongue to simulate a cock, dipping in and out of her juices. Her hands grasped at his head, urging him deeper before they fell helpless at her side.

He sucked as if she were the most exotic thing he'd ever tasted.

I could imagine what she was going through. Thoughts of my time with my invisible lover, his tongue playing with me, licking at me, driving me to the point of madness before I orgasmed. Mina must have felt the same.

Her cries of delight built until I saw her muscles tighten. I knew she was coming.

Dracula pulled back, letting her recover while he shed his pants. He turned slightly, and I could see his physique better. His hard cock, ramrod straight, made him a gorgeous sight in the moonlight. Even Armand's eyes widened with lust.

Mina turned her head and caught the gypsy's expression.

"He's beautiful," Mina said to him. "Exquisite."

"He is," Armand agreed with a cattiness meant to irk Mina. "A beautiful creature that I've seen many times."

She pouted a moment, put off by his attitude, but then stood, wrapping a lazy arm around Dracula.

"Would you like to touch him once more?" Mina asked as she lightly kissed Dracula. He grinned, pleased by her bawdy suggestion. "After all, he's about to mine forever. I can share him a bit longer."

Dracula fixed his gaze on Armand, commanding him with unspoken words, and Armand crossed to her.

"He says I am to pleasure you on this night. Not him." Armand stared at Mina and lifted his eyebrows suggestively. "If you would like that, of course."

"I don't know," she said, her breath catching audibly when Armand gently stroked her nipple. "But if it's what my love wants…"

"I will have you forever," Dracula whispered, sitting behind her on the bench. "Enjoy this last tryst with the boy. It will never be quite the same again."

"If you insist."

Mina gripped the front of Armand's trousers and undid the laces at his waist. With a firm tug, they dropped the ground, revealing the gypsy's erection. Her fingers crept up his torso, pulling the shirt he wore until it was over his head, and Armand was naked.

"Beautiful," Mina whispered. "Such a physique. No wonder he finds you delicious."

Armand smiled, pleased at her words, but he kept looking at Dracula as if searching for some signal. The vampire ignored him, intent on seeing to Mina's happiness. He caressed Mina's ass as she studied Armand.

"May I?" she asked, taking Armand's cock into her hands without waiting for his assent. Her hands slid smoothly up and down the hard member. Armand closed his eyes, letting her stroke him so that he grew even more swollen.

Mina went to her knees. Her tongue teased and tormented the tip as if it were a delicacy that she'd been denying herself. Then she wrapped her lips around Armand's cock and sucked on his hardness, her hands clutching his ass. He hissed low, his fingers in her hair while his eyes shut. So slow it must have been agony, Mina worked his shaft, her eyes shut, contentment on her pale face. He thrust against her, begging to be swallowed deeper.

"Whoa," I whispered. "This is not a woman saying 'no' like Bram Stoker would have us believe."

"Mina was a wanton woman." The Present Dracula standing next to me sounded proud. "For her time, she was quite…progressive in the bedroom."

"No kidding. I bet if anyone had found out they would have been shocked."

"Why do you think Bram Stoker chose to paint her as a victim? Someone did find out, Maisy. Look in the window."

One of the curtains of the second story window parted, revealing the shadow of someone standing there. I didn't know who it was. Bram? Jonathan?

Mina stopped, and Armand let out a low breath. He hadn't come yet, and his cock gleamed in the moonlight. The gypsy stared down at Mina, a dazed expression on his face.

"Have no fear," she whispered. "I'm not done with you yet. I only need a little something for myself. Lie in the grass."

He did as she asked, lying on the lush lawn. Mina pounced, taking him between her lips again, bending over him while her ass lifted in the air, begging for Dracula to fill her from behind. He got the message, and while she sucked greedily at Armand, Dracula inched into her tempting, wet crevasse.

"Mina," Dracula groaned. "The things you do to me…it's beyond me to maintain my control. We must join our souls soon."

His words spurred her on. While he took his time, Mina bobbed her head up and down, her lips tight around the cock before her. Soon, Armand cried out, his hands clutching the ground on either side of him. He came hard and fast, but Mina did not free him from her hold until every drop he'd released was gone.

When she lifted her head, Mina gave Armand a little wink as if they shared a great secret now or were somehow kindred spirits. He nodded. Dracula pulled Mina back so that she sat on him, his erection still deep inside her.

"Thank you, Armand," Mina said, her head lolling back onto Dracula's shoulders. "I hope you enjoyed that, as well."

"I did." Armand slid into his trousers while the lovers continued. "It's almost time to start the ritual." Neither of them saw the disappointment and hate cross his face as he returned to his supplies.

Mina and Dracula turned their attentions back to each other. His arms wrapped around her tightly as her back pressed against his chest. One hand stroked her side, caressing her breast lovingly.

"Mina." The raw tenderness in his voice touched me. "I must ask again. Are you sure?"

"Oh, yes, my darling!" She thrust up and down, breathless from riding him. "Yes. I am yours."

"Armand, you may begin," Dracula commanded. "Start the ritual."

Chapter Eleven

The gypsy stared with a calculating eye, taking in everything—the tall shrubs of the garden, the sleeping honeysuckle vines entwined with the roses, the soft babble of the fountain which accompanied the moans of pleasure from the ardent couple on the bench. He glanced around the area as if he wanted to ensure their privacy one final time. Then his expression hardened.

"What's that about?" I asked Present Dracula. "He's up to something."

"That is the reason we are here today." His face took on a sad, unhappy look. "Long ago, I'd made a pact with the gypsies. They would help me, provide protection when I needed it, and in return, I would provide them money and supplies. I would also never kill or bite one of their kind. It was a solemn oath. One doesn't break oaths with the gypsy clans."

"But you didn't bite him," I said.

"Armand was in love with me. He'd begged me to turn him, but I'd refused." He shrugged. "I didn't understand what unrecognized love can make a person do."

Armand chanted, and a little glow of light flickered to life in the silver pot. He picked up the silver knife and went to Mina, still too busy pleasuring herself to really notice him. Taking her hand, he pricked one of her fingers so blood dripped from it to the ground. He collected some of it in the little bowl and then did the same thing to Dracula. Armand swirled the blood, mixing it together while he chanted, his eyes hard as he watched the rutting couple.

Dracula opened his mouth, revealing tiny, pointed fangs. Mina stuck her bleeding finger between his lips, and he clamped down greedily, drinking the blood as if it were a sweet nectar. His cock thrust deeply inside her, his eyes turning bright red. The taste of her must have been too much because he rose, still holding her on his shaft as he pinned her to the ground. Her hair splayed all around her on the grass, and she wrapped her legs around his waist, matching him thrust for thrust.

"This is where the curse begins," Present Dracula whispered. "Armand is chanting a binding spell, but not the one I requested."

The light from the little silver bowl expanded and drifted over Dracula and Mina, blanketing them.

"Want her for the rest of your long life, but she will never be yours. I curse you, Dracula. Your blood will taint hers so in every generation after her, you will sense the love that almost was, but you will never be able to force it. They must choose you to break this curse, but every woman in this line will drive you mad. Your blood mixed with theirs will repel them. Only death will break the bond, and you will wield destruction on every generation. Eternal loneliness awaits you, your burden to carry for crossing those with power."

Armand crept silently back to the lovers who had not heard his words. He held the bowl to Dracula's lips while he paused, lifted his head, and drank, Mina's body still pinned beneath him. He offered the bowl to Mina, and the young woman lifted her upper body and willingly sipped from it. Blood dotted their lips, the scent of it sharp in the air.

"And it is done," Armand whispered, stepping back.

The light disappeared.

"You must drink from me now." Dracula slowed his thrusts, causing little gasps of pleasure to come from Mina. He bit at his wrist and then pressed it to her lips.

Mina latched on, slurping eagerly at the crimson liquid, letting it gush in her mouth.

"Careful, love," Dracula said. "You don't want to overdo it."

Something changed.

Mina shuddered and arched back. For a moment, I thought she was coming, but then she opened her eyes, confusion and horror in them. She turned her mouth away, spitting and retching at the taste of his blood.

"Oh, god," she cried out. "What have I done?" Her hands beat against the vampire, trying to get him off of her.

"Mina, what's wrong?" Dracula asked.

"Get off me. I don't want this. You're hurting me."

Dracula stilled. His eyes opened wide as he stared down at the woman struggling beneath him. "What are you saying? The ritual is almost complete."

"Help," she screamed, her voice filling the garden. A light bloomed behind one of the curtains. "Somebody help me."

Dracula sprang off her, his face wild with confusion and anger. Blood dripped from his mouth, giving him a frightening appearance.

He turned to the gypsy. "What have you done?" he yelled. "What madness is this?"

"You broke your oath to me," Armand hissed. "I was to be your next companion."

Someone shouted from the porch. Hysterical, Mina snatched at her nightgown, the picture of the damsel in distress as she tried to cover her nakedness.

"What did you do to us?" Dracula grabbed Armand by the neck, lifting him up so his feet dangled about a foot off the ground. "What did you do?"

"Only what I would do to anyone who crossed a gypsy. I gave you something to remember me by." Armand had the nerve to smile while being choked. "You will always remember this night as the night you almost had love. But I took it."

Dracula let out a roar and snapped Armand's neck. He dropped the lifeless body to the ground.

Mina screamed.

"Mina, calm down. It's me. Your love."

"Stay away." She held out a hand as if to ward him off. "You are evil. You have raped me. Soiled me. I am unholy." She started to cry.

The vision faded, and before I knew it, we were back on the bridge, far from the late 1800s, back to my current reality.

"And now you have seen how it came to be," Dracula said softly. There was no mistaking the tears in his eyes. "I am cursed to love you, drawn to you by blood and a gypsy's prayer. You will never love me, and I cannot force you, though I've tried with many of your ancestors. My anger always gets the best of me."

"What do you mean by that?" Rising fear made me take a small step back. "How does it get the best of you?"

"I…I kill them." The pain in his voice tempered the fear I felt at this confession. "I can't help it. The curse overwhelms me. The fear, the loathing, they all feel just when they finally start to confess their love for me—it's too much for even me to bear. In all these years, only one has escaped death at my hands."

The agony in his eyes was pitiful. He was talking about my mother.

"Why didn't you kill Momma?" I asked.

"Because of you. You stopped me."

"How? I don't remember much about that day."

"It's not important how," he said evasively. "You're here now. It's your turn to face this. Perhaps your gift will save us again."

My gift. So I'd used a thrall against him.

"Have you ever tried to have the curse reversed?" I asked.

"The gypsies will have nothing to do with me. Over the years, we've developed a solid hatred for one another."

"Have you ever explained this to the other women in my line, my ancestors?"

"They all grew up knowing the legend of what I am, of what I've done. They were all influenced by those tales. There was no convincing them of anything."

"The gypsy said only death will set you free." I imagined the faces of all the dead Harker women who'd come before me, chilled by the thought of what they'd suffered. "Doesn't seem to be working for you."

"He meant *my* death, of course. Only going to the sun or staying in the light without protection until I burn and die will appease this curse."

I took a deep breath, trying to think it through, battling feelings of sympathy for him. "Look, I think you were given a bad deal, but you had said our time is short now," I said. "What does that mean?"

"You're ready. Your soul is ready to make the choice just as all the others have done. I can feel it."

Something in his features changed. The sad man I'd been speaking with disappeared. There was a cold, predatory vibe about him now. I took a step back, frightened.

"Maybe there is something that can be done." Dracula touched my hair, a gleam in his eye similar to what I'd seen only moments before when he'd been kissing Mina in the past. Heat enveloped me as it had every time I'd sensed any sexual tension from Dracula. Only this time, it was different—more powerful, more forceful.

Suddenly, my head filled with thoughts of how hard his cock had looked, at how tight his muscles were. What would it feel like to have him naked beneath me for real and not in some dream?

Dracula leaned forward and kissed me, his tongue gently flirting with the seam of my lips.

Breaking free, I gasped. "What are you doing? I can't…do this. I'm not ready."

"Too bad. You are a victim of this curse, too. You feel heat, passion. But can you handle it? The Institute thinks you have a choice. They think you can choose to be with me, and I kill the ones who don't choose me because of my rage.

"Truthfully, it doesn't matter what you choose. That's the secret the Institute doesn't know. The curse will make you hate me in the end even if you do pick me as Mina did." He grabbed my waist and pinned my body to the rail of the bridge with his own. I could feel his hardness against me, his breath hot on my neck. "I approached you once before, you know. But you were much too young, not at all ready for eternal love. I watched you thrall that boy, and I wished it was me making love to you."

"Maisy!"

Astonished, I jerked my head to see Jensen running toward us. Something was in his hand. A knife maybe?

"Who knew that boy would turn out to be a guardian? Or that you would marry him?" Dracula sneered. "Guardians are such a hindrance."

"Get away from her," Jensen shouted.

Dracula kissed me again, taking my breath away.

"We'll talk soon, Maisy," he said. Bitterness colored his words. "There is no escape for either of us now."

Then he shot straight up into the air and out of sight.

"Are you all right?" Jensen ran up and put his hands on my shoulders, examining me. "Let me look at you."

"What do you care?" I snapped, reeling from the kiss, from Dracula's revelations. "You wanted me to become a vampire. Well, guess what? I don't think it's even possible for me to really choose that. The damn curse can't be broken. Apparently, at the last moment, I'm going to refuse him even if I want him. He'll kill me when I do that. Every choice is death it seems."

"Oh my god, Maisy. Is that what he told you? Did he say that's why he has killed them in the past?"

Jensen shook his head. "I was right all along."

"Well good for you! Give yourself a gold star. I'll bet the Institute knows the truth, too." I started to stomp off, and he grabbed my arm. "Let go of me."

"No. You have to listen to me. I don't know what that blood sucker told you, but I'm the one who loves you. I'm the one who will do whatever it takes to free you from this curse." The fury on Jensen's face was truly alarming. "And despite what you might think, I don't believe the Institute does know what really happens at that pivotal moment. They believe Dracula kills the woman because they reject him. I know the Institute would have spoken up if they knew the truth about the curse, maybe even been able to do more. It's just no one has ever been alive to tell us what happens."

"Except for my mother," I pointed out.

"But she's so far gone mentally that she'd never been able to give the Institute any help. She might as well be dead," Jensen said. I glared at him, hating that he could be so callous. "Not that I want that. It's just that she's been grilled hundreds of times and never says anything new. You've seen her. You know that whatever happened to her took every bit of sanity away."

"So what am I supposed to do here?" I snapped. I didn't like the thought of my mother being an empty shell. What if I ended up like that, too? "Do I just lie back and take it? Fall in love with him?"

Jensen's eye narrowed. "What did he tell you to do?"

"Do? He told me I had no choice. All roads lead to death."

"What else did he say?"

"He showed me how the curse began. He broke the heart of a gypsy boy, and that's why we're cursed."

Jensen stared at me, surprised. Then he started to laugh.

"What's so funny?" I demanded.

"His excuses for the curse get better and better."

"What do you mean?"

"The curse wasn't started over a broken heart. Dracula slaughtered the boy's entire village and forced the boy to help him bond souls with Mina. That's why the gypsy put a curse on him."

Oh shit. Dracula hadn't mentioned anything about that. Was that true? Had Dracula lied to me, manipulated the vision for his own needs?

And just when I was starting to like him.

Chapter Twelve

Jensen took me home.

On the ride, I fell into a light sleep, lulled by the steady rhythm of tires on the road.

Visions passed through my head, tumbling into one another and mixing with things which had happened to me in life. I dreamt Momma and Mina studied me through a mirror, their faces a grim mixture of hate and desire. I saw Momma and Jared kissing, and then Jared on the ground with a knife in his stomach, his eyes wide and lifeless. Images of Dracula and my neighbors took over, and I could envision the vampires they might become in the near future—beautiful but deadly women.

And I saw my Rebecca as a grown woman. I couldn't help but wonder about my options. Be killed by Dracula and let my child go through all this? Or was I to try the method Momma attempted on me?

No. I couldn't do that. I would never harm Rebecca.

"Maisy." Jensen woke me as he guided the car into the driveway. "Did you ever invite Dracula into our house?"

"No." But as I opened the car door, I remembered how I'd awoke from the first sex dream and had seen the shadow of a man in the room. "But I did have a couple of dreams where he was in the house."

"As long as it didn't happen in real life. Sometimes he can create the illusion of being in the room. It depends on how deep his connection is with his victim." Jensen unlocked the front door. "But he can't really get in without an invitation."

"I know. Apparently, when I was kid, I invited him in," I said. "Momma told me it was all my fault. None of this would be happening if I hadn't invited him in."

"Maisy, I know she's your mom, and I shouldn't be saying this, but that woman is a raving lunatic. You were a child. No one can blame any of this stuff on you."

Inside the house, Jensen turned on the lights, but his guarded posture warned me we could be the victims of a vampiric home invasion at any second. Maybe it was part of his job, but I'd never seen this side of him. Not even when we were teens and he would show up at Pops bruised and banged up. He'd still been the laid-back version of himself I was most familiar with. But now, that boy was replaced by this man who emitted a raw energy that was both frightening and sexy.

After a few tense moments while he checked the house, Jensen relaxed.

"Everything okay?" I asked.

"Sure." He headed for the living room bar and pulled out the vodka bottle. Jensen frowned as he shook the half empty bottle. "Uh…did you have some drinks this afternoon?"

"Yeah. And I'd like another one since you have it out." I sat on the couch and watched him. "I told you the dildo lady was here. Actually, her name is Bianca, and she is a gypsy."

I know I'd promised not to mention her name, but

all this talk of gypsies had gotten me to thinking about a few things.

"Bianca? Bianca Rivera? You met her? She was in this house?" Jensen stopped pouring the vodka to give me a severe look. "The Institute is not going to like that."

"What do I care? At this point, I don't like the Institute. And neither does Bianca. Which makes her A-Okay in my book."

"Bianca holds a grudge against us."

"Not me. She wants to help me."

"I'll bet." Jensen laughed bitterly. "She has some interesting ideas."

"What's that supposed to mean?"

Jensen handed me a drink. "Bianca used to work for the Institute, but she had a falling out with the head. She is a vampire sympathizer."

"Is she a descendant from the clan of gypsies Dracula worked with?"

"You mean slaughtered?" Jensen sipped from his drink. "Yeah, actually she is, which makes her defection from us and the accusations she made even stranger."

"What kind of accusations?"

"I can't tell you." Jensen sighed. "You don't have clearance."

Well that sucked. Considering that it was my family heritage that built the damn Institute, it seemed only fair I should have access to everything.

"Tell me about the slaughter of these gypsies then. Or is that something I can't know, either?"

"Come with me. There is something I want to show you in my office."

Silently, I followed him upstairs, unable to keep from checking out his butt encased in tight jeans. Even though a part of me was angry at him for keeping secrets, all the sex stuff Dracula had shown me with Mina had me kind of revved up. Seeing into the past allowed me to understand how easily one could fall into a thrall and do things that you might not normally do in other situations.

Jensen wouldn't have slept with me all those years ago if I hadn't played into his feelings, if I hadn't seduced him by the lake. Just thinking about it made my heart ache. My feelings for him right now were so mixed up and yet there was no doubt how much I wanted him. I would have to be careful from now on with my powers of persuasion, careful not to take advantage of him.

"Jensen," I said as we entered the room. "The other night I saw a trunk in here, a box full of knives."

"Yeah, it belonged to my uncle." He shot me a sideways look, gauging my reaction. "Jared."

"So it's true. Pops and Jared. They were brothers. Pops was your dad."

"Yep." Jensen sat down, not meeting my eyes. "Pops was my father."

"Why didn't you or he ever tell me? I mean, I don't see how that would have mattered to the Institute if I knew you were related."

"It had nothing to do with you. Pops and my mother were divorced a long time ago. She didn't approve of the Institute even though her family actually started it. But Pops...well, he believed in the idea of fighting evil in the world. Mom didn't like that, so she thought keeping me away from him would prevent me from joining up," Jensen said. "I never knew my father until I was a teenager, just a few years before you came into the picture."

"I see."

Maybe this was why my mother-in-law wasn't my biggest fan. Being my guardian would have dragged her son into danger. As a mother myself, I couldn't blame her for thinking like that.

Jensen tapped at the keys of his computer. "I don't understand why Dracula told you what he did. He knows we have proof he is a mass murderer." I guessed we were done with the family chat. "He must be changing his strategy, going for the sympathy vote."

"Is he? Or is the Institute's plan working. I haven't been as influenced by these stories about him. Maybe my mind is more open to the truth." I was reluctant to give the Institute any kind of validation on their decisions, but some things couldn't be ignored. "Maybe to some extent, they were right to keep me in the dark."

"He's a vampire." Jensen swiveled in his chair. "They all lie to get what they want."

"Doesn't everybody?"

The screen behind him clicked, and an image appeared. Grainy and old, the image was still clear enough to make my heart pound, yet I couldn't turn away.

Bodies were strewn haphazardly about in what appeared to be a field. At first glance, a few appeared to be sleeping, but the longer I studied them, the more my brain translated the horror of what I was really seeing. Many of them had their throats ripped out and blood gushed from the wounds. At least two of the bodies were headless.

Silent, Jensen scrolled to the next set of pictures, watching my reactions.

The rest were equally faded photographs of severed heads with wide, terrified eyes. A few showed the women naked, their bodies coated in blood. One of them had her hand stretched out in the shape of a claw. Marks streaked the ground where she'd been digging in order to crawl away from her attacker.

One picture was of a baby, its neck twisted, bite marks clearly visible on its torso.

"Dracula did this?" Shocked, I could hardly breathe. I closed my eyes, trying to focus. "He did this by himself?"

"Yes."

"He did this before the curse was placed?"

"Yes. This is one example of his destruction, one small part of the gypsy clan. He traveled through Europe, doing this same thing to dozens of other groups after the curse—all part of his revenge." Jensen clicked the screen and brought up other images, all of them just as horrific. "Take a good look, Maisy. This is the creature the Institute wants to stop, the creature you are attracted to."

I looked away, unable to meet his eyes.

"You are attracted to him, right? Even six years ago, you must have felt something, thrall or no thrall." Jensen pushed on, letting out the tension he'd been holding back. The easy going attitude I was so accustomed to had fled, replaced by tight shoulders, a flushed face, and an accusatory glare. I'd never really seen him angry, and it stung that this new emotion was directed at me. "You said you've been dreaming of him, and from what I saw this evening, he is becoming more aggressive. That was some lip lock I caught you in."

"I don't—I don't know what I feel toward him. And you said yourself that my genetic whatever makes me attracted to him. I can't help it," I snapped. Who was he to judge me, to make me feel so weak? "I had no warning about any of this."

"You had warnings, Maisy. You just never allowed yourself to see them. Didn't you ever think maybe your mother might be telling the truth about the demons she saw? Do you really not remember the day she tried to kill you?" Jensen studied me. "I've always wondered about it. The files on the event are detailed, but you never talk about it much. When you do talk, the things you remember don't seem to match up with what we know happened."

"You've got files on me?"

"Of course." He said it like it was no big deal, but it was a big deal to me. Talk about an invasion of privacy. "We study our wards carefully to find out how best to protect them."

Now I was his *ward*, an object to protect.

"What do these files say, Jensen? How much of my private information do they contain?"

"They're confidential."

"They're about *me*. I have a right to read them. I can't believe these…these…assholes you work for think it's all right to invade my privacy and then keep me in the dark about what's really going on." I crossed my arms and leaned against the edge of his desk. "Is there a file on you? Do they keep tabs on all the guardians who sleep with their thralled wards?"

"I assume so," he quietly.

179

"Then I want to read your file."

"No." Jensen's face turned red. "That's confidential, too."

"If you get to read my stuff, shouldn't I be able to read yours? Or do you have personal stuff in there I might not like to find out about you?"

Jensen stood so fast he nearly knocked me off the desk. He paced the room, shoulders hunched, angry energy radiating off him in waves. I didn't care. Let him be pissed. Now he knew how I felt.

"Dammit. You are the most frustrating person. I've shown you the man you are lusting after has killed entire masses of people, and all you care about is reading my file? What's wrong with you? Don't you see Dracula has to be dealt with? He's a killer." Jensen fumed. "And if he doesn't get you, he'll go after Rebecca. The whole cycle will continue."

His words stung. "Jensen, I—"

"No. I'm your damn guardian. I'm going to do something about Dracula whether the Institute likes it." He turned to me, the fury in his eyes as I'd never seen before.

It smothered the outrage festering inside me, transforming into concern for his personal safety. Anger was making him reckless.

"I made a vow to you on our wedding day," he said, "but I had made another way before that. I took on the role of a guardian because I wanted you. I knew the risks. Everyone told me I was crazy. But I knew you were the one for me. I'm not losing you or Rebecca to some vampire. Got it?"

I swallowed hard, remembering his declaration of love at the restaurant. Joy, excitement, desire—all these emotions welled inside me, hitting me so fast I couldn't make sense of them, but they were quickly followed by sadness and fear. The women in my line hadn't had good luck in romance. Why would I be any different? Wasn't this the same sad love story most of them had experienced with their guardians?

And there was another big difference here—I had thralled him into loving me. He'd had no choice. That wasn't really love.

"I said do you get that?" he demanded when I didn't respond. "Do you understand me?"

"Yes. I get it." Better than he probably thought. This was the moment to tell him that what he felt wasn't real. That I'd unwittingly tricked him. I opened my mouth.

"Good. Now, I'm pissed, and I can't think straight, so I need to go take a shower and regroup." He started to stomp away, but turned back one last time, shaking his finger at me. "We aren't done talking about this."

The words I should have said died on my lips. "All right."

His anger trailed after him, a perfume both terrifying and intoxicating. Every woman wants to feel like their husband cherishes them, but how many women have husbands that would slay vampires for them?

Not many.

And this is how guardians get killed. Their passions overtake their sense of reason.

I didn't want Jensen to go crazy and get himself killed, trying to protect me. Considering the mood he was in, I was half afraid that was what he might do. I turned off the light in the office and followed him to our room, worried. The water was running in the shower, and I heard him muttering. Briefly, I entertained thoughts of stripping down and surprising him. What better way to keep him focused on me and not killing Dracula?

But he was also incredibly upset right now, and so was I. My emotions and my head were out of sync. I wasn't sure sex was the best option at this moment.

Sleep, Maisy. Now is the time to rest.

Exhaustion hit me hard. Unable to resist, I slipped on my nightgown and slid beneath the covers of our bed. I could rest a minute and then figure out how to handle my messed up life of certain death and possible vampiric activity. Maybe I could cuddle up to Jensen when he came to bed. Maybe the cuddle would turn into heavy petting which would turn into mind-blowing sex. I'd sort the love stuff out later, figure out how to give him back the free will I'd stolen.

Before I could torture myself with more thoughts like that, I fell asleep.

****

"Maisy, come here," Momma ordered.

I knew that tone of voice. It meant if I didn't obey in ten seconds or less, my backside was going to feel it for much longer. I scooted into the bedroom.

Momma sat on the edge of the bed, her favorite white, silk robe in a swirl around her thin body. Her pale face was accentuated by the tight ballerina bun she'd fixed her hair into. Bloodshot blue eyes were the only bright spot of color in all that stark white, and they were startling in their brilliance. Despite her depression and years of hard living, Momma would always be a beautiful woman.

"Yes, Momma." I stood outside the doorway to her room. There were shadows on the floor as the sun started to set outside. "Why did you call me?"

"Come here." She sounded strange, breathy almost. "I need to show you something."

Curious, I went to her, inhaling the soft scent of her perfume. She placed her hands on my shoulders and looked at me.

"Maisy, I love you. Having a child is the most important thing I've ever done." She took a deep breath. "But the world has gone crazy. I have to do something about that."

"What do you mean?"

"There is darkness coming for me. You've seen it in my drawings. I can't stop sketching his true face." She spoke so quietly I had to lean closer to hear her. "The demon is coming for us."

I'd seen her drawings. They terrified me.

"You're scaring me." I tried to edge back, but her strong fingers gripped my shoulders tight. "Let me go."

"I'm going to let you go. I'm going to end this curse, baby." Momma smiled, but there was no warmth in it. Her eyes swirled with despair and madness. Even at the age of ten, I knew something was very wrong with my mother. The last few months had been especially telling. Her drawings were darker, more evil.

"Just remember I do this because I love you," she said.

Like lightning, her hands were around my throat. I struggled, scratching and clawing, kicking with my feet. I couldn't breathe. The edges of my vision started to go dark until all I could see was the penetrating blue of Momma's eyes.

Something knocked us off the bed, forcing her to release me. I gulped in air, trying to fill my lungs and crawl away at the same time. Voices argued behind me.

"What the hell are you doing?" Jared shouted. "She's a child."

"It's for her own good. I've rejected him. I don't know what happened. One moment I wanted him so badly and the next...he repulsed me, sickened me. That monster is biding his time now, toying with me. He let me go so he could have his fun, hunting me down when he's ready. He's so angry. But if she's gone, then he can't get her, too. I can end this curse for everyone. First her, then me," Momma screamed. "Get out of my way, Jared."

Momma lunged for me as I crawled away, her hand grabbing my foot and dragging me back. My fingernails scraped at the hard wood floor as I tried to find something to grab onto.

Luckily, Jared stopped her before she could get her hands on my throat again. "No. Elizabeth, you can't."

"Don't tell me what I can or can't do. You and that damn Institute have been lazy for too long. It's my turn now. I will take control of my destiny." Momma slapped him.

Jared grabbed her hands so she couldn't do it again. Immediately, her body swayed against his, all the defiance going out of her as she sobbed.

"Let go of me. Please, let me finish this. It was hard enough to gather my courage in the first place."

"This isn't the solution. Killing your child isn't the solution." Jared struggled to keep her under control. "Killing the vampire? That's the solution."

"Then why haven't you done that?" Momma

wailed. "Why haven't you done that? Instead, you and the people you work for have allowed him to drive me crazy over the years."

"Every woman in your line reacts differently to the genetic mutation."

"Mutation?" Momma scoffed. "It's an abomination. It's evil. It makes me want to do crazy things—anything to end the visions. And Maisy? Her mutation allows her to control people. That can't be allowed to continue. Just look how she has you wrapped around her finger."

"I know, I know, but Maisy isn't out of control with it. She doesn't even understand her power. You've had it the worst of any of the others. Most of them don't have...mental issues. They don't see the demon behind the human mask he wears," Jared said. "But it's okay now. I'm here. I'm going to protect you."

"Still...if the Institute had killed him all those years ago..." Momma was crying now. "I never would have been born. I never would have had to see those demons in my head or draw them."

"I know, I know, baby." Jared crooned. "I know."

I was all but forgotten in the corner, listening to the adults in my life argue about things I didn't understand. Genetic mutation? What was that? And my mother had mental issues? Did that mean she was crazy? Her art certainly was. I knew Momma had talent, but why she chose to only draw darkness mystified me.

And nothing was in my control. What was she talking about?

My throat hurt, and I wanted water. I coughed.

Momma's eyes opened wide with realization.

"Maisy." She limped toward me. "I'm so sorry, baby."

I crawled away, terrified she would hurt me.

"Oh, sweetheart," she cried. "Jared, bring her back to me."

I made it into the hall where I stood on shaky feet and stumbled to the living room. Call for help. That's what I had to do.

"Maisy, honey." Jared stood behind me. "Don't worry. I've got this. Your momma wasn't feeling well, but she's better. You go on into your room. I'll check on you in a minute."

His face was so sad, defeated almost, and when he looked at me, there was sympathy. I trusted Jared. I meant to do what he told me.

Behind him, I heard glass break. Momma screamed in the bedroom. Something thumped against the floorboards. Jared entered the room, slamming the door shut behind him.

What should I do?

The phone. It was right there on the wall. So close. I picked up the receiver and dialed 911.

"Maisy?"

The person on the other end of the line knew my name. But I'd dialed 911. I was sure of it. How could they know my name already?

"Maisy. Hold on. Help is coming," a female voice said. "Where is your mother?"

I couldn't speak. My throat hurt too much. I stared at the phone, confused and frightened. The person on the other end kept calling my name, but I let the receiver dangle off the hook. The sounds in the bedroom were loud, and I could hear my mother screaming.

What was happening?

And then came the silence. Everything stopped. The house held its breath, and even my heart seemed to stop beating for a moment.

Dazed, I crept back to my mother's bedroom.

The door was now slightly open. I pushed it wider.

Shattered glass from the window was everywhere, almost as if a tornado had swept through the room, overturning the chest of drawers, flipping the mattress off the bed. There were dents in the wall where the plaster cracked.

Jared lay on the floor, eyes sightless, blood creeping from the edge of his mouth, the iron scent of it almost overpowering. A large knife protruded from his chest. I covered my mouth, unable to scream even if I'd wanted to.

Something slurped—a wet, nasty sound which reminded me of when our dog sat on the couch and licked at his paw for no reason. It came from the side of the mattress.

I glimpsed Momma's feet before I saw the rest of her. They peeked out from the side of the bed. Her toes wiggled a little.

Unable to stop myself, I went to see what the rest of her was doing.

Someone was on top of her.

A man had his face to her neck, and she had her arms wrapped around him, her gaze on the ceiling, rare contentment on her face. I couldn't understand it. Jared was dead on the floor. She'd tried to kill me. And now this…man was kissing her neck.

My knees gave way, and I fell.

Momma blinked and looked over at me. "Maisy,

run," she said weakly. "Run."

The man lifted his head. Slowly, he turned his head so I could see him. His eyes were red and blood dripped from his mouth, covering his chin and the front of his chest.

Terror gripped me. It felt like Momma was strangling me all over again. I couldn't breathe.

"Stay away from her," Momma gasped as the vampire started toward me. "You promised to leave her alone. Please. Have some mercy. I would love you if I could."

The vampire was inches from me. He tilted his head to the side, studying me, a ferocious expression on his face.

I stared back, my eyes wide, wishing he would go away, that he wouldn't hurt my mother.

"It...it doesn't have to end in death," Momma whispered.

Something changed in his expression. A flicker of compassion flared in his eyes. I was unable to look away even if I wanted to.

I forced myself to speak. "Go. Away." The words were strong, and I meant them with every fiber of my being. "Don't hurt my mother anymore. Don't kill her."

His fangs retracted, and he tilted his head to the side, clearly confused by something.

"Forget this encounter," he whispered with a slight shake of his head. "I won't harm your mother with death. There are other ways to torture her for not loving me."

I blacked out.

Chapter Thirteen

"Momma!" I woke up, unable to keep from calling out to the woman who'd given me life and then tried to take it away.

The past flooded back, for once a clear stream of thoughts and memories. I sat up in bed, clutching the blanket tight, trying to catch my breath.

Dracula had made me forget all those years ago. No wonder I had never fully been able to remember. But not anymore. Maybe that was part of the effects of the curse.

I'd woken up after that horrific scene with my mother in a hospital. They'd told me Momma had experienced a psychotic break and had killed Jared. She'd been put in a psychiatric ward, and suddenly, I'd become a ward of the state. Within days, I'd begun bouncing around from foster home to foster home.

I'd had no memory of what had really happened until now.

"Psychotic break, my ass," I grumbled.

So many things were suddenly clear to me.

My mother had been a little off her rocker. Jared had called it a genetic mutation as a result of the vampire gene. He'd said everyone experienced something different. What other dark gifts had the women in my family experienced as a side effect of the gypsy curse?

I looked over at Jensen's side of the bed, thinking I should let him know what I'd learned. But Jensen was gone. The covers were still smooth as if he'd never come to bed.

A little tingle of fear worked its way into my stomach. What if Dracula did something to Jensen while I slept?

What if he's dead on the floor like Jared?

I slid out of bed, chilled in my thin nightgown. The first place I checked was Jensen's office.

It was empty, but the window was wide open, and I could hear someone giggling.

Peeking out, I couldn't quite figure out what I was seeing, but then I heard the familiar hum of the hot tub and saw the lights turn on beneath the fizzing jets.

Okay, I know he's stressed, but why would Jensen get in the hot tub in the middle of the night?

I could see him down there, settling in, the bubbles surging around his body.

Three people converged on the hot tub. I recognized them immediately though they were all dressed in long, flowing nightgowns.

Sophia, Jane, and Zero to Sixty circled the tub, staring hungrily at Jensen.

"What's going on? You...you shouldn't be here," I heard him say. "You should all be at home."

"And you should be snug in your bed, too." Sophia's light laughter chilled me. "Instead, you've decided to play with us. You answered our call."

"No. I—I didn't." But Jensen didn't sound too sure. "I wanted to be alone."

"Are you sure?" Zero stroked his head.

"Go away!"

"Don't be so mean," Jane purred. "I know you were thinking about us in the shower."

"No." Jensen tried to stand but fell back into the warm water. "This is a vamp trick, a thrall. You've been with him, with Dracula."

"He's so cute," Zero said. The others nodded in agreement. "He called us vamps."

"Look, ladies, it's not too late." Jensen managed to stand this time and moved to the opposite side of the tub. "You don't have to be under Dracula's control."

"Says the man who is so obviously under a vampire's control. How do you really think you got out here? Who really put the idea in your mind to join us in the hot tub?" Zero laughed. "Our master is a talented man."

"He's not a man," Jensen protested.

"But you are." Jane slipped her silk nightgown free, displaying her full, naked glory in the light of the hot tub. "A man like you should be able to have whatever he wants."

"Oh hell." Jensen groaned, but he didn't cover his eyes at the sight of Jane's nakedness. Nor did he turn away when Zero and Sophia shimmied out of their nightgowns, too. "Oh God."

"Shh…" Sophia soothed as she entered the hot tub. "It's going to be all right."

Jensen tried to leave, but Zero and Jane blocked his path. I could see the dilemma in his eyes. Was it all right to knock three naked women out of his way?

They entered the tub, surrounding him.

"Now don't be afraid, darlin'," Jane drawled. "We won't bite."

"Much." Sophia laughed. "Maybe a nibble."

"Ah, but where will that nibble be?" Zero countered. She touched his back. "Will it be here?"

"How about here?" Sophia tweaked his nipple.

"Or how about here?" Jane's hand disappeared beneath the water, and from the low groan Jensen gave, I knew exactly what she touched. "Oh, yes. I think here."

"That's really not necessary," Jensen said as Jane lowered herself into the water. "What about your husband? Won't he be pissed about this?"

"After the sex we had tonight, I don't think my husband is ever going to wake up again," Jane said.

The other women laughed maliciously.

Jane sank beneath the water. Seconds later, Jensen's body grew rigid with tension.

"She's such a show off," Sophia said. "Personally, I prefer not to get my hair wet."

She caressed Jensen's chest and then kissed the taut flesh.

"Um, both of you are married." Jensen's voice quavered. So much for the big bad vampire hunter. It only took three horny neighbors to disarm him. "Don't tell me your husbands won't be waking up, either."

"My husband is still out of town." Zero pressed her breasts to his back, stroking his side. "But I can't wait to show him a few tricks when he gets home."

"And as for my husband...I think you all know the truth about him." Sophia smiled. "He's really just my brother."

"I knew it!" My exclamation was a little too loud. They all jerked their heads up, spying me in the window. Jensen pulled Jane out of the water.

"What?" Jane sputtered before seeing where

everyone else was looking.

"You bitches better get your cheap, trashy hands off him before I get down there," I shouted.

I marched out of the room and down the stairs. On my way to the back yard, I stopped in the kitchen and grabbed the butcher knife. Yanking the French doors open, I gripped the knife, ready to kill my neighbors if they didn't get out of my hot tub.

But they were already gone.

Jensen stood in the water, an expression of disbelief and fading lust in his eyes. He raised his eyebrow when he spotted the knife in my hand.

"And what the hell were you going to do with that?" he asked. "You don't know the first thing about killing fledglings."

"That's because your shitty Institute never bothered to train me. If they had, perhaps I wouldn't be waking up in the middle of the night to the sight of my husband getting a blowjob from a bunch of bitch ass, vampire wannabes!"

"I was putting a stop to it," Jensen grumbled. Despite my anger, I couldn't help but be impressed at the sight of him naked and aroused as he got out of the tub. "I wasn't going to fall for their charms."

"You were already getting the feel of their charms on your cock."

"I was under a thrall."

"Fine. Don't be so judgy from now on when I tell you Dracula's been doing the nasty with me in my dreams. At least those are imaginary." I stomped back into the house. "Asshole."

"Maisy." Jensen slammed the door behind him as he hurried after me. "Come back here."

"Why should I?"

"At least put the knife down."

It clattered on the table. I marched up the stairs, fuming.

"I've had enough of this," Jensen muttered, following me. "You're right. The Institute doesn't know what they're doing."

He stopped me outside the bedroom door by grabbing my arm. His eyes were fevered in a way I'd never seen before, but I knew what he wanted. I wanted it, too.

Seeing him with those women....it had stirred desire in me. It may have been the completely wrong time and place, and there were certainly bigger issues plaguing us, but I'd never wanted Jensen as badly as I did right then.

"Listen to me, Maisy Harker." His voice was rough and raspy as he pinned me against the doorframe. "You are mine."

"I know," I whispered. "And you are mine."

His eyes widened as if I'd surprised him.

"That's right, you big idiot," I said. "No stupid half-vampire neighbor gets you. Only me. And just so you know, this is me talking. The real me. No thralled co-ed who had always harbored a secret crush on you, who would have done anything to be with you."

His eyes widened.

"Yeah, you heard me right. Let's be clear. I'm not thralling you right now. If this is going to happen, and believe me, I want it to, Jensen," I said. "The choice has to be yours this time."

He kissed me, one of his hands touching the side of my face. His lips were soft but forceful, creating an electric current between us which ran all the way to my toes. My head leaned against the doorframe, my knees weak. Tentative, I slipped my arms around his naked, wet body, and he wrapped his free arm around my waist, flooding me with warmth, filling me with security as his tongue chased mine—a drowning man searching for air.

"God, I've wanted this for so long," he whispered, breaking off and looking in my eyes. "You have no idea."

"And you have no idea how many times I almost jumped you in the shower."

My confession of desire was cathartic for me and any inhibition slid away as he grinned, happiness shining from his eyes, echoing what I felt in my heart.

He swept me off my feet, picking me up like a delicate flower.

"I swore to protect you," he whispered. "Tonight, the only thing you're not safe from is me."

I swooned a little at his words. I'd wanted this for so long. Finally, the man of my heart wanted me back.

He carried me across the room and set me on my feet next to the bed, his fingers running along the thin straps of my nightgown. "Take this off. I want to see you."

The gown puddled on the floor as I slipped it over my shoulders. He stared at my body, the awe on his face causing me to blush.

"You're as beautiful as when I last saw you like this." Jensen grinned. "And that was a long time ago. Unlike you, I don't spy on people when they're in the shower."

He kissed me again, his touch as soft as butterfly

wings. Those strong hands of his, the ones I'd longed to feel on my skin for the past year, slid up and down my arms. I kissed the smooth line of Jensen's collar bone, thrilled when little goose bumps broke out on his skin because of it. Stroking the small of his back, I felt his hardness pressed against my lower abdomen, begging for attention, but there was no rush. For now, we enjoyed exploring each other's bodies, discovering the hidden sweet spots while we pressed together like puzzle pieces finding their long lost mate.

"Lay down."

I did as he asked, though I couldn't help but think about the difference in his tone versus Dracula's when he'd forced me to stay and watch him with my neighbors. Jensen didn't command me. He didn't need to. This was mutual. We both wanted the same thing.

Each other.

I lay on my back, easing the cool sheets against my over-warm body. For a moment, Jensen stared, drinking in the sight of my curves, the bends of my legs and feet. Then he stroked one of my legs, lifting it up and kissing the bottom of my foot, sending sparks flying to my core, making me wet. He propped the leg up so it rested on his shoulder and then kissed my calf.

I was open to him, dripping with eagerness, wondering what he would do next. He stroked between my legs, dipping his fingers lightly into my folds before pinching my clit. For a wild moment, I thought I might orgasm right there.

His cock—so big, so hard—was in the right position. If I scooted forward, I could claim it before Jensen knew what hit him. I couldn't wait to feel it deep within me.

"I know what you're thinking, Maisy," Jensen said. "But you can't have it yet."

I pouted, pretending to be miffed but he saw through me.

"I want to see you like this," he said. "I want you to come for me first."

Who could argue with that?

Gently, he stroked my clit, dragging the wetness, making me crazy with need. I never noticed how long his fingers were until he inched one inside of me. In this position, leg up, spread apart, open for him, I felt helpless to do anything but enjoy the moment.

My little gasps of pleasure made Jensen smile wider. "You like that?"

"Oh yes," I breathed.

"You're so wet." He slid his finger out. "I bet I could make you wetter."

He put my leg down but grasped my legs to drag me to the edge of the bed. Sinking to his knees, he bent to the wetness he'd created, running his tongue from back to front. My skin flushed with heat, and I cried out as his finger glided inside of me, thrusting while his tongue teased and tormented my clit.

My restless hands stroked his head but then crept upward. I cupped my breasts, caressing the nipples, adding to the fire he was creating. He must have liked the sight of that, because he flicked his tongue faster and fingerfucked me harder, building the need so much it was almost painful.

My climax sent waves of warmth running through me, and every muscle in my body contracted and released.

"Oh, Jensen," I cried out. "Oh god."

As I came back to Earth, he chuckled and climbed on the bed, pleased. He shifted me away from the edge, wrapping his arms around me so my back was to his chest. His hot breath whispered on my neck as he kissed me there, and his cock twitched against my ass, waiting for its turn to be pleasured.

"There's no rush, Maisy," Jensen whispered. "Just recover. Enjoy what just happened. I know I did."

"You did?"

"Seeing you orgasm like this has been a part of my fantasies," he said. "I've dreamed about doing that to you for a long time."

Jensen's body covered mine. My hands roamed aimlessly across the edges and curves of his wonderful back while he kissed me, taking my breath away. His cock nudged my clit, searching for its home, and I lifted my hips, adjusting my body, wanting more than anything to be helpful.

The hard head found what it wanted, penetrating my core with a slow thrust which made me moan and shiver all at the same time. I wrapped my legs around his waist, guiding him deeper, loving how he groaned in ecstasy at the depth this allowed him. In and out, deeper and deeper he dove, driving us both into a frenzy.

But I didn't think he should do all the work, and I wanted his passion to last longer.

Catching him by surprise, I rolled him over, sitting astride him, watching the excitement grow in his eyes. His hands grasped my hips, but I quickly pinned them above his head with my own. In this position, I was the one in control. I took full advantage of it, something he didn't appear to mind if his deep moans were any indication.

I ground my clit against him, taking all of him into me before slowly lifting back up to the point where the tip of his cock almost broke free. Then I slid back down, watching his face twist in pleasure. Over and over I did this, driving him crazy by prolonging the moment.

"You are a devil," he whispered. "I never knew you could be such a tease."

"We have a lot to learn about each other."

He broke free of my hands, grabbing my waist and thrusting upward, no longer willing to be my submissive. I bucked wildly against him, ready to feel him come inside me, ready to come again myself as the pull of an orgasm had me gasping. My breasts ached for his touch, and I dangled them above his mouth, letting him latch on. Another wave of passion crashed through me as his tongue caressed the hard nipples. Our bodies were drenched in pleasure, and my muscles tightened around him, milking his cock.

He rolled me over, continuing to thrust, stroking a spot I'd never known existed. Heat and fire mixed together inside us, and I wrapped my legs around him tight, not wanting to let him go. His eyes clouded with lust, and tension rocketed through his body as his cock swelled before he found release. Jensen shuddered as he came, and the pulse of it brought me to a slow orgasm, flooding me from head to toe, stealing all rational thought.

"Maisy," he murmured, lost in his orgasm. "Oh, baby."

We lay there, catching our breaths.

"That was amazing," he said and then looked at

me, stroking the hair out of my face. "Are you okay?"

"No."

Immediately, he was concerned. "Did I hurt you? I'm sorry, babe—"

"I'm wonderful. I'm great. I'm every word in the dictionary which means happy."

He relaxed and kissed me.

"Me, too," he said.

We didn't say anything else for a few minutes, content to recover and stare at each other. Jensen had always been there for me. I'd always wanted this man even though Pops had tried to steer me away. He'd probably been worried about what the future would hold between his son and the crazy woman he'd sworn to protect. But then again, maybe Pops had realized there was no fighting destiny. That's why he'd made us get married, knowing our fates were intertwined.

It was a lot to think about and not something I was ready to do right then. Basking in the glow that was after sex with Jensen—that's what I really needed.

"I'm thirsty," Jensen said. "You want me to get you something to drink from downstairs?"

"That's okay," I said. "I can come with you. I'm recovered now."

"Already? I didn't do my job right then."

"Uh…you did your job just fine."

Laughing we headed downstairs, not bothering to get dressed. We both sipped from the same glass of water, teasing each other, happy to have reached this point in our relationship.

But my man wasn't satisfied with talk.

Jensen's eyes became smoky and dark. His cock twitched and swelled as if whatever he was thinking had him excited all over again.

"I have a new idea," he said, running a finger across one of my nipples. "If you're ready for round two."

"Can't wait." I said. "What else do you have in mind?

"Let's give the neighbors a show."

I suddenly hoped Dracula was spying on us. He needed to see *I* was master of my destiny. Not some curse.

With a wink and a smile, Jensen took my hand and led me into the backyard. The night air cooled my naked body, but I understood his intention immediately. The hot tub hummed in the moonlight, steam rising softly.

"What about the neighborhood vampires?" I asked. "Your fan club could come back."

Jensen pressed the jet button. The water bubbled, and the lights turned a soft pink.

"Fuck 'em. I can handle the three evil sluts," he said. "And as for Dracula, I want him to see he doesn't know the first thing about fucking my wife."

"Still, isn't this dangerous?" I asked.

"I've got you."

Who was I to protest? I slipped into the tub, loving the feel of the water bubbles against my breasts. Jensen floated behind me, his hands caressing my nipples. His cock, hard and ready, rubbed against my lower back.

"Here." He spread my legs with his knee and lifted me. "Try this."

Jensen's cock surged inside me, and I relaxed against his chest, the steam coating us. His fingers stroked and tweaked my nipples as his cock kept a steady rhythm. My head lolled back against him, and he teased at my ear with his tongue before he maneuvered us toward one of the jets, holding my lower body against it.

"How's that?" he whispered.

A throbbing stream of water hit my clit, and I squirmed against his hard erection, pinned in place.

"Fantastic," I whimpered. "But I'm going to come again too soon."

"Good. Relax," Jensen urged. "Just let it happen. I love feeling you let go."

The jet applied exquisite pressure right on the perfect spot, and I couldn't hold back. My clit ached from the steady massage of the stream of water and my heart raced as once again the delicious warmth of an orgasm built. I craved it, wanted it to be never-ending, wanted it to explode through me and surround Jensen's cock.

My breath came faster, and I gripped the side of the tub as I pressed my clit harder against the stream of water. Arching back against him, the orgasm ripped through me. I clung to the side of the hot tub as if my life depended on, not caring if my cries awoke the whole neighborhood.

Eyes closed, I let the bliss of it run through me.

When I opened them, I met the hard gaze of Dracula, standing in the shadows of the yard. Angry, he watched me and Jensen, and yet I could sense the longing in him.

You are mine, Maisy. Not his.

Jensen eased me back from the jet, whispering soft words of love in my ear. His hard cock slipped away, but as out of breath as I felt, I wasn't done with him.

Facing Jensen, I guided him onto the sunken bench lining the wall of the hot tub, keeping Dracula in my eye line.

Lust blossomed in the vampire's eyes as he watched me ride Jensen's cock. His eyes dilated a bit, revealing the crimson telltale sign he was aroused. I moaned and tossed my head back, thrusting my breasts up. Jensen grabbed them and the sensation of his tongue caressing my nipples almost made me come again. I rode him a little harder, a little faster. His cock pulsed like he was going to explode at any moment.

"Oh god, Maisy," Jensen breathed, leaning back against the wall of tub. "What have you done to me?"

Eagerly, I slid up and down on his cock, faster and faster, excited by his deepening groans, the quickness of his breath. He cried out when he came, but I didn't stop until I was certain he was spent.

Through the haze of steam coming off the tub, I could see Dracula was gone. I had a moment of worry as I thought about the anger I'd seen flash in his eye. The curse had wormed its way into him, twisting his mind away from rational thought. What would he do now that he'd seen me with Jensen?

I'd deal with it tomorrow. This night was for my husband.

We eased from the tub, both of us a little unsteady. Laughing like two school kids, we hurried into the house and up the stairs to our bedroom. Jensen collapsed on the bed, his gaze on me.

"That was...amazing." He looked a little sheepish. "You sure I didn't hurt you."

"Baby, you didn't hurt me. I loved every minute of it."

"Good." He turned down the bed covers. "Come on. Lie down."

I did as he said, cuddling up to his body, feeling safe and cared for.

"Maisy, no matter what, I'm here for you," he whispered. "We'll figure out what to do about everything else tomorrow. I promise."

"All right," I said, already nodding off.

Tomorrow we would take on the world, figure out the important shit.

Tonight, we would recover from hot sex.

Chapter Fourteen

I awoke to Jensen gently sucking on one of my nipples, causing shivers to zip through me and straight to the vajayjay. My body craved his hands and his mouth touching other places.

"Hmm....what are you doing?" I asked sleepily.

Lying on his side with one hand propping up his head, his other hand slipped between my legs, stroking me until I was wet. What bliss. What ecstasy. His expert fingers manipulated my clit until I practically purred in delight.

"Good morning," Jensen said with a smile. "I see you like being woke up this way."

He rolled on top of me, his cock finding its way. Delighted, I moaned, but he covered the sound with a kiss and proceeded to thrust deeply inside me. My legs wrapped around him, allowing him to take whatever he wanted.

Our lovemaking wasn't as long as it had been the night before, but when Jensen came, happiness overwhelmed me. Tears sprang into my eyes. I tried to turn my head so he couldn't see, but I wasn't quick enough.

"Darlin', are you okay?" His concern made me cry harder. "Oh god, Maisy. I'm sorry."

"No...it's fine." I wiped at my eyes. "I'm just...happy."

His smile was full of understanding. "I'm happy, too," he said, kissing the tip of my nose. "So happy."

Of course, that's when the guilt reared its ugly head. Last night I'd allowed myself to be swept away, to embrace the love I'd craved so badly from the one man I'd always wanted it from.

Everything is so romantic in the dark hours of night, when inhibitions are low and desire is high. I'd pretended Jensen's feelings of love were real, but the reality was that they weren't. I'd commanded him to love me. Just like I'd commanded Dracula to leave my mother alive and alone. If my thrall had lasted all this time on a vampire, a creature who'd been around for over a century, then it sure as hell had lasted the last five years on Jensen.

The thought of having to tell him the truth, of having to see the love fade out of his eyes when I unthralled him—it was the only decent thing to do—it terrified me. The last thing I ever wanted to do was hurt Jensen.

"I don't want anything to happen to you," I said.

"It won't." He studied me. "I'm tougher than I look."

"I know. But I know we have a lot of things to think about—"

"Stop." He cut me off. "We'll figure those things out."

"Will we?"

"Yes. I promise we are going to live a long and happy life together."

"None of the other women in the Harker clan have."

"What about your mom?" Jensen pointed out.

"She's outlived all the other women in your family tree."

"She's in an institution for the mentally insane. And last night, before the gruesome threesome almost had their way with you, I finally remembered what happened the day Momma tried to kill me, the day they carted her off to the mental institution," I said.

"Um, about that... Your mother is not a patient at a real mental institute." He shifted in the bed. "That place in San Antonio is one of the Helser Institute's safe houses. It looks like a medical facility, but it's under our protection."

"What?" Yet somehow, I wasn't completely surprised by the revelation. "Are they studying her or something?"

"Yes. Her escape from death is an anomaly. No other Harker woman has done it."

I told him about the memory that had come back to me the evening before. Recounting how Momma had tried to kill me and the way Jared had died was hard. It made me think about Jensen and what could happen to him as my guardian.

The fear only grew as I recalled Dracula's face and our encounter when I was a child. Despite the tenderness he'd shown me then and even the evening before on the bridge, he was a vampire who killed without regard for anyone.

"You were told to forget by Dracula." Jensen nodded, his face full of wonder. "It makes sense now. I guess with the reappearance of him in your life, the memories are coming back. But you said you were able to thrall him into not killing Elizabeth?"

I nodded, watching his reaction.

"Pops theorized that's what had happened," Jensen said. "Before Jared died, he'd told my father that he believed you were able to thrall people from time to time, but we've kept that a secret from the Institute. Pops was worried what they might do to you."

Until that moment, I hadn't thought about what the Institute could do to me if they found out about my mutation. Would they put me in a lab and examine me, too? Would I end up in some safe house if I survived this curse?

The thought of having my freedom taken away did not sit well, and suddenly, I was relieved Jensen was my guardian and not next in line anymore to take over the Institute. When you're the head of an organization, there are more people to answer to, more people to oppose your actions.

"I think...I think Dracula was trying to help me," I said. Jensen frowned, ready to protest, but I stopped him before he could start. "When I was a kid I mean. All I asked him to do was not kill my mom. He didn't have to make me forget the most awful day of my life. He took those memories away as a kindness."

"Maybe." Jensen shrugged. "You can't trust his intentions. They are never what they seem."

I didn't say it out loud, but I thought the same was true for the Institute. How was I supposed to trust a group who'd made some major decisions about my life without my knowledge? Again, I wondered what they would do if they knew I could thrall people.

"Has any other Harker woman had my mutation?"

"I don't know," he admitted. "Some of the women have been a touch psychic, some are artistic like your mom and able to see a demon even in their human disguise. Others have been a bit hyper-sensitive. More than one has had true mental issues, but we attributed that to their knowledge of the curse as well as the effect of Dracula's blood."

"So it's kind of a crap shoot." I sighed. "Fate rolls the dice for us Harkers and then genetics decides how to mess us up."

"Maisy, your mother outlasted all the other Harker women. None of them lived past the age of thirty. And now there are three generations alive at the same time. That's unprecedented." Jensen touched my cheek and then pulled me into a hug, the sheets slipping down around us. "I'll bet that scares the hell out of Dracula."

I thought of something else that scared the hell out of me, something I still hadn't figured out how to deal with—the fledging vampire neighbors living on all sides of us. "We have another problem."

"What's that?"

"Our neighbors are vampires, too."

"Not yet," Jensen said with a frown and slid out of bed. I admired the curve of his butt as he walked into the closet. He came back out with a pair of boxers in his hand which he stepped into and pulled up. "And by the way, it would have been nice to know Dracula had been using his thrall on them."

"Sorry. We were so busy talking about other things I forgot to mention that. Besides, you sort of figured it out on your own last night."

He had the grace to blush. "Um…about that…you know I would never have…well, you know…"

"Shut up, Jensen. I know you would have fought those sluts off as best you could." I rolled my eyes. "Right after they had their nasty way with you."

"Touché."

"So what do we do to them? Do we kill them or something?" Wow. I'd reached a new point in my life. I could calmly plan the murder of my neighbors without batting an eye.

"No," Jensen said. "We have to get Dracula's power over them to fade. Fledglings can be saved."

"How do you become a fledgling? I assume you have to share blood with a vampire." I didn't recall seeing any of the neighbors drinking from Dracula during the sex fest I'd witnessed, but I hadn't been there the whole time. I did know he had drunk from them, causing some sort of passionate thrall. Not that they'd need much encouragement. I shivered, thinking how close I'd come to joining them.

"Yes, but in order to become a full vamp, you have to die with vampire blood inside you." Jensen sat on the edge of the bed. "Something in the vamp blood is what causes the transformation. The Institute is still studying this. However, the good news is that if you are a fledgling you may feel vampiric urges, but as long as you don't die or if you're separated long enough from the vampire for the blood to lose its power, then there is hope you won't turn into a creature of the night."

My neighbors had been so turned on by Dracula, so needy in their desires. Would they want to be turned back to the way they were? I wasn't so sure.

"Easier said than done," I said. "These girls are so sex-crazed I don't think they will want to let go of him. And it sounds like appealing to their husbands for help is out of the question."

"We need to find out if that's what really happened to Seth and Michael."

"Hey, does this mean the 'no being an asshole' ban is lifted?" I asked.

Jensen rolled his eyes and grinned. "For now."

"Cool." I stretched, letting the covers slip down. "I'm going to take a shower. Then we can figure out a plan."

"I have a plan," Jensen said, eyeing my breasts. "A good one."

"As much as I've enjoyed your plans, I need a little recovery time."

Jensen grinned and kissed me, copping a quick feel by tweaking one of my nipples. Playfully, I smacked his hand away and got out of bed, making a beeline for the shower. I heard him whistling as he left the room.

I caught sight of myself in the mirror. There was a glow to me that I hadn't seen before. It's amazing what super awesome sex can do.

The hot water on my skin felt good. I hummed a little, thinking about Jensen and the last twenty-four hours. As I scrubbed every inch of myself with this special pomegranate cleanser I love, a little idea started to form in my head.

A gypsy had put this curse on my family.

I happened to know of a gypsy who liked to defy the Institute. True, she also liked vibrators and creams for your ass, but hey, who doesn't have their quirks? Bianca might be the solution to all our problems.

Maybe she'd give me a discount on lubricants, too.

****

"You want to get Bianca to help lift the curse?" Jensen looked at me like I was crazy and ran a hand through his already mussed hair.

We stood in his office. The late morning sun shone

through the window, landing on his bare chest and highlighting every sculpted muscle there. Trying not to drool, I focused on his green eyes. I'd slipped into my favorite blue sundress after the shower, deciding worn shorts and raggedy T-shirts weren't the way to keep a man you'd just started sleeping with interested. I'd even dabbed on a bit of makeup. The appreciation he'd had in his eyes before I had opened my mouth and explained my plan had been worth the effort.

"The Institute won't allow it," he said. "They don't trust her. She's a traitor in their eyes."

"Why is that? She never told me why she left," I said. "Something about some accusations she made?"

"She claimed to have discovered the Institute was manipulating history, sort of changing it in the archives to make themselves look good." He shook his head. "It wasn't true, though. Pops and I both checked into it."

"So they kicked her out?"

"More like she walked out and took a bunch of files with her."

"But if she helps us break the curse, this could be a chance for redemption for her." I sat down in one of the plush chairs in his office. "I would think the Institute could overlook a few things she's done if she saved their asses."

"She and the head of the Institute no longer see eye to eye."

"I see." I thought about the way Bianca had tensed up when talking about the head of the Institute. Perhaps the head felt the same hostility toward her. "So we don't tell your boss that Bianca is helping us. We keep it quiet."

"That's going to be a challenge."

"Why?"

"They have eyes everywhere. Don't worry," Jensen glanced at me, reading the worry on my face. "I've checked the house for listening devices. We're clear. I even have a special program running which blocks them from using any type of satellite to check up on us, too. It was part of my conditions."

"Conditions?"

"For when we got married."

There was so much I wanted to know about that.

"Tell me your plan again. What do you think Bianca can do?" he asked, changing the subject back to Bianca and my plan. His face grew serious as he slipped into a more professional mode. This was the attitude of a man used to be in charge or giving orders.

"If a gypsy can place the curse, why can't one remove it? I bet she has some ancient text somewhere that can undo this. Or maybe she can put down a new curse in place of the first one."

"You really watched way too much Buffy and Angel back in the day." Jensen gave a hollow laugh. "It's never as simple as it seems."

"It was never simple for Buffy and Angel, either," I snapped. "But at least we are trying to do something other than kill him—which let me point out, has never worked. Hell, I'd have better luck trying to thrall him out of killing me than you guys have had at plunging a stake through his heart."

Jensen held up his hand, his face tight and unreadable as he took a moment to think over my plan. Finally, he nodded. "Look, I'm not saying this gypsy curse removal thing isn't worth following up on. Call Bianca."

I dialed her number, but she didn't answer.

"Hey, it's Maisy Harker," I said when her voice mail picked up. "I really need to talk to you about an idea I've got. Call me when you get this."

I paused, looked at Jensen's shirtless body, and then added as an afterthought, "And can I get some of that strawberry-flavored lubricant? Thanks."

Jensen raised an eyebrow. "All righty then."

He went to the closet and emerged, carrying the small weapons trunk I'd been looking for in his office. It hadn't even occurred to me to search for it in there. "In the meantime, I want to go pay a call on our neighbors."

"Where did you hide that? Is there a secret compartment or something in the wall?"

"Yep." He opened the trunk and produced a sharp knife.

"Most people just bring a bottle of wine or something over when they go visiting," I studied the knife and shivered, thinking about what I'd seen Jensen do with a weapon in those videos Bianca had shown me. "We're not going to really kill them right? That would just turn them into vampires."

Jensen pulled on a tight black T-shirt and pair of jeans from the closet. I couldn't hide a small sigh of disappointment that he was so well-covered now. His bare chest had been a nice distraction. He didn't answer my question though, and anxiety fluttered in my stomach.

Maybe he was preparing for both options—having to kill them to keep us safe and then having to kill them again because they had become vamps. What a mess.

"Stay here." He sheathed the knife and stuck it in

the back of his pants so that his untucked shirt covered it. "This shouldn't take long. I'm just doing a little reconnaissance. I don't plan to kill anyone."

"No way. What if you run into the vengeful sluts again? You need protection."

"I can handle them." He smiled grimly. "It's my job."

"Um....you were having some trouble last night."

"This is serious. You could get hurt."

"So could you. Please, Jensen. Let me help."

His eyes dilated, and slowly, he nodded his head.

Oh shit. Did I just thrall him again? What is wrong with me?

I had to be more careful about that. Picking up an axe from the weapons box, I said, "Sweet. Let's do this."

The sun blinded me when we stepped outside the front of our house. I held up a hand, shielding my eyes. Normally, kids would already be running around, shooting water guns at each other or something. But all the houses were still, the shades clamped down tight.

Across the street at Zero's, there was no sign anyone was home. At the SOS house, both cars still sat in the driveway—a bad sign since Seth was usually gone by this time of morning. Over at Jane's, the motorcycle was parked out front, its rider nowhere to be seen.

None of that was especially mysterious, but I couldn't shake the feeling something was very wrong.

"Where do we start?" I asked.

"Seth and Sophia's."

The shades were pulled down tight in the front windows. I knocked on the front door, hearing the sound echo through the house. Where were their kids? Usually, one of them would be hollering about something.

There was nothing but silence.

I turned the knob, surprised when it opened easily.

"Let me go first," Jensen said. He stepped in front of me, knife in hand.

We walked down the entry way hall and into the living room where everything was tidy and in its place. There were only empty rooms and no signs of violence.

Where were they?

Once we were satisfied no one was home, we headed back outside.

"I don't understand," I said. "Both cars are here. Where could they be?"

"I don't know." Jensen's mouth set in a grim line. "Let's go to Jane's next."

It was more of the same. No signs of trouble. Everything in its place.

"I don't know what to make of this," I said. "Should we even bother going to Zero's?"

"I wonder...well, I wonder if they're all at his house," Jensen said.

I knew who he meant though he didn't say the name.

Dracula.

"What are we going to do?" I asked anxiously. I couldn't help but think about the last time I'd been in Dracula's lair and the things I witnessed, the things I'd almost been tempted to do. What if that happened again? What would Jensen think of me?

"We need to send in a team." Jensen took out his cell phone. "Extractions like this require serious manpower. Our goal is not to kill anyone, but sometimes…accidents happen."

Accidents happen? I swallowed hard and tried to keep my face neutral.

He spoke curtly to someone on the phone, his tone leaving no room for the person on the other end to argue. I'd never really heard him sound so confident. Once again, I was reminded of how much I didn't know about the man I'd married.

He listened a moment and gave me a strange look before turning away so I could no longer see his face.

"What do you mean?" he asked, lowering his voice. "How long has she been gone?"

He listened to the person on the other end, his shoulders hunching with tension.

"Your job was to make sure that if something like this happened we would be prepared. Having her disappear at this crucial time doesn't bode well. If something happens to her, your ass is on the line. Are we clear?" He turned so I could see the angry line of his profile. "I said, are we clear?"

I didn't know who he talked to or what they'd done to mess up, but I knew I wouldn't want to be in their shoes. Jensen's barking tone meant business.

"It's taken care of," he said to me after ending the phone conversation, a frustrated look on his face. "There will be a team here in fifteen minutes."

"Everything okay?" I asked.

He smiled, but it didn't reach his eyes. "We're all set."

"Cool. Do I get to see the Institute in action?" I didn't ask what I really wanted to know. Would I get to see Jensen in action? It was one thing to view it on video, another to see it live and in person. The very thought of him chopping off one of our neighbor's heads made me queasy.

"No. You'll stay in the house."

"But—"

"But nothing. You'll stay in the house. And don't think you can thrall me into this one like you did a few minutes ago." The look he gave me didn't allow for argument, and I flushed with embarrassment. "Let us handle this. Things could be messy."

Visions of Jane, Zero, and Sophia getting slaughtered drifted through my head. Ugh. They didn't deserve that. And what about their families? If they were over there, would they witness that? Or had something happened to them already? "What's going to happen? Is this team going to...well, you know. I mean...you said they could still be saved. Shouldn't that be the focus?"

"Depends on what they find."

I followed Jensen back into our house, sick to my stomach. As much as I joked about my stupid neighbors, I wouldn't want to see them killed. The reality of it was they were really innocent bystanders, sucked into this saga of Dracula's by me and my heritage.

Guilt pricked at my conscience.

Jensen was on the phone again, barking orders as he went to his office, closing the door behind him. I stood on the other side, unable to help listening in on what he was saying. It sounded like he was preparing for war. I leaned my head against the door, letting the wood cool my forehead.

Then something in his tone changed, and I could

tell he was on a new call.

"Yes, sir," he said. "I understand."

There was a long pause while I strained to hear more.

"She's always been gullible," he said. "We've used that to our advantage before. I see no need to stop now."

Who was gullible? Me?

"At this point, sir, I really think she will believe whatever truth we give her," he said. "Keeping her secure is the most important thing if we want the curse to take its natural course."

Natural course? Was he talking about the Institute's plan to let Dracula turn me into a vampire? Had Jensen…lied to me? Was last night all an act, an attempt to make me believe he was on my side? I backed away from the door, unable to catch my breath. He was keeping me secure, keeping me prisoner, making sure I didn't run before I could be turned.

No. That couldn't be right. Dracula's vision had shown that the curse would not allow me to choose him. He would kill me when I refused. Was that what Jensen wanted then? Me dead?

Or was Dracula the one lying? Had he influenced the vision so that I saw what he wanted? Maybe he was trying to sway my sympathy?

I didn't know who to believe. Loneliness and fear stole my breath. There wasn't enough air in the hallway. I swayed, almost collapsing as if my legs were jelly.

"We'll use deadly force next door." His voice rose, and even from where I now stood in the middle of the hall, the words were clear. "Based on what I've seen,

I'm not taking any chances."

And he was going to kill my neighbors. Devastated, I made my way down the stairs and tried to calm down.

Jensen lied to me. I can't trust him.

The betrayal spurred me to action.

If there was still hope of saving the others by killing Dracula, then I couldn't let the Institute barge in, guns blazing. It would be as if I'd murdered them myself. And that wasn't fair. All the neighborhood sluts had wanted a few nights ago was to have great sex and buy a few vibrators. So maybe they'd gotten a bit more than they bargained for. It wasn't their fault. They didn't deserve to be punished because a vampire who could make himself look like their favorite movie star wanted to have his way with them. That was all just a diversion while he waited for the main attraction.

Me.

I couldn't let the Institute kill anyone because of me.

Even though it was risky, even though I might be forced to have sex with Dracula's slutty minions or maybe even get killed myself, I knew I had to do the right thing.

Hoping Jensen was still busy bossing people around on the phone, I hauled one of the kitchen chairs into the backyard. Placing it against the fence, I stood on it and hoisted myself up, swinging one leg over. Using all the grace and charm of an elephant, I managed to fall into Dracula's backyard. For a few seconds, I lay there, struggling to catch my breath, but the urgency of the situation spurred me into action.

I crossed the yard and opened the back doors of

Dracula's house, cautiously peeping in. Hearing and seeing nothing alarming, I entered. Unlike the other houses I'd just visited, this place showed serious signs of yuckiness. Dishes were stacked everywhere in the kitchen. Trash littered the floor along with empty soda cans and newspapers. Sticky little hand prints made out of peanut butter clung on the table.

Little handprints? Sophia's kids were here somewhere.

"Hello?" I called out. "Anybody home?"

There was a sound in the living room. I recognized it, though I couldn't quite put my finger on what it was. Following the noise, I prayed I wasn't about to walk in on a bloody mess or a massacre like I'd seen in the Institute's pictures.

The television blared the theme music to Mario Kart in the living room. Jane's husband, Michael, was seated on the couch next to Sophia's husband. Seth's fair hair stood up on his head like he'd been shocked or something. Both men had deep circles under their eyes and gripped the steering wheel controller so tight their knuckles were white. Intent on the game, they never even spared me a glance.

"Michael?" I asked.

Nothing. With his buzz-cut brown hair, I could see sweat gleaming on his scalp.

"Hello?" I waved a hand in front of Seth's face. "Seth? Can you hear me?"

His eyes squinted a little as if he were trying to see the television better.

Weird. It was like they were under a spell or something.

Or a thrall.

Looking around, I spotted the SOS kids in the corner of the room. Each child was huddled over a book. In fact, there was a stack of books all around them as if they were going through them one after another. The titles of the books ranged from *Jane Eyre* to *Twilight*.

"Hey, guys," I said. "Everything okay?"

"Quiet," one shushed. "We're reading."

As if one, they all said, "We love to read."

"Okay," I said, stepping back. "Where is your mother?"

In unison, they all pointed up the stairs. Dracula's bedroom. I was tempted to go up there, to see what was happening, but I figured I probably only had a few minutes until the Jensen's buddies arrived. I should save the kids first.

"I hate to interrupt your reading time," I said to the kids. "But you really need to come with me."

"No. Must keep reading."

Wow. Their devotion was impressive.

"All right." I tried to get Seth and Michael's attention again. "Gentlemen, you need to stop playing your games, get your kids, and come with me. You're all in danger."

None of them responded.

I tried to take one of the Mario Kart wheels away, but Seth wasn't about to let go. He wrestled it back, and without missing a beat, he continued playing. He and Michael looked exhausted. How long had they been playing anyway?

I would have tried the thrall thing but none of them would look me in the eye.

"Damn," I said. "I guess I'm going to have to

appeal to those bitches' better nature."

With a sigh, I headed up the stairs.

All three of my neighbors were strewn across the bed. They wore the nightgowns they'd had on the previous evening when they'd tried to seduce Jensen. Their faces were so pale that I wondered if they were even still alive.

I saw no sign of Dracula.

"Jane," I whispered. "You have to wake up. You're in trouble."

"Leave me alone." She groaned, rolling away from me. Her smeared black eyeliner stood out on her white face, giving her an odd Goth look. "I'm so hungover."

"You're not hungover. You're changing."

"Don't talk so loud," she said, covering her ears.

I tried Zero. A little red drop of something stained the skin right below her lips. Blood? Wine? There was no way to know for sure right then. Like Jane, her skin was cool to the touch and pale like marble.

"Alexis. Hey. Wake up." I shook her hard and her red hair swished to one side like a glossy curtain. "We've got a problem. You're all in danger."

"Uh...*mlkhk*."

I couldn't even begin to decipher what she'd said. Like Jane, Zero wanted nothing to do with me. Okay. That left Sophia.

"Sophia, your kids are in trouble." Maybe the bonds of motherhood would help me get through to her. "They need you."

"They're fine," she muttered, but opened one blue eye. Her blonde hair was up in a slightly messy ballerina bun. "I thralled them into doing all their summer reading."

"Really? *Twilight* is on their summer reading list?"

"I threw that one in as a bonus."

"Well, come unthrall them. These people are coming over here and they might accidentally hurt the kids." I shook her again as her eye shut. "Please wake up."

"Seth. Get him," she said.

"He's under your thrall, too."

"Are they still playing Mario Kart?" she asked, opening the other eye.

"Yes."

"Good. Then leave me alone. I need rest. I'm exhausted from all this sex." She closed her eye and drifted back into sleep.

"Shit!" I fussed. "Shit. Shit. Shit."

The house came alive with shouts and glass shattering as men in dark shirts and pants burst in. A few of them even crashed through the windows of the bedroom, their guns drawn and ready for action.

"Get down," one of them shouted, pointing his weapon at me. "Get away from the vampires."

"Um...they aren't quite dead yet," I tried to explain, standing in front of the bed. "They're still fledglings. Please don't kill them."

All sorts of loud noises were coming from downstairs, and the kids started crying. Their angry wails drifted up the stairs, causing Sophia to sit straight up in bed. Her eyes opened wide and her hands stretched out like claws. She threw back her head and opened her mouth, revealing small fangs as she hissed in protest.

"Get back," the soldiers ordered.

"Don't touch my babies." Sophia jumped from the

bed with a speed I wouldn't have thought possible. She barreled past the armed men and down the stairs.

I followed, uncertain what to do.

"Give them back their books, you bastards," Sophia screamed and attacked one of the men who held a copy of *Salem's Lot* in his hand. "They want to read."

Sophia raked her nails across his face and then hurtled him through the air. She gave a menacing glare to another guard standing nearby. He had the good sense to drop the book next to the kid he'd taken it from and back up a few steps.

"Sophia," I said, raising my hands in what I hoped was a soothing manner. "You've got to calm down."

"Where is the Master?" she asked. "He'll take care of this."

Master? I couldn't believe they were into that sexist shit.

"I don't know," I said. "I think he bailed a long time ago."

"No. The Master wouldn't do that." Her eyes turned wide and pleading. "I need him. I must have him."

"He's a vampire, Sophia. Trust me. He's not good for you or your marriage."

"I can't live without him."

"Ma'am, we've got this." One of the soldiers stepped up. "Let us handle the situation."

Before I could say no, the soldier shot Sophia with a dart. She gasped and fell backward on to the floor, her nightgown fluttering around her legs.

I rushed to her. "Sophia?"

I looked at the man who shot her. "What did you do? She isn't dead, is she?"

"No. She's knocked out. We can take her out of here safely."

Thank god. Maybe the "use deadly force" comment I'd overheard from Jensen had been intended for Dracula.

The Institute took over. One of the soldiers escorted me into the kitchen, forcing me to wait there while my neighbors were rounded up. I think they shot Zero and Jane with darts because they were motionless as the soldiers carried them downstairs.

Even the husbands put up a fight.

The moment the television switched off, they started throwing a fit and had to be shot with darts, too. It only took about fifteen minutes for all my neighbors to be packed away and taken off.

"Where are you taking them?" I asked one of the soldiers.

"To the Institute. They'll be good as new in a few weeks."

"Weeks?"

"It takes time to undo a thrall. The blood has to thin out a bit and the brain has to be rewired."

Rewired? What the hell did that mean? Would they be subjected to weird experiments? Chilled, I couldn't get coherent words out. "That's...that's..."

"Crazy?" The deep, British voice came from behind me, catching me off guard.

I turned and faced the speaker.

He gave me a grim smile that immediately made me wary. From the top of his dark, wavy hair to the lean lines of his black suit, this man radiated power. He had one of those perfect Roman noses, and his piercing hazel eyes took in everyone and everything around him at once. My guard went up. It's hard to trust someone who knows everything, or at least thinks they do.

"Who are you?" I asked.

"Victor Wales," he answered with a small nod of greeting. "I'm the head of the Institute."

Chapter Fifteen

"Maisy, it's good to see you in person," Mr. Wales said. His keen gaze studied me as if he knew every secret in my head, making me self-conscious.

Standing in the messy kitchen, I became aware of how small the space felt now that this man was in it. He looked my outfit up and down as if he was making mental notes on my appearance.

I fought the urge to smooth down the skirt of my blue sundress, to make sure a bra strap wasn't showing. His GQ fashion put most of the men I knew to shame.

Coolly, he dusted off a piece of lint from his shoulder. "The pictures of you in our files don't do you justice."

I didn't know what to say to him. Here was the man who ran the organization in charge of keeping me in the dark about my past, the man who'd manipulated my life without me ever knowing. I'd expected someone much older. This guy looked like he was in his early thirties and could have been a male model for a men's perfume ad.

Yet, I didn't feel any kind of attraction to him. Not the way I did for Jensen or even Dracula. Every fiber in my being objected to this prissy man who so easily intimidated me with his snobby British accent. Had he been the one Jensen had talked to on the phone? The one he'd assured I was gullible?

"First of all, let me say I'm sorry for all the lies you've been surrounded by." His face grew serious. "I'd hoped you would be able to live a normal life. We thought living without the constant threat of the vampire would ease the stress many of the women in your line have experienced."

"A normal life?" I rolled my eyes, seriously irritated with this guy. "My mother tried to kill me, was hauled away to some mental ward provided by the Institute, and I ended up being shuttled around from home to home in the foster care system before finally being taken in by a man who I just recently found out worked for you guys. That's not a normal life."

"I know. I kept tabs on you," he said and adjusted the cuffs of his sleeves. "I watched you for a long time, observing how you might be different from the other Harker women. I've often wondered what gift you inherited from Dracula."

Don't tell him. He doesn't need to know yet.

However, if Jensen had been lying to me, it was possible he had told the Institute that I could create a thrall. I pressed my lips together, trying to hold back the smatter of frustration I felt from showing on my face.

"Your mother's gift wasn't particularly helpful to her," Mr. Wales continued.

"Yeah, the gift of craziness isn't exactly what anyone would wish for."

"Tell me, Maisy," he said, his gaze turning shrewd. "When was the last time you spoke with your mother?"

Hmm…did he mean in reality or in my dreams?

"Why?" I asked. "What does that have to do with anything?"

"Did you speak with her today?" he persisted.

Why did he want to know so badly? If she was in an Institute facility, couldn't he just check the visitor log or something and see when I'd last been there? I bet there were videos of our visits, too. The Institute didn't impress me as a group who believed in privacy.

A little tingle of suspicion went through me as I recalled the conversation Jensen had on the phone. Someone had gone missing. What if that someone was my mother? It would be just one more thing my sneaky husband had lied to me about. I couldn't help but seethe over this even as I worried about my mother's intentions.

Was Momma coming to find me, to finish the job she'd failed to do so long ago? I shuddered inwardly and fought against the current of anxiety slowing making its way through me.

"I haven't spoken to my mother in months," I told Victor, hoping my fears didn't show on my face. "And I don't see why that matters right now. Just tell me what you are going to do to assist me in killing Dracula."

"You're going to kill him?" Mr. Wales smiled patronizingly. "My dear, you lack the necessary skills."

"And whose fault is that?"

"I'd heard you were feisty."

"I know what you want. You and your Institute buddies want me to give in, let him turn me into a vampire so you can kill us both." I shook my head. "Well, you can count that plan out. I'm not turning into a vampire."

"Of course not. I only stated it as a goal in order to keep certain over-zealous members of the Institute in line. And I doubt your Jensen would ever allow it to happen anyway."

My Jensen. Ha! Where was he? I glanced out the kitchen window to the back yard where other people from the Institute still lingered. It wouldn't have surprised me if he'd been the first one bursting through the windows upstairs. I hadn't seen him, though.

Probably a good thing. I can't wait to give him a piece of my mind.

Mr. Wales narrowed his eyes. "I think different measure will have to be taken to kill Dracula. You'll need some training, and I'm willing to give you what none of the other women had."

"And what is that?" I asked sarcastically. "A knife in the back?"

Mr. Wales tsked as if I were a petulant child. "I don't blame you for thinking that, but no."

"Then what?"

"Every resource the Institute has at its fingertips." Mr. Wales crossed his arms.

I couldn't help but wonder why he was making me this offer now. If he was so progressive compared to the other Institute members why hadn't he reached out sooner? I mean, here he was basically handing me the keys to the kingdom which should have made me happy, should have comforted me. Instead, it alarmed me, seeming almost too good to be true.

"Prior to my appointment to this position ten years ago, the previous leaders of the Institute had some rather old-fashioned ideas regarding women and their ability to fight or even problem solve. I am not stodgy in my thinking. I believe the Helser Institute must move forward in order to keep up with the competition."

Competition? Were there other organizations out there, fighting evil? Was he going to make me into a lean, mean fighting machine? I didn't have time to find out. A little inner voice told me to get away from this man. I had more important things to consider right now like where the hell was my mother? What would I do if she came after me? Was she going to try and kill me again? Not to mention the pesky little problem of possibly being bested by a vampire.

I edged toward the kitchen door. "Well, it's been lovely chatting with you, Mr. Wales, but this is a discussion I'd like to continue another time." I forced a smile. "I've got to be going now."

"Where?" The surprise on his face would have been funny if it had been another time or place. "I've just offered you every resource the Institute has, and you don't want to at least discuss it?"

"I'm going home. I appreciate your offer of help, but I've got my own plans to deal with this mess. I'm pretty sure it's too late for me to utilize much of the Institute's resources."

"And may I ask what those plans are?" Mr. Wales stepped toward me, anger flashing in his eyes. "You must be careful. Now that the curse has ramped up, it is more difficult to predict Dracula's moods. More than likely the silver-tongued charmer he may have presented to you has faded, replaced by the fearful predator of legends. He will try to draw you in now, try to convince you to turn into a true companion."

Fearful predator? Great. Just what I didn't need. I waited to see if he would confirm that the curse wouldn't actually let me give in, but he only stared, his gaze penetrating and harsh.

"Thank you for your concern," I said, taking a deep, steadying breath. "But I can handle myself."

"Are you sure?" He gripped my arm tightly. "Are you prepared to meet death?"

His hand was cold. A little flare of pain zipped up my arm from his too-tight grip.

"Let. Go. Of. My. Arm." I stared, making each word its own sentence. His eye dilated from my command, and he released me. "Thank you."

I left, but not before I'd seen a trace of anger on his face. Had I just made a new enemy?

****

"Jensen?" I called as I entered my house. "Are you here? You better be, mister. We have some serious shit to talk about!"

An odd quiet settled around the house. Something was off. I thought for sure he'd be waiting back home, ready to convince me that the Institute knew best or something. There was no sign of him.

Had he been with the soldiers at Dracula's house? I didn't think so. I couldn't remember seeing him there, and I felt sure he would have confronted me immediately about not following his orders.

Then where was he?

My cell phone rang. I stared at the unfamiliar number of the caller. Normally, I would have ignored it, but my gut told me I should take the call.

"Hello?"

"Ah, Maisy, my darling," Dracula's silky voice purred in my ear. "I was hoping to catch you."

"Where are you?" I asked, glancing out the bedroom window at his house.

"I'm not home right now," he said. "A fact that the members of the Institute are probably unhappy about."

How had he even known they were going raid his

home?

"What do you want?"

"To talk."

"I'm listening," I said.

"Oh, no." He chuckled. "Not on the phone. We should meet in person."

Visions of his hands and lips on my body danced through my mind, warring with my instincts.

"I don't think that's a good idea," I said.

"It's a wonderful idea. Even Jensen thinks so."

No. The blood drained from my head and an awful coldness shrouded me. I may have been pissed at him, worried that he'd done nothing but lie to me, but I loved him and panic made my heart beat faster. The curse was starting to come true, and it never ended well for guardians.

Please let him still be alive.

"What do you mean?" A sinister silence was his answer, and fear ricocheted through me, causing my hand to shake as I held the phone to my ear. "Where is Jensen?"

"Don't worry. Your love is right here. A little dazed but safe. He didn't expect me to be dressed as a member of the Institute team he'd ordered to invade my home. Removing him from the fight was easier than I expected. You can have him after we chat." His voice softened. "The curse will wait no longer. Come and meet your fate." I could swear there was a trace of regret in his words.

"Where and what time?" I struggled to keep my voice calm.

"Ten o'clock at the cemetery by the lake."

"A cemetery? Really?"

"Some clichés are cliché for a reason." Dracula chuckled. "I'm sure it goes without saying you don't tell the Institute about this. We don't need them interfering in our business."

"Of course. How will I find you?"

"Head toward the back of the cemetery. I'll find you."

He hung up.

Jensen was with him. And what fate did guardians usually meet?

Death.

I collapsed on the carpet, my shaking legs unable to hold me. Tears welled, but I refused to let them fall. Crying was useless right now, and it wouldn't do Jensen any good. No matter how upset I was with him, the blame for his kidnapping fell on my shoulders.

I'd baited Dracula by having sex with Jensen in front of him. Now, that little act was coming back to bite me in the ass. Dracula may have shown me a softer side in his visions, but I wasn't stupid. He didn't get a reputation for being the most famous vampire in the world by cuddling kittens. Jensen would pay for our indiscretion last night, for riling Dracula's anger. Victor Wales had been right. The charming creature I'd almost been seduced by was gone, leaving a cold predator whose actions I couldn't predict.

And it was all my fault. If something happened to Jensen, if he died...how could I survive?

Bianca. I needed Bianca and a gypsy curse.

I dialed her number again.

"Maisy? I was about to call you—"

"Bianca, do you think you can create a curse which might break the one on me and Dracula?" I asked.

I heard her take a deep breath. My heart pounded in fear as I waited for her answer.

"Maybe," she said, hesitant. "I'm not as powerful as my ancestors."

"You were powerful enough to punch a hole in the fabric of time, Bianca. What's one gypsy reversal curse? Do you think it could be done?"

There was a long pause, and I could barely contain my frustration.

"It's worth a try," she said after an eternity passed. "What kind of curse? What do you want it to do?"

"Meet me at Trudy's Bar in an hour. I'll explain there."

She agreed. As I hung up, hope blossomed inside me. Maybe I could change my fate.

Maybe I could save Jensen's life.

****

The light laughter of small groups having fun bounced off the walls of Trudy's Bar and should have been a balm to anyone with wound-up nerves. But not me. Having so many people around made me nervous.

I kept thinking how easy it would be for someone from the Institute to mingle with the other patrons, to get lost in the swirl of cigarette smoke which clouded the air. The long, mirrored bar at one side of the room would be an ideal way to view the plush booths lining the opposite wall or the round tables in the center.

Bianca sat across from me in the booth, her black bobbed hair perfect as ever. Her martini glass left sweat rings on the dark wood of the table, and occasionally, she would run her finger through the moisture, deep in thought. Several men passed our table on their way to wherever, each of them glancing at the swell of her breasts rising from the tight, low-cut blouse she wore. I guess when you're a hot, sex toy associate you get used to strange men giving you the once over in bars because Bianca never glanced their way.

I, on the other hand, was impatient to get on with it.

"Bianca, I need you to find a way to break the original curse."

She swirled her martini. "Dracula actually tried to get the gypsies to reverse the curse, but they weren't going for it. The Institute had already poisoned their minds."

"What do you mean?"

"Jensen showed you those photos, right? The ones of the gypsy massacre?"

"Uh-huh. They were brutal."

"Yeah. They were, but the story behind them is not what you think."

Oh, boy. Another twist in the story. Was this more proof that my husband had lied to me? Jensen put his faith in the Institute and Victor Wales. Bianca held no love for them at all. I didn't know where I stood yet, but it bothered me there were multiple stories for every event.

"What do you mean?" I asked.

"The Institute wanted to make sure Dracula would always be feared in the gypsy culture. They used those old photos to frighten my ancestors, to ensure Dracula would never be able to use them as an ally again," Bianca explained. "Prior to the events of Dracula and Mina's little love story, the gypsy clans were loyal to Dracula. They used their powers to help him. I'm certain he wasn't the one to slaughter the clans—not even after the curse was placed. The Institute knows that, but they didn't want to take a chance on the gypsies helping him ever again."

"Why?"

"Because with the gypsies, Dracula was powerful. Too powerful. No one could touch him. The Institutes' original intent was to strip him of his allies, and the photos helped them do that."

"Wait a minute. If Dracula didn't slaughter those gypsies, who did?"

Bianca shifted in her seat, not quite meeting my eye. "The one who gave them the photos in the first place. The Institute didn't take those themselves, you know. They were given to them by an outside party, and more importantly, they were given to the Institute *after* the curse had been placed. They were a tool used in the following generations to instill fear. But it doesn't matter now," she said, sipping her drink. "What's done is done."

She was hiding something. I could feel it. Why wasn't she telling me who the outside party was? Bianca was covering for someone.

"How did you discover the truth?" I asked.

"I told you, I once worked for the Institute. Like so many others, I grew up in that culture. I was trained to use my gifts to help them fight against evil, but one day, I got nosy. Too nosy." Bianca glanced around the crowded bar as if worried about being overheard. "I discovered evil may very well be in the Institute."

"You mentioned not liking the head of the Institute. Is Victor Wales up to something?"

"I can't say for sure, but I do know Thomas King was also suspicious of the head." She took a deep breath. "I think his suspicions may have gotten him killed."

"Pops was murdered by the Institute?" Stunned, I sat back in my chair. I fanned myself with my hand, aware of how hot it had become. "You've got to be kidding me."

"I can't prove it," Bianca said. "But I think it's a real possibility, one even Jensen may not be aware of. I know he and Thomas had followed up on some of the claims I made, but I expect they found no evidence to support me. However, about a week before Thomas died, he contacted me. He mentioned that he thought my theories about the Institute were correct."

"What were your claims?" I leaned forward. "What did you find out?"

"I believe the Institute has manipulated its history." Bianca studied her drink again, an uncertain expression on her face. She wanted to tell me more—I just knew it—but was warring with herself over whether or not she should. "It's too long a tale to go into right now. We need to focus on getting Jensen back."

Jensen. I swallowed and glanced at the clock above the bar. Though I was disappointed in not getting more out of her about the Institute, Bianca was right. We could hash out who may or may not have been behind Pops death later. Pops would have wanted me to focus on the most important thing right now—protecting Jensen.

"Okay. Let's stay on point," I said. "When Dracula tried to get the curse reversed, none of the gypsies would help?"

"No. They'd all seen or heard about the massacres courtesy of the Institute." Bianca drummed her nails on the table. "For the kind of curse reversal we need, you're going to have to be pretty close to him. Like the kind of close Mina was when it was originally cast."

Oh. Hell. No.

I couldn't be intimate with Dracula. Not when I'd made love to Jensen. And yet I could still feel the tingle of desire when I thought about the vampire in that way. I still wondered what it would be like to…*be* with him.

Damn curse.

"Um…I don't think I can do it." I fanned myself again. "That's risky."

"Do you want him to stop killing your descendants? Do you want him to leave your child alone?" Bianca tapped her nails on the table as I nodded. "Then you're going to have to spend close, quality time with him."

"Oh god. Okay. Tell me what exactly I need to do."

"The first time around, Mina was in love with Dracula. She made the choice to run away with him, to become a vampire, to bind her very soul to his. The soul binding was especially important. In fact, it's the key to this whole mess. He'd tried to create companions before, but something happens when you become undead. The humanity Dracula finds so attractive dies. It changes the personality. He didn't want that with Mina. I believe the true power of this curse lies in the feelings they had *prior* to drinking the blood," Bianca explained. "If we could channel that love again, repeat the ritual, we could undo this. The problem is that the curse states no Harker woman will ever choose him willingly."

"We may be attracted, but we can't ever open our hearts to him," I mulled.

Bianca smiled and leaned forward. "But you can fake it. At least enough for me to channel Mina's soul."

"Death is what breaks the curse." I remembered what the gypsy, Armand, had said. I'd thought he meant Dracula's death. Maybe he had, but perhaps there was a little loophole they gypsy had overlooked. "So when Mina died, the curse lost its grip on her soul?"

"I believe so."

"Then she could pledge herself to him now."

"That's the idea. It would also be an opportunity to get close enough to kill him if you had to."

Kill him? Could I really do that? Would Mina's spirit even allow me to?

"Did Dracula kill Mina?" I asked.

"No. He wasn't responsible for her eventual death."

"Good. So there's no chance that even in death, she could hold a grudge about that." I sighed, relieved to know he hadn't kill Mina. Her feelings for him would still be pure. "I still think I should talk to him before this whole seduction thing happens. Maybe explain the plan to him. Don't you think he might want to be rid of the curse, too?"

"No one knows what goes on in the mind of a vampire." She shrugged. "Does he have any feelings besides lust?"

I remembered the sadness Dracula exuded when he showed me his last memories of Mina, the love I know he'd felt for her. In our short time together, he'd even expressed genuine amusement at the stories I told him about the neighbors. If I wasn't mistaken, I think he'd been merciful when he took my memories as a child.

I nodded. "I bet he experiences all kinds of

emotions. I have to find what they are."

"Or you can just pretend to be attracted and sleep with him." She smiled slyly. "I doubt it will be too hard to fake that."

I blushed.

"I should warn you about something," Bianca's pretty face turned grim. "We are going to channel Mina's spirit and put her in your body for a short time. That means you will feel everything she felt for Dracula prior to the curse."

Foreboding over took me. Feel everything Mina had? This sounded like trouble. And Dracula? What would he do when his love's soul was gone again? Sounded like the perfect reason for him to kill me.

"This is really risky," I said.

"Yes," Bianca agreed. "But sometimes you have to take matters into your hands in order to serve the greater good."

Could I have sex with Dracula and say it was for the greater good, knowing it might hurt Jensen? What would he think? Could I even trust Jensen? I doubted he would encourage me to go through with this plan.

But like it or not, that's exactly what I was going to do.

And if nothing else, maybe I could thrall Dracula into not killing me.

Chapter Sixteen

Breaking a gypsy curse has its challenges.

Apparently, you need a lot of horrible smelling stuff and little silver bowls and masher thingies. You also have to have faith in magic and powers that seem completely unfathomable in the modern world.

Faith was something I felt a little low on.

A rotten egg smell permeated the small and dingy motel room we'd rented a few streets away from the cemetery. The odor came from the little collection of herbs Bianca produced from her purse and had laid out on the worn bedspread which matched the orange-and-black paisley curtains covering the windows. The scratched wooden chair in the corner beneath an old, drop-down light completed the look of a place possibly frequented by serial killers and aging men needing a quiet spot for drugs and prostitutes.

Or in our case, a meeting between gypsy and Dracula's possible future meal.

As the time of my meeting with the vampire drew near, my stomach kept twisting in knots. Nervous jitters prevented me from relaxing, and even though Bianca and I had been over the plan a million times, I couldn't quite stay focused.

The idea of being intimate with Dracula frightened and titillated me. He was so masculine, so seductive. I couldn't deny the attraction I'd felt for him from the beginning.

I wanted to have control over my feelings, to not fall into the curse so deeply that I couldn't separate myself. With that in mind, I tried to thrall myself.

"You will not feel anything for Dracula." I stared at myself in the mirror. "You will feel no revulsion for him. You will be in control of your passion."

My eyes dilated the tiniest bit.

I'd decided there would be no tricks, no games. Honesty with this seductive vampire would be the most important part of the game. He had to know what I was up to, and he had to agree to our plan. My hope was that knowledge would prevent him from doing anything rash like killing me or Jensen. I hated to sound like Luke Skywalker, but I believed there was still good in Dracula.

"We can't trust him," Bianca argued. "He is a vampire."

"That's the ingrained words of the Institute talking. He's not all bad." I leaned my head out of the bathroom. "Look at what he did when I was a kid. He actually stopped himself from killing my mother, and in his own way, he tried to help me. To some extent, taking my memory away was probably for the best. At least I didn't have to relive him biting my mother over and over again."

"He helped you because he knew he might need you later." Bianca rolled her eyes. "And if I understand what you've told me, you actually thralled him into not killing you or your mother. He had nothing to do with it."

She had point. But damn. I needed to have some hope.

"Bianca, stop being a pain in the ass." I bit my lip, unsure if I should bring the next subject up. I ducked back into the bathroom so I didn't have to look her in the eye, though I could still see her in the mirror. "You...you haven't by chance heard anything from my mother, have you? You said she might have used your cousin Belinda to make contact with me in that dream. Where does Belinda live?"

"I couldn't reach Belinda to ask about your mom, and she's in San Antonio, about an hour away from the facility your mother is in. Why? Is something wrong?" Bianca stood in the bathroom doorway. "Did she try to contact you again?"

"No, but I don't think she's still at the Institute."

She raised an eyebrow but said nothing before going to sit on the bed. "So are you ready or what? Come out and let me see the full effect."

"I guess so." I stepped out of the bathroom of the small motel room and showed off my outfit. "What do you think?"

Critical, she tilted her head to the side, surveying the long, old-fashioned nightgown I wore. She'd happened to have one in her arsenal of sex supplies. Made of a light blue silk, it clung to my curves, leaving nothing to the imagination. Hopefully, it would remind Dracula of Mina and make him willing to go along with our plan.

"Hot stuff, Maisy," Bianca said with admiration. "Let's hope he lets you explain the plan before he gobbles you up."

She sprayed me with perfume that smelled like a sickly sweet combo of vanilla and candy.

"Geez," I complained. "What's that called? Baby

Prostitute?"

"C'mon," she said and led me out the door.

The cemetery wasn't far from the motel, but we chose to drive there instead of walking. Bianca parked the car beneath the trees lining the main entrance. The wind whispered around us as we entered the main area of the graveyard where the lawns were lush and well maintained, bordered by gray tombstones.

"Did he say where exactly you were supposed to meet him?" Bianca asked, glancing around.

"Head toward the back. He'll find us."

A marble mausoleum loomed in the distance. I guided us toward it, thinking it might offer privacy for what we had in mind. No sense in getting freaky by the road where everyone and their brother could see.

As we drew near it, a sense of *déjà vu* overwhelmed me. I could make out a bench in front of the mausoleum, reminiscent of the one I'd seen in Dracula's vision of the past. I couldn't help but remember the things he'd done to Mina on the bench. My skin warmed. Would the same things happen to me?

A tiny part of me, the part the curse still had a hold on despite my thrall, hoped so.

I sat on the bench, waiting for something to happen while Bianca prepared everything we needed for the curse.

"Maisy," a voice whispered in the night, the sound skittering across my skin, startling me. "Welcome."

And then *he* was standing there, imposing and starkly handsome in black jeans and tight black T-shirt. However, something about his face was off. I could still see hints of Adam Levine, but they were mixed with the face he'd worn in the past with Mina. What really caught my attention was the torment in his eyes.

He couldn't fight this curse. Unlike me, he wasn't able to thrall himself.

"What have we here?" Dracula nodded his head at Bianca. He'd come in so quietly she'd yet to notice him. Bianca yelped as she spied Dracula and scrambled to her feet. "Have you brought a friend to play with us?"

"Where's Jensen?" I asked. "I want to see him."

"He's fine. I left him in the mausoleum." Dracula smiled. "He's quite a fighter, but I thought this final bit of business was best kept between us."

Relief made my body limp for a moment. He was a creature of the night, a murderer, and I didn't completely trust him. Yet I didn't think Dracula would kill my husband unless Jensen interfered in some way. A small kernel of hope rooted in my heart that maybe he might make it out of this alive.

Dracula edged toward me, but I held up my hand to stop him. "Before you go putting on all the vamp moves you're known for, we need to talk."

"Speak quickly. The curse is overwhelming my senses. Time is short, and I can't control myself forever." He studied my outfit, a sly smile curving his sensuous lips. "I like what you're wearing."

He crept closer, the heat rising between us. Dracula stroked my cheek. "You feel the desire between us. Why fight it? I know I'm tired of the battle. Every time I tell myself this time is going to be different. But you…you are special, Maisy. It really could be different this time. I hope for the best."

I shivered.

He kissed me, catching me off guard. Those firm lips teased at mine, searing me with heat. Unable to help myself, I responded. My body tingled, anticipating what might come next. This was how it worked. The magic of the past was taking hold, and I couldn't breathe. Desire made me dizzy, and my thrall wasn't as strong as I thought.

"Maisy," Bianca warned me. "Stay the course."

"We… we can't do this. I have a plan, a plan which could maybe reverse the curse," I managed to say. "If we broke this curse, you would be free, right? The need to attach yourself to my family would be gone. You could go on with your life, pursue other interests."

"But it can't be broken." Dracula frowned. "I will always hunger for what I can't have, and the women in your family will always deny me."

"What if you could have it? With Mina?"

He stared at me, his body so still he could have been a statue.

"That would be a dream come true," he said after a moment. "One I don't deserve. When you live as long as I have, there is plenty of time to contemplate your sins. I've done too much evil. I've succumbed to the blood lust far too often. I deserve to meet the sun and die a real death. I've promised myself that if you refuse me, I will do just that."

I don't know if vampires have a soul, but if so, he was baring his to me. It must be lonely to never have companionship, to outlive everyone you know. I couldn't imagine what that would be like, but I did know that if our plan worked, it might mean that he could find some happiness. Bianca, Jensen—hell, even my mother—would probably argue that he didn't deserve that. Maybe he didn't. All I knew is that one way or the other, this curse had to end.

I swallowed. "Our plan is to reenact the original binding spell."

"For what purpose?"

"We're going to call Mina's spirit here. This time, she will bind her soul to yours."

"But then what?" His bitter laugh pierced the otherwise quiet cemetery. "A soul is a fleeting thing. Once or twice, I've met an entity without its body, what you would call a ghost, but they cannot sustain their place here on Earth. Mina will be the same. Am I to be bound to her, but never with her?"

Good point.

"You aren't with her now," I pointed out. "You're just doomed to repeat the past over and over. You might be bound to her, but you would be free of the obsession of loving women who can't love you back. You'd be free to move on, to attempt relationships with others who might be able to love you in return."

I could tell the idea interested him. The air around us cooled slightly as his mind shifted from sex to freedom of a sort.

"What if the curse still holds her, even in death?" His eyes were soft, full of a pitiful anxiousness. Again, it seemed I was seeing a rare side of him. "What if she…she doesn't love me?"

My heart ached a little for him. How awful to be in love with someone and know they once loved you but they can't feel that anymore—the passion once shared erased in an instant. And all on the jealous whims of a young gypsy.

"Please, we have to try," I begged. "We won't

know until we do that. The gypsy had said, 'Death breaks the curse.' He meant for you to kill yourself, but I think it means death breaks the curse even for us Harker women."

"So I could be free," he mused. "If this spell works, I would be with Mina in death. I won't continue on in this world if I can't have her."

"That's a big decision to make," I said. "You should think it through."

"And the binding spell, you know what it entails. You remember what I showed you," he murmured, standing. Predatory, he circled me. "You understand the…intimacy of it?"

"It frightens me," I admitted. "I—I'm very attracted to you, and it's tricky business."

He smiled, pleasure in his eyes.

"But I don't love you," I said.

The pleasure dimmed, but his smile remained.

"I know," he said. "It is always the same. My desires are never met. That's the problem with this plan. As soon as we begin, the curse will take hold and then…I can't control my actions. No matter how gentle I am, how seductive I am, you will reject me. The rage will take over, and I will kill you. The curse will start anew. You'll never have the chance to get Mina's soul."

"You didn't kill my mother." I pointed out, sounding more confident than I felt. "You were able to beat the curse to some extent."

"You thralled me enough to allow me time to regain control."

"See? Changes can be made. If need be, I can thrall you again and stop you from killing me."

"Perhaps." Dracula glanced at Bianca. "You'd need a gypsy to reverse the curse. No gypsy will ever help me."

"Meet Bianca." I gestured to her, and she stepped forward, wary.

"I remember you," Dracula hissed softly. "You were at Alexis's the other evening."

"I was." She crossed her arms. "I knew you right away."

"You're kind always does, my dear." Like lightning, Dracula leaped to stand in front of her. "And they usually run in the opposite direction."

"I'm not like them." Bianca stayed calm despite his sudden closeness. "My mind hasn't been completely poisoned by the lies the Institute spreads about your relationship with the gypsies."

"Interesting." Dracula stroked her cheek, obviously trying to sway her as he did so many women. "And why is that?"

"Because I know who really runs the Institute." She tilted her head, appraising him. If she felt any affects from his thrall, there was no sign of it. "And I suspect you do, too."

They exchanged a look of understanding, but I was confused. Didn't Victor Wales run the Institute?

"Careful, little gypsy," Dracula whispered. "You don't want to let anyone know that truth."

"So you know, too?" she asked.

He gave her a slow smile but didn't answer her question. More secrets. My distrust of the Institute grew even more. When this was all over, *if* we survived this, Jensen and I were going to have a serious "Come to Jesus" meeting about the place he worked.

"Tell me more about your plans," Dracula said to Bianca.

"The feelings you and Mina shared were crucial to sealing the curse in the first place."

"And the blood," Dracula reminded her. "The gypsy boy was originally going to bind us in death. Our souls were going to be connected. You have to have blood for that."

"I think he did make that happen to some extent. After all, you've been attracted to every Harker woman in the last century. A piece of Mina has lived on through them. But you're right. We need fresh blood to recreate the spell."

"How did Mina die? I know you didn't kill her, so what happened?" I asked. "Bram Stoker's book indicated she and Jonathan lived a long life. They even had a child named Quincy. Is that true?"

"No." Dracula looked away, but not before I'd seen the flash of anger in his eyes. "She died nine months after the curse was placed."

"Nine months?"

Plenty of time for the blood they'd shared during the originally binding spell to become unviable.

"Just in time for her to deliver Jonathan Harker's child." Dracula looked back at me, his smile grim. "The child was a boy, but Mina was too frail to recover from the delivery. She died a day after the birth of the baby. Harker never realized he'd aided the curse by allowing his son to live. I'm sure it would have given him great pleasure had he known."

"So the son went on to have children of his own?"

"Yes, but they weren't all daughters. There were times when I was able to live without the torment of the curse. But every time a woman was born into the family, I knew. I could feel it in my blood. Her soul called to me, blocking out rational thought," Dracula said. "These last fifty years have been extremely difficult. Having three Harker women alive at once has been like lighting a match beneath my skin. The cravings, the desire, the lust for death—it's stronger than ever with three."

"Yet you managed not to kill Mina or my mother," I pointed out. "Or me."

"Don't imagine I'm a saint." Dracula crossed his arms. "There have been plenty of others who have lost their lives because I chose to take my anger out on them. My bond to Mina would never allow me to hurt her. The others couldn't thrall me into seeing reason as you can."

He drew himself up to his full height, every inch the frightening creature which haunted the dreams of men and women. I shivered, unable to help the stab of fear in my gut. He'd taken his anger out on guardians like Jared.

Or Jensen.

"The question is, Dracula," Bianca said, interrupting my morbid thoughts. "Are you willing to take a chance with your self-restraint and see if we can reverse the curse?"

He paused, and I thought he might answer no.

"Yes, I would end this curse, and then I will go meet the sun. It's time for me to find out what happens next."

He surprised me with his soft words. In that moment, it was easy to forget what he was and instead see him as the mortal he might have once been. I knew nothing about how he became a vampire or what he'd done in the years prior to the curse, but he'd gotten stuck in this loop just as the women in my family were. Maybe death would be a welcome relief.

"Then we should begin," Bianca said. "Maisy, sit on the bench."

Nervous, I did as she told me, wondering how this was going to work. Dracula stood to the side, watching Bianca's preparations to summon his long dead love. She grabbed a handful of dirt from a nearby grave and tossed it into one of the little silver bowls she'd set up. It had pungent, earthy smell. Lighting a match, she touched the flame to each bowl.

Bianca closed her eyes and started to chant. I couldn't begin to decipher the words or their meanings. Her voice was low at first, building in rhythm and intonation as she got more into whatever she was saying. I felt hypnotized by her words, by her tone, unable to make a sound.

Wind moaned through the cemetery, and the hair on the back of my neck stood on end. Something was coming, I could feel it. A force rolled toward us from the past.

Mina.

Chapter Seventeen

Mina's spirit. Her soul. It surrounded me in the cold graveyard, poking gently at my body, pinning me down so that I couldn't resist even if I wanted to. Mina's essence sank inside of me, and my own soul was cast aside, my consciousness replaced by her spirit. Feelings of loss and love surged through me, a rushing tidal wave of emotions stealing my breath as I was cast outside of my body, helpless, no longer a participant but a voyeur.

"Dracula?" My lips moved, but the words weren't mine. Even the voice no longer belonged to me. "My love?"

I can't even begin to describe how strange it was to be standing outside of my body, watching the two of them. Sure, he may have been a vampire, but there was no denying his appeal. He and Mina—or I guess me—made a striking couple. One dark and deadly, the other fair and blonde.

Dracula stared, disbelief on his face. "Mina?" he whispered. "Can it be?"

"Where are we?" Mina asked. "What is happening?"

"Go to her," Bianca instructed, watching the scene with wide eyes. "She doesn't know what has happened. Her soul is confused."

Dracula needed no urging. "My darling," he

whispered, gathering Mina in his arms. "How I have missed you."

"Hold me," she cried. "It's dark where I've been. So dark and cold."

He held her tightly, kissing her forehead. She leaned into him, pressing her body to his as if he were a life preserver.

"Dracula, you must…you have to…" Bianca cleared her throat, nervous. "You have to recreate the intimacy. That's how the curse uses its power."

"I can't." He turned to Bianca. "I can't bear the revulsion in her eyes again."

"It's the only way," Bianca said softly. "And I don't think the curse is on her now. She's been…gone for a while."

"Revulsion? To what do you speak of?" Mina pulled back, her delicate face a mask of questions. "I don't understand what's happened."

"Do you trust me?" Dracula asked.

"Of course."

He kissed her deeply and whole heartedly. Her arms entwined around his neck, forcing him closer. Her nipples hardened, jutting through the fabric of the nightgown.

"Mina," Dracula whispered when they broke apart. "Is it really you? Are you mine once again?"

"Always. Take me," she urged. "I need you."

His hand inched up the material of the nightgown so he could touch her bare skin. Her hands teased at his chest, dragging up the bottom of his black T-shirt. He stopped kissing her long enough to let her slide the shirt over her head. She tossed it away, her hands roaming freely over his torso.

Dracula was more restrained. Maybe he feared the rug would be pulled out from under him again. Patient, he remained still, letting her touch his body, a dazed look on his face when she cupped his face in her hands and softly kissed him.

I glanced at Bianca as she watched the couple. She reminded me of a doctor trying to maintain a clinical interest in the proceedings. A small, silver knife glittered in her hand, and she held one of the silver bowls in the other one as she waited for the pivotal moment.

Dracula slipped the thin straps of the nightgown down, kissing Mina's bare shoulders before yanking the material down, baring her breasts. The vampire smiled as he took her in, and like smoke, a hint of wild abandon lit in his eyes.

"Mina," he whispered, stroking one of her breasts. "You are so lovely."

"My prince of the night." She ran a hand through his silky dark hair. "You are still the most handsome man I've ever seen."

Swiftly, she stood and let the rest of the nightgown slide to the ground. Stepping out of it, she held out her arms, a silent invitation. Dracula stared, transfixed by the woman in the moonlight.

She may have been using my body, but I did not see myself when I looked at her. Her skin was pale and her features fine in a way I could never hope to be. Something about her made me think of those enchantresses in story books who always find a way to get what they want.

"Come to me," she urged. "I'm ready for you."

Dracula stood. Mina's hands worked the button on

his pants until he was free.

Damn, but he was fine. All muscles and taut skin. His hard cock jutted straight out, begging to be touched and tasted. God, how he radiated lust.

I figured he would take her now, maybe put her on the ground and have his way with her. But no. Her hands stroked his cock gently before she wrapped her lips around his hardness. He sighed with pleasure as she sucked, her fingers sliding up and down his shaft as she took him deeper into her mouth.

A sound from nearby startled me. The others didn't seem to notice, but I walked a few yards toward the sound to see what it might be.

The door to the mausoleum cracked open slightly.

Jensen peered out. Disheveled and bruised, he gripped the edge of the tomb door, trying to collect himself. His eyes widened at the sight of Dracula gripping Mina's head as she took him deeper in her mouth.

"See? She is totally falling for his charms as we did," a woman said.

Someone else was in the tomb with him. I crept closer. A face appeared in the crack above his left shoulder.

Sophia.

What the hell was my neighbor doing here? Hadn't the Institute packed her and the others off?

"Let me see." That was Jane's voice. "I want to see them, too."

"Hush," Zero's admonishment carried a note of warning. "Our job is to guard lover boy here."

How had they gotten away from the Institute? What were they doing with Jensen?

"I told you she would give in to him," Zero said, smugly. "She's not special, Jensen."

When he watched Dracula and Mina, he didn't see Mina's spirit.

He only saw his wife, giving a blowjob to another man.

The look on Jensen's face... Hurt and misery took the wind out of him, and his body sagged against the door. He may have lied to me about a few things, but seeing his pain...I couldn't help but question his lies. Maybe there was a reason for them, a reason that would make it all okay.

Please let that be the case.

"Jensen, I'm here," I said, but the words fell on deaf ears.

"Oh, god, Dracula," Mina moaned. I looked over to see Dracula lift her up and lay her on the bench. "Please take me. Make me yours. Give me the gift of eternal life you promised."

Dracula slid his cock into her.

Jensen swallowed hard and closed his eyes.

Oh no. No! This can't be happening.

But it was. And judging from the moans, it was going well between Dracula and Mina.

Bianca must have thought the same, because she stood and crossed to the fornicating couple. "It's time," she said softly.

Dracula maneuvered Mina so she sat on top of him.

"Once again, my darling, we must take the blood in order to be bonded," Dracula said. "Are you still willing?"

"Yes," she said and held out her arm to Bianca.

Using the knife, Bianca cut her forearm, capturing

the blood in the silver bowl. She repeated the action with Dracula. She stepped back, swirling the bowl and mixing the blood.

Then she chanted words again in a language I didn't understand.

The bowl lit up with an ethereal glow.

To my surprise, I found myself being snatched away from Jensen and toward the light. I shivered and a great wave of energy ran through me. But it wasn't the kind of heat one would typically experience on a warm June night.

This was a sexual heat.

"Sorry, Maisy," Bianca whispered though I doubt she knew exactly where I was. "I tried to keep you separate, but Mina's soul can't stay. She has to go back. You have to take her spot back in your body to complete this."

"No!" Dracula grabbed Mina as if sensing their time was nearly at an end. "Stay with me, Mina. Claim this body for your own and we can live as we intended."

Wait a second. That wasn't part of the plan. What would happen to me? That traitor.

"I can't live without you," he whispered. "Please stay here."

"I can't," she sighed. "I'm not strong enough."

She wrapped her legs around Dracula. I could feel myself settling back into my body. For a moment, my soul merged with Mina's, and I tasted her love and lust for Dracula as she orgasmed. It overwhelmed my senses, leaving me breathless. The depth of her feelings for this vampire were so strong, so emotional. She truly loved him and would have given up her life to be a part of his world. As she drifted away, energy surrounded us, a tight chain which made my heart race.

The curse. It's the curse's energy.

But suddenly, it lifted away from us.

As I settled back into my body, I stared into Dracula's eyes and saw wonder. He could feel the horrible energy leaving, too. Bianca's spell had worked.

The next thing I knew, Mina and the energy were gone.

But I wasn't.

Dracula's cock was deep inside me. I couldn't help but arch against it, wanting to know just once what it felt like. I don't think he noticed. There was a dazed expression on his face.

"The spell is complete," Bianca announced. "You are free, Dracula. Your soul is bound to your one true love."

"No!"

The shout shook the air. At first, I thought it was Jensen, but the deep voice didn't belong to him. The air around us shook. Dracula broke away from me, and I scrambled to grab the nightgown and cover myself.

The acrid scent of smoke tickled my nose and throat. Then the mausoleum shook, along with several headstones nearby. Terrified, I looked to Dracula for an explanation.

"We have company, Maisy." Dracula slid into his pants, tugging the shirt over his head. "Prepare yourself. You're about to meet the real reason for this curse."

"Real reason?" I asked, watching the mausoleum. Had I missed a step somewhere? Confusion battled with the fear coursing through me. "I thought it was the gypsy boy's fault. Don't tell me you had another jealous lover out there?"

"I did get around a lot in my day."

I turned to Bianca who stared at the mausoleum with wide, frightened eyes. Something jumped out from behind her, forcing her to the ground. I screamed as I realized what I was seeing.

Zero to Sixty had ripped out Bianca's throat. She lay on the ground, shock and horror frozen in her lifeless eyes. Zero's body twisted and bent in an unnatural way as she leaped on to Bianca's body.

Jane and Sophia ran from the mausoleum.

"Brad Pitt," Sophia screeched when she saw Dracula, her face a mask of terror. "Run. The Master's after us."

Jensen stumbled out, his hair streaked with dirt from the tomb and one hand clutched to his neck. Blood gushed from beneath his fingers, dotting his dirty and torn clothing. Was he trying to attack the neighbors? Kill them?

"Run, Maisy," he gasped. "Get out of here right now."

Behind him, the marble door of the mausoleum flew off, landing with a heavy thud inches from where Zero was greedily licking the blood from Bianca's neck. She glanced up, but then went back to her meal, ignoring the commotion.

A dark shadow formed in the doorway of the tomb, reeking of rot and decay.

"Jensen is right." Dracula glanced at me. "You need to run, Maisy."

"What is it?" I asked, backing away, covering my nose from the horrible stench, afraid that even breathing it in would be inviting the creature's attention.

"Real evil."

Jensen crawled toward us, determination on his face. I ran to him, grasping his hand, helping him to his feet. The strange shadow behind him hissed.

"No." Jensen shook his head, shoving me away. "Get out of here. I'll meet you at home. And don't trust anyone who says they're from the Institute."

"Sssstay," the thing hissed. "Ssstay."

"Yes." Zero grabbed me from behind, shoving me toward the creature. "Stay and meet the Master."

I broke free and turned to Zero. Dark eyeliner ran down her cheeks, and she smelled like she'd been on a non-stop drinking binge. Bianca's blood covered her mouth, chilling me to the bone.

She smiled, revealing two sharp fangs.

"What's wrong?" Zero asked, grinning wider. "You look flushed."

"I guess fucking a vampire will do that to you," Sophia said, flanking me on the right.

"And to think, she was so pious and pure." Jane closed in on the left. "We all saw you screwing Dracula just now."

"That…that wasn't really me…" I said. "It was Mina Harker's soul."

The three women smiled, their fangs gleaming.

"Now you can be one of us." Jane put a hand on my shoulder. "Our new master wants to meet you."

I glanced at Dracula, but he was gone. And so was Jensen. That left me with three neighborhood sluts and one scary looking…thing. I wasn't sure what to call it just yet.

Where was Jensen? Hurt, he couldn't have gotten

far. God, how much more worry could I take? Then again, Jensen was supposed to be a bad ass trained by the Institute. From what I'd seen in the videos, he could handle himself.

But could I? That remained to be seen.

"I've already met Dracula." I prepared to make a break for it as I scanned the area for Jensen, hoping to see some sign of him or even Dracula. Any extra help would have been appreciated. "I don't think he really wants me that much anymore."

"Dracula?" Sophia laughed. "He's not the Master. He's a pawn in a much bigger game."

The ugly, hissing shadow chuckled softly.

"T-t-t-take her, ladiesss," it ordered. "We need the little bitch that broke the curse. She needs to be punished."

Oh shit.

Jane lunged at me.

I screamed and sidestepped her. Jane's head made contact with the tombstone I'd been standing in front of, and her yelp of pain spurred me into making a decision. No way was I sticking around to be a late night snack for Zero and Sophia. The thought of their pointy teeth sinking into any part of me kicked my adrenaline into high gear, and I did what anyone girl in my position would have done.

I hauled ass out of there.

Chapter Eighteen

I ran past Bianca's car like one of those lame chicks you see in a bad horror movie and wished I had grabbed the keys. I'd managed to slip back into the nightgown before the mausoleum door had burst open, and it clung to my sweaty body. The pounding of my heart echoed in my ears, reminding me of how much I hated running and that I was currently fulfilling a saying I always told the PE coach at school—*I don't run unless someone is chasing me.* Maybe that was a saying I would need to rethink for the future, considering how badly my lungs ached from the short distance I'd covered.

I should go back for Jensen. I know he'd told me to run, but at the same time, I can't leave him there. Where is Dracula? Why isn't he helping me fight off that thing in the cemetery?

Then again, if Dracula was actually free from the Harker curse, why would he stick around to help me?

Luckily, I wasn't too far from the motel Bianca and I had been at earlier. I could probably get some help there—or at least call someone for assistance. My sides ached from running, and I knew the evil triplets were probably close behind me.

The lights of the motel were a welcome sight. I slowed, daring to glance behind me. No sign of my neighbors.

I tried to catch my breath, but when I turned to keep moving to the motel, I bumped squarely into a firm, masculine chest.

"Maisy." Dracula put his arms around me. "Be calm. I've got you now."

"What the hell did you do to my neighbors? What was that thing?" I sounded hysterical. "And Jensen…oh my god, I left him behind. I didn't see him anywhere."

"Put your arms around me," Dracula said. "Hold on."

"I don't think so. We've already been a little too chummy tonight."

With a sigh, he grabbed my arms and forced them around his neck.

The ground fell away.

Terrified by the sudden rush of cold air, I couldn't help but scream. We were flying. Actually, I think we were bounding or jumping or something. I closed my eyes and leaned into him.

After a few minutes, it stopped. Cautious, I turned my head away from his chest. We were in my front yard and the moon shone down on us, illuminating the whole area.

"What are we doing here?" I struggled out of his arms so I could see his face better.

"Jensen asked me to bring you here. He said to go to the weapons chest."

"Where is he? Did you hurt him?"

I couldn't imagine Jensen trusting Dracula. Not after all the warnings and the things he'd told me. Could Dracula be lying to me?

Cautious, I stepped away and glanced around for something to use as a weapon, just in case.

"I took him while you were dealing with your neighbors. He is not far." Dracula's pale face was grave. "He was bitten, Maisy. The ladies did quite a number on him. For fledglings, they've caught on quick to the vampiric way of life."

"Will he be okay?" I asked. "Is he...a vampire now? Did he share blood with that thing in the cemetery?"

Oh god. What would I do with a vampire husband? Would the Institute try and kill him? No. No way. I wouldn't let that happen. If I had to thrall every last Institute member, they wouldn't touch him.

"You must be calm." Dracula put his hands on my shoulders, forcing me to look at him and ignoring my question. "Hysteria will not help."

"Calm? Are you kidding?" I jerked away, crossing my arms. "What was that thing back there?"

Dracula narrowed his eyes. "An old creature."

"What about my neighbors?" I glanced at Zero's house across the street. "He ordered them to bring me to him. Why?"

"Because he controls them."

"I thought you did. I mean, you seduced them. You were turning them into fledglings, right?"

He laughed. "Definitely not. I enjoy sex as much as the next vampire, but if there's one thing I've learned, it's that you never create new vampires. Too much responsibility. A little nip to satisfy hunger is all I care to do with women like your neighbors." Dracula's laughter died away. "I've tried to create companions before. I wouldn't even have considered doing it to Mina if she hadn't agreed to the soul binding."

"But you had to have known what was happening

to the other girls. Why didn't you stop it?'

"I'm a vampire. Not an all-seeing being, Maisy." He rolled his eyes. "I bought the house behind you, but I don't actually live there. Far too risky to sleep there all the time with the Institute always around. It's more a place to crash when I want to be with mortals. My last tryst with your neighbors was the one you decided not to join yesterday morning."

Had that only been yesterday? So much had happened. It felt like a life time ago.

"What are you saying then?" I asked.

"This new creature had plenty of time last night and today to turn the ladies into his new playthings. Fledglings are surprisingly easy to create," he said. "It only takes a few drops of shared blood to start the transition."

I could see how it happened. While Dracula is a way, the Master will play. It seemed an awful risk to take, though. How would the Master know that Dracula wouldn't come back to the house? Or had that been what he'd hoped for? A confrontation?

"But that means…" I tried to sort it all out. "Well, he's been here all along. Watching us. Watching you."

"Yes." Dracula frowned. "The Helser Institute has gone to great lengths over the years to hunt me down. Yet I have sensed a new presence among them the last few months, something that taints even their pious beliefs."

"They did go out of their way to make it appear you were responsible for the massacre of the gypsy clans."

"I didn't do that." There was no mistaking the anger in Dracula's voice. "The creature you encountered did that. He killed those innocents. I'm certain of it."

"Why? Why would the Institute frame you? Why do they spend so much time chasing after you and not him?"

Dracula's eyes glittered with anger in the moonlight. "Because my dear, that creature runs the Institute."

For about ten seconds, all I could do was stare open mouthed. Victor Wales was a vampire? That disgusting monstrosity had been the immaculate Victor I'd seen just this afternoon? All the thoughts in my head rushed out at once.

"No wonder they've always been after you," I said. "This curse was convenient for him. If all the attention is focused on you, then the Institute would never realize that a vampire was actually running everything. That's why the neighbors were at the cemetery tonight, too. Victor didn't have them taken anywhere," I babbled. "And Bianca. She knew. She said she had a falling out with the head."

This had to be the allegation she'd made to Jensen and Pops, the one they'd check into. Victor Wales must have been very good at covering his tracks if neither man had found out about him. Except maybe Pops had been on to something, and Victor Wales had killed him.

Bastard.

Dracula nodded. "It's only been in recent months I figured out a vampire—this Victor Wales—might be in charge of the Institute now. He had to be the one to give them those gruesome photos of the gypsy clans long ago. However, I don't think he was part of the Institute back then. Somewhere along the way, he learned to disguise himself well enough so that no one would detect his secret when he made the move to take over as Head of the Institute. With the curse controlling my actions, I never felt compelled to investigate him further or find out his motivations. But now that it's lifted…"

Anger turned his eyes blood red.

I stepped away, afraid he would lose control. The sympathy I felt for his situation was real, but I knew better than to completely forget the power he had, what he was capable of. How badly hurt was Jensen? I didn't think I had a chance of stopping Victor without him, and Dracula hadn't answered my question about his condition. Was it to shield me from pain or just to keep me in the dark?

I hated to admit it, but I needed Dracula on my side. Victor Wales was going to come after me. The fury Dracula felt could be useful—as long as it wasn't directed at me.

"The curse has lifted, hasn't it?" Furtively, I looked around for a makeshift weapon just in case he wasn't able to keep it together. "When Mina and I were…exchanging spots, so to speak, I felt something pulling away from us."

"As did I. And I do feel different. Bound to Mina, ready to meet the sun to be with her."

A few hours ago, that had sounded like a great plan. Meet the sun. Die. Get out of my hair. But now…the Big Bad Dracula needed to hang in there a little while longer. Hell, he owed it to all the women in my family to help me now.

"Really?" *Play it cool, Maisy. Don't pressure the guy who could rip out your throat in the blink of an eye.*

"You're going to go ahead and do that?"

"I've lived a long time. I'm not sure I can live being bound to her but never have her again."

"That's how I feel about Jensen," I said, softly, admitting out loud what I'd only ever thought in my head. "I helped you become one with Mina. Will you help me save my love? Will you help me get rid of Victor?"

Dracula reached toward me, and I forced myself to stand my ground. One of his long fingers stroked the side of my face. To my surprise, I no longer tingled at his touch, no longer felt the throb of lust. A huge weight lifted from my shoulders. My mind, my will, heart—they were all my own. What a relief.

"It would be my pleasure to help you," he said. "After all, I owe you a favor or two. There is still plenty of time before the sun rises."

For a second, I thought he might kiss me once more, but there was movement out of the corner of my eye. We both turned to see what it was.

Uh-oh. My neighbors staggered down the street, their gaits' wobbly and unsteady.

"You must go inside and arm yourself," Dracula instructed when he spotted them. "Hopefully, Jensen will be here with help soon. Keep what I've told you about the Institute to yourself. Let me deal with Victor."

Hopefully? What if Jensen was a vampire now? What if he was like my neighbors?

"Go," Dracula ordered. "Hurry."

I obeyed. Taking the spare key from beneath the rock where we had hid it, I let myself in. I shivered, afraid I might not be alone. Victor Wales could be hiding anywhere. I'd never invited him in, but maybe Jensen had.

Be brave. Turn on a light and get to the weapons.

Taking a deep breath, I flicked on the lights and hurried up the stairs to our bedroom closet. The trunk was right where we'd left it earlier. Deciding which weapon to use was easy. I settled for another ax and a short dagger.

Going past Jensen's office on my way downstairs, I heard the computer ping with an incoming message. Curious, I went in to see what it said.

Emergency message to all Institute Members: Possible security breach with Jensen Helsing. Consider him non-human until further notice. Approach with caution.

Non-human? Oh god. My head swam with the implications.

Terrified, I ran back out of the room and down the hall to our bedroom where I barricaded the door. Would Jensen try to kill me? Was he a vampire? Had Victor Wales turned him with the intention of killing me, thinking it would be a good way to make it look like again Dracula had triumphed?

Outside the house, my neighbors called to me, begging to be let in.

"Maisy," Sophia yelled. "We know you're up there. Be a good girl and let us in."

"Go away," I yelled, drawn to the window. They writhed and wriggled against each other. I scooted back, forcing myself to try and think rationally. "I don't want to be one of the undead. Why is that so hard for you people to understand?"

"C'mon, Maisy," Jane's pleading voice floated up

to me. "We just want to…talk."

They all three cackled as if what she'd said was hysterical.

Strange noises erupted outside—popping mixed with grunts and moans of agony followed by loud silence.

"Maisy?" Jensen called, startling me.

He was in the house. Downstairs. My mouth went dry. Unsteady on my feet, I staggered away from the bedroom door as I heard his light tread on the stairs. I wanted to trust him, wanted to believe his lies were told because he'd been under the influence of the Institute. But what if turning him into a vampire had been part of Victor Wales' plan? Maybe he was here to turn me or kill me?

"Maisy?" Seconds later he was outside the door. "Are you in there? Let me in."

"Go away," I shouted. "I know you're a vampire now."

"I'm not, Maisy. I swear. Let me in."

"No way. Not until you can prove you're still human." I ran into the bathroom, locking the door.

Why the hell had I ever let him guilt me into hanging out with our neighbors? None of this would be happening right now if I'd just continued to be an asshole. Dracula would not have gone after them. They wouldn't have been changed into vampires by Victor Wales.

"Let me in." I heard him slam against the bedroom door, trying to break it open with his body. "C'mon Maisy."

"No."

"C'mon, baby. It's me."

I didn't believe him.

Something tapped at the bathroom window next to the large marble bath tub. Two pale yellow eyes glared in at me through the frosted pane. A crack spidered against the length of the glass. Whatever was on the other side was about to come through.

The window shattered.

Chapter Nineteen

Victor Wales dove through the large window and into the bathroom, landing gracefully on his feet in front of the toilet. Broken glass sprinkled everywhere, dusting the ceramic tile of the floor and the top of the black marble sink. His face still held a hint of the man I'd met earlier in the day. But his eyes...they swirled with malice, and his face was contorted like the demons my mother had so artfully drawn. Even through that ugliness, there was something else that struck me as familiar about him, as if I'd met him somewhere besides Dracula's kitchen.

"Maisy," he hissed. "The little bitch that broke the curse I labored so hard to keep intact all these years."

Terrified, I backed toward the door, my fingers gripping the counter for support. How did you get in here? I thought you had to be invited."

"Your sweet little daughter was kind enough to invite me in the other night when she heard me on the roof. A trusting little thing, isn't she? So easy to thrall." He smiled, revealing the sharpest pair of fangs I'd ever seen. "I will devour you whole and then finish off your little lover boy in the other room. Last but not least, I'll get that darling girl of yours."

Jensen broke down the bathroom door. He staggered into the room looking like a wild creature. Blood covered his torn shirt, and his hair and face were dusty with filth from the mausoleum. Without a second thought, he hurled a knife, landing it squarely in Victor's chest.

The vampire's faced contorted into a cruel smile. Calmly, he plucked the blade free and dropped it to the floor. With one hand, he lifted Jensen up by his neck and pinned him to the wall.

"Aim for the heart, boy," Victor sneered. "You really should know better."

Did this mean Jensen wasn't a vamp? Oh god.

"Jensen," I screamed and started toward him.

Victor grabbed me with his free hand and yanked me against him, trapping me with his arm. "Be still, my sweet. I'm holding you like this so you can't thrall me. I'm on to your little tricks now," he rasped in my ear. "I only want to rip out your throat. You'll hardly feel a thing."

The stench of his rotting flesh made me gag. "No." I twisted in his embrace, trying to free myself. "Can't we talk about this?"

"Talk? I've never believed in conversation with a woman. Useless creatures, full of terrible, inane ideas. I loved watching the women in your line fall apart because of dear old Dracula and that ridiculous curse. They were perfect examples of why the weaker sex is just that—weak," Victor said. "You've spoiled my fun by lifting the curse. Time to take your punishment."

I could see his reflection in the mirror. His mouth opened, exposing the jagged and sharp teeth. He reared back, ready to sink them into my neck.

"Armand, you really shouldn't play with your food."

Victor stopped, wonder on his face as he slowly

turned to see who had spoken. Dracula perched in the window sill, a bored expression on his face. I let out a slow breath, processing what he'd just said.

Armand? As in the gypsy boy who had placed the curse? But Dracula had killed him. I'd seen it with my own eyes. There was no way he could have turned into a vampire unless he'd drunk Dracula's blood. Dracula had made a point of saying he would only do that with Mina, and I believed him. So how could Armand the gypsy be Victor the vampire?

Dracula shook his head as if addressing a small child. "This is why we could never have nice things, Armand. You were always so greedy for instant gratification."

"Dracula." Armand shoved me down and released Jensen in his haste to greet his old enemy. Jensen fell to the ground as limp as a rag doll. "You look well."

"I wish I could say the same about you." Dracula's scornful graze raked over him. "I see time hasn't been kind for everyone."

In an instant, Armand transformed from horrific demon to the young handsome boy of the past.

"Better?" he asked. "You always did prefer youthful partners."

"But I didn't choose you as an eternal one," Dracula pointed out. "How did you overcome death?"

"I sipped from the blood in the ritual bowl while you were busy with Mina." Armand smiled triumphantly. "You should have turned me into a vampire when I asked. I might not have been as jealous of you and your whore then. Placing the curse was fun, but helping her die, paying a midwife to cut her during the birth of her child so that she bled to death shortly after…now that was real entertainment."

The air in the room grew cold, and Dracula's beautiful face transformed into a full on demon. His distorted features thickened and pulsed with rage as he lips drew back to show his fangs. Seeing his true form paralyzed me, and I forgot how to breathe as I stared.

"Invite me in, Maisy." He glanced at me, his voice harsh and brutal with his demand.

This was the creature of nightmares, this was the boogeyman that came for you in your sleep. And now there were two of them. What would happen if they were both inside? Would Dracula turn on me once he was done with Armand?

I glanced at Jensen, passed out on the floor. What would *he* do in my position? Whatever was needed to take down either vampire. Invite one in and hope one of them killed the other off. Think about how to get rid of whichever one was left. Okay. I could do that, too.

"Come in, Dracula." My voice shook, and I braced for what was coming.

Dracula's eyes turned scarlet, and he lunged at Armand. Ready for the strike, Armand grasped him, driving both of them into the bedroom. They crashed into a wall, the plaster crumbling around them.

I scrambled out of the way, trying to get to an unconscious Jensen. He bled profusely from the neck and from bite marks all over his stomach. It was as if a bunch of wild animals had nibbled at him. His pale face was too still and already a ring of purple bruises formed around his neck from Armand's grip.

"Jensen, wake up," I said.

He moaned, and his eyes flickered open.

"Thank god," I whispered, tearing up. "You're

alive."

Behind us, the two vampires grappled at each other, destroying the bedroom furniture in their wake. Glass shattered, and shards of it hit me. I had to get us out of there, had to get Jensen to safety before the vamps turned on us.

"We have to get out of here," I whispered, trying to shield him from a tossed chair as it splintered against the wall. "Can you stand?"

Jensen didn't answer, but he started to haul himself up just as Armand grabbed Dracula and heaved him out the window. I hoped he would follow, but instead, he turned back to us. I stood in front of Jensen, my arms out to shield him.

"I'm going to kill you now, my sweet," Armand hissed, his face transforming back to that of a demon. He gnashed his teeth, and the blood red of his deep set eyes glowed, a contrast to the scaly green of his face. "That will teach my old friend he ought to treat me with respect."

He lunged.

"Jensen," I screamed as Armand's sharp fingernails tore into my shoulder. The odor of decay assaulted my senses, and his hot breath singed my neck.

I closed my eyes, waiting for those long teeth to rip out my throat and complete the cycle of destiny that befell all Harker women.

Armand howled in pain and released me. I opened one eye to see him staring down at an arrow in his chest. His brow furrowed as if he couldn't quite believe what he saw. Whoever had shot it hadn't missed their mark as Jensen had. Grabbing the end of the arrow, Armand stumbled backward toward the window.

Where had the arrow come from?

My mother stood in the doorway of the bedroom, a small crossbow in her hand which she kept trained on Armand as she loaded another arrow. She looked impossibly thin in a gray T-shirt and matching baggy sweat pants dotted with dirt and sweat. There were scars on her face which hadn't been there before, and the deep circles under her eyes made her look much older than she was.

That's when it hit me.

Momma was in the same room I was.

There was no nurse or guard standing nearby to prevent her from hurting me. I should have been frightened, but understanding better what she'd gone through now changed how I viewed the events of the past. A vitality sparked within her that I'd never seen before.

Momma fired an arrow from the cross bow again. It slid into his chest right next to the first one that had pricked at his heart. Armand screamed and fell backward through the window.

It occurred to me how right this was, how perfect that she was here to finish this. All the women who'd come before me had suffered, but Momma had suffered and survived, living with a mental illness she had no control over.

She'd risked a lot to leave the Institute, to fight this vampire, but I knew she'd done it not only for herself, but for me, too. You don't look evil in the face for people you don't care about.

You do it for the people you love.

Momma didn't speak to me as she strode to look out the window. I joined her, and together, we stared down at the twisted creature below. The arms were turned back and the legs splayed too far apart. Armand's head lolled to the side, revealing an indention where he'd landed.

"Is he dead?" I asked.

As we watched, the body caved in on itself and disintegrated to ash.

"Yes." Momma crossed herself. "Yes. I believe Dracula is finally gone."

"Dracula? But—"

The hope in Momma's eyes made me stop. I couldn't tell her the truth. In that moment, I would have told every lie possible to keep from seeing my mother withdraw back into herself.

"It's over." Momma backed away from the window. "The curse...it's gone. I can feel it. Earlier today, something snapped inside me. I felt strong, strong enough to find you. I knew you needed me. At last, I could help you. I could make amends for the horrible thing I did. And then, just as I was almost here, this beautiful feeling of peace overwhelmed me. An invisible chain broke, and it was like my mind cleared completely."

I'd never seen her look so happy. A great darkness had fallen away. Her tired eyes sparkled with an awareness I hadn't seen since I was a child. It made my heart ache for all the things I'd wanted when I was small—the touch of her hand on mine, the smell of her perfume next to me, the warmth of her hug as she held me tight. Her lips curved into a smile as she looked at me, a smile of hope and longing.

"Momma?" I knew what I wanted to do, but fear prevented me from hugging her. What if she rejected me?

She held out her arms, and I ran into them, both of us crying.

"How did you get here so fast? Where did you get a crossbow?" I sobbed. "San Antonio is several hours away. You don't even have a car."

"I know a gypsy who works at the facility I stayed at part time. She can do amazing things with a pinch of dirt and a little squirt of toothpaste." Momma's face was so earnest I didn't have the heart to question her means of transportation or how they'd given her access to a weapon. I was just glad to see her safe and grateful for what she'd done to save my life.

Jensen cleared his throat.

I turned, concerned about the battered and bruised man I saw. He swayed slightly but gave us a half smile. Breaking away from Momma, I put a supportive arm around him and led him over to my mother.

"Momma, you remember Jensen," I said. "You met him when we visited."

She stared at him, but I got the feeling she didn't really see my husband.

"Jared," she said finally. "You have his eyes."

"It's nice to see you again." Jensen nodded and turned me, his voice crisp and formal. "Maisy, the Institute people are coming. I need you to tell them exactly what I say."

The next few minutes were a flurry of activity. People filled our house. There was a general sense of celebration now that the news of Dracula's demise was out. Neither of us bothered to correct them.

Jensen accepted the hearty congratulations of his colleagues, but his smile of thanks didn't quite reach his eyes. From time to time, I saw him pull over a few people to talk to privately. Judging from the expression on their faces, whatever he was sharing was shocking information. I figured it must be the truth about Victor Wales.

I was dying to ask him questions. Where was Dracula? Where were my neighbors?

"They are under containment right now," Jensen explained when we were finally alone. It was around four in the morning and the house was silent. I'd tucked Momma into Rebecca's room for the night since she was still with her other grandmother. Jensen had sent the remaining Institute people away, promising to be at work later in the morning to debrief them on what would happen next. "We are taking them back to the Institute. After a few days without exposure to Victor, they should start to return to normal. They weren't full into the transition yet."

We sat at the kitchen table, both of us exhausted. There was so much I wanted to ask, but Jensen was recovering from the attack. It didn't seem fair to pepper him with questions when he'd almost lost his life for me.

Still, there were things I had to know.

"Did you suspect Victor was a vampire?" I asked.

"Not at first. I knew there was something off about him, but I didn't know he was a vamp until tonight. He and the other girls attacked me in the tomb while Dracula was…talking with you."

Talking? You mean having wild, passionate sex with me?

His face grew pinched, and I knew he was reliving what he'd seen. Oh, how I wished I could wipe that from his memory. Maybe there was still some way to make him understand.

First things first, though.

"Why did you lie to me?" I asked, softly. "I heard you on the phone saying I was gullible, that you had to secure me. I thought...well, it sounded like you wanted me to let the curse take its natural course and let Dracula kill me."

"Oh, Maisy, no. I never wanted that." He shook his head. "You misunderstood. I was talking about your mom. Due to her illness, she tended to believe all sorts of things. I was concerned about her interfering in our plans to stop Dracula. I didn't know how she got out, but I authorized my men to tell her whatever was necessary to get her back to the safe house. I did mean for the curse to play out the way it always does, but this time, I was going to make sure Dracula was stopped before he could kill you."

Thank god. I'd never felt so grateful in all my life.

"Jensen, about what you saw at the cemetery," I said, slowly. "That wasn't really me, you know. Mina was in control of my body."

"So I gather." He crossed his arms, uncomfortable. "All part of the binding spell."

"I know it hurt to see me with him." Guilt brought tears to my eyes. Hurting this sweet, brave man was so not what I wanted. "It really was just part of the ritual."

"I know. I really do, but there was a tiny part of me that couldn't help but think I'd been wrong about what the curse would and would not let you do," he admitted. "I thought there was a possibility you were choosing to turn into a vampire, that maybe you really loved him."

"If it meant saving you, I would have," I said. "I

would do whatever it takes to protect you and Rebecca. But I...I love you, Jensen."

"I love you, Maisy."

Okay. Here it was. Truth time. I needed to unthrall him and take the consequences that would bring. I hated the thought of it, but I loved him too much to keep him in the dark.

"No, Jensen. You don't." I looked down at the table. "I thralled you into loving me that night at the lake. I told you to love me. That means I took your free will away. What you're experiencing, those feelings of love—they aren't real."

Jensen laughed.

Startled, I met his amused gaze.

"You are silly, Maisy," he chided. "I loved you before that night at the lake. I loved you the moment I met you, and that was way before Rebecca's conception. You have always been my heart. Always. It's true you might have broken down my resolve that night about not sleeping with you until you felt the same way about me, but I didn't do anything—I didn't *feel* anything—that I hadn't already wanted or felt."

My heart leapt with joy.

"Are you sure?" I asked, tears welling up. "Are you really sure you love me? Weird, crazy, me?"

"I love you more than anything in this world."

He smiled and took my hand across the table before using his other one to wipe away a stray tear from my cheek.

"Darlin', you know what we need? A real vacation," he said. "To the beach or something."

"I think that sounds great," I agreed, sniffling. "But would you settle for a trip to the hot tub in the meantime?"

Jensen grinned. "Can I have some recovery time first?" he asked, patting the wound on his neck.

"Sure. You should get some rest." I winked. "You're gonna need it."

"Why's that?"

"Because I'm never going to let you go."

I kissed him, leaning across the table to reach him and loving the spark between us, loving that I didn't have to wonder anymore about his feelings. Jensen truly loved me.

I snuggled into our bed a few minutes later, feeling like the luckiest girl in the world.

****

The hot tub bubbles tickled me in all the right places. I sank into the water, letting my muscles relax. Even a week later, they were sore from everything I'd been through. The night air was warm, and there were still several weeks of summer left. Jensen was busy putting Rebecca to bed, giving me a few minutes to myself.

I listened to the whir of the hot tub, and then strained to hear anything else that might be echoing around the neighborhood. My neighbors were still away on a "vacation" provided by the Helser Institute. I had no idea when they would be back or what I would say when they returned. How does one bring up the subject of vampires and wild sex in the neighborhood? It's not something that's covered in the bylaws of our local Home Owners Association.

"Hello, Maisy." Dracula stood on the opposite side of the tub.

"Hi." I couldn't help but jump at his unexpected

appearance. "Where have you been? I was worried."

"How kind you are." He smiled. Gone was the Adam Levine glamour. I assumed I was looking at the face he'd had as a mortal. That chiseled jawline and strong lips would have made me swoon in another time and place—okay, last week—but now I couldn't see him quite the same way. "Are you well?"

"A little worse for wear, but I'll survive."

"You're a Harker. Women in your line can be tough. I should know." He smiled and fixed me with one of his penetrating stares. "I wanted you to know I didn't abandon you the other night. Victor tossed me out the window, and I was climbing back up when your mother took matters into her own hands. I felt it best to stay out of sight since she thought it was me she had killed."

"A wise plan. What will you do now?" I asked. "The Institute thinks you're dead. Victor is gone. What's next?"

"I don't know. But I look forward to finding out."

Quicker than I could blink, he was at my side.

"I have a little parting gift for you," he whispered and kissed me. His lips were so soft, so sweet as they teased at my own, but I didn't have the urge to kiss him back. All of my passion was saved for someone else now.

Jensen cleared his throat, and Dracula and I sprang apart. Shirtless and clad only in the tight fitting jeans, he crossed his arms and lifted an eyebrow.

With a sardonic grin, Dracula took off into the sky. I watched him disappear across the rooftops.

"Maisy—"

"Jensen, I love you. You're the only man for me." I

gestured in the direction Dracula had taken. "He was just saying goodbye."

Jensen didn't crack a smile.

"Come here." I stood, revealing I hadn't put on my swim suit. "Let me show you that you're the only one I want."

Jensen tried to stay stoic, but the corners of his mouth lifted up a little. He stepped to the side of the tub, and I ran a finger down his bare chest, stopping above the button of his jeans. Jensen sucked in his breath as I unzipped his pants, delighted to find there were no boxers barring me from his cock.

Since my lips were right at the level of his pants, it wasn't any trick to take him with my mouth. He moaned and gripped my shoulders for support. I ran my tongue along the length of him while my hands held on to his firm ass.

"Maisy," he whispered. "Oh god."

I ran my tongue up his stomach, up his chest so I could kiss him. He plucked me from the water, lifting me so my arms circled around his neck, my legs around his waist. His cock slid home, causing me to moan with delight.

"I love you," he whispered. "I never want to see you kiss another man again."

"You won't," I said. "Ever. You're my heart."

He kissed me and carried me into the house, into our future.

Epilogue

We have a new neighbor behind us. I haven't met him. Don't even have plans to spy on him.

Yep, it's a whole new me.

It's been six weeks since the ordeal with Dracula. Life has pretty much returned to normal. Jane, Sophia, and Zero have all come home. They don't seem to remember much about their experience. They believe Bianca gave them acid at the Lovely Lust party, and they all had bad trips from it.

I notice Zero is a bit more withdrawn than the others, and from time to time, I think I see the telltale tint of red in her eyes. Jensen assures me that in order to truly be a vampire, she would have had to die herself. Her infamous neck shredding trick on Bianca was part of the early stages of transformation. Victor Wales/Armand's death stopped her total transformation.

I don't know if I believe that. Something about her is still off. She'll never be the same.

Of course, all three of the women are interested in meeting the new neighbor. Apparently, he's single.

My days and nights are filled with family and getting ready to start a new job in a few weeks. I gave my notice at the school yesterday.

I'm going to work for the Institute.

It's a decision I didn't make lightly. But when the head of the Institute asks you to do something, it's hard to say no.

Especially if the new Head is none other than your husband.

Jensen took the reins reluctantly. With his family name being Helser, he's practically a legacy, and he had been everyone's choice before Victor Wales came along. He will fix all the things that are wrong with the place. And I'm going to help him.

Jensen told everyone Victor Wales was killed by Dracula, and no one knows what that vindictive creature did with Victor's body. The vamp died before he could tell us the truth. People actually appeared to have bought that story—except for the chosen few Jensen let in on the secret.

My mother is doing well. She has taken up drawing again, but now I like what I see in her work. Momma mainly draws pictures of a little girl, a happy child with twinkling eyes who has no idea what true darkness is—Rebecca.

I wonder about Dracula—where he is, what he's doing. Did he go to the sun? Someday, people may find out that he's not dead. I hope to be able to protect him if that happens.

Sometimes, I still dream about him, his scent, his touch, the way he could make me burn with desire with a look. But I can't tell you what we do in my dreams. I can't even tell Jensen.

I'll leave it to your imagination.

Sleep well.

About the Author

Esmae Browder enjoys writing in all subgenres of romance. A native Texas, she enjoys martinis, good books, and a sweet talking man to cuddle with.

~*~

Visit Esmae at
www.esmaebrowder.com

~*~

To chat with Esmae Browder and other Wild Rose Press authors of erotic romance, join us at
www.groups.yahoo.com/group/thewilderroses.

Also Available

Last Enchantment

by

L.M. Connolly

http://a.co/bXyqfYL

An agent for CAT, the Central Agency for Talents, Tegan Gibbs was a powerful sorcerer until she was attacked and her virginity stolen along with her powers. Now she's a normal human being with a thirst for revenge. To discover and capture her attackers, she must work with the Earl of Derrington, the only man to ever stir the desires she so carefully kept tucked away. But he's an ancient vampire, and while once his equal, she now has nothing. Or so she thinks.

Oliver Derrington aches to bring Tegan back to life and into his bed. What starts as a rescue quickly turns into a passionate affair. They set fire to the night, but with the differences between them, Oliver fears his time with Tegan is limited. Yet, he'll fight to protect her—and to keep her.

Danger threatens from an unexpected quarter, and if they don't stop those responsible for stealing power from other Talents, they won't have a future—together or apart.

Melt in Your Mouth
Mocha Magic

by

Skye Kohl

http://a.co/5iZaW0o

After her parents are forced to sell their bakery due to the economy, Elizabeth Carpelli wants security, and that means a dependable man with a college education and a stable job. No matter that her degree in marketing is being wasted in a coffee shop. She wants it all. But then, with the help of her boss, and the most deliciously sensual chocolate, she discovers lust beyond her wildest dreams in a no-commitment arrangement with an uber fit carpenter—a blue collar worker.

Having his heart ripped in two by a cheating fiancée, Hank Lehman wanders into Mocha Magic to drown his sorrows in a steamy black brew. When the sweet and sassy barista gives him an offer he can't refuse, chocolate body paint and a canvas of silky flesh with no strings attached, it may just help him forget his past and turn his future toward a more tasty adventure.

www.ingramcontent.com/pod-product-compliance
Lightning Source LLC
Chambersburg PA
CBHW051523260626
47170CB00003B/754